MILO'S BURDEN

I0633681

Peggy Hogan

MILO'S BURDEN

DOUBLE DRAGON

Dedication

For my father,

John Larracey Hogan
(1927 – 1976),

who continues to inspire.

Chapter 1

A blanket of stale smoke hung over the event like a foul-smelling fog. Revulsion and excitement danced back and forth on the faces of the crowd that had somehow congealed into a single blurred mass. Fear and sweat thickened the air and mingled with the odour of overcooked sausages and onions from the food vendors to form a truly disgusting concoction.

Jon took a deep breath and erupted in a spasm of coughs. He shook his head to clear it and noticed the blank sheets of parchment forgotten in his lap. He groaned. He was here to record what he saw and had not written a single word.

It seemed a lifetime ago that Jon had been given this assignment, thinking that the new event added to the monthly market was some sort of sports contest. His work so far as an Apprentice Historian had mostly consisted of rewriting some ancient, boring story into current language. He could deal with that. Or, sometimes, he would be asked to attend a Council meeting accompanied by other Apprentices. They would all diligently record what transpired, then return to a classroom to critique each other's work. Theoretically. The critique was more like a free-for-all where his so-called colleagues would gleefully tear his work to small pieces. He could deal with that too. But this assignment was like something from a nightmare and for the first time he wasn't certain that he could accomplish his task.

Jon would never have imagined—and he

thought he had a pretty good imagination—the loathsome struggles he witnessed today. He gritted his teeth, summoning his determination to deliver an accurate account. His reputation as a budding Historian rested on how well he did. He knew that many in the School expected him to fail, students and teachers alike. He was, after all, a dock rat skulking among his betters. His dormitory mates had tried to torment him into quitting from the moment he walked through the door but they were no match for the abuse he had survived at the hands of the bully-boy gangs along the waterfront. Jon had learned when to hide, when to run, and when to fight. His slim frame hid a tough, wiry body and more than once, one of his much larger tormentors at the School had limped away from a fast and vicious lesson that Jon had administered, however reluctantly.

The blaring horns announced the final contest. He gave fervent thanks that this was the last one in a morning that seemed to never end.

The pair of monstrosities stood motionless, each a few paces beyond the sturdy gate through which it had been unceremoniously shoved. In a well-practised motion, the beast handlers used small crossbows to embed barbed darts into their hides. Agitated, the beasts began to move towards each other.

They were 450 pounds each, the weighing-in made certain of that, but any other resemblance ended there. The many-legged creature with the red paint smeared on its back stood no more than two feet high at the shoulder. Its scaled head rose to a crest that covered half its body. At the front and to either side of the head were its primary fighting tools: three cavernous mouths each equipped with razor sharp sets of teeth, extendable downwards to hold its prey and outwards to stab or slice. Its six stout legs ended in claws that glinted dully where the light caught them. It had no eyes, no ears, no tail, no visible genitalia.

Its opponent, with blue streaks of paint down its upper limbs, appeared emaciated by comparison. It stood over seven feet tall, the legs easily two-thirds of that, but most of its weight was in the massive arms that twitched and quivered with tension. It bounced more than walked on the two stick legs, and above a small but heavily muscled torso was a head from nightmares. A horny beak with a serpent's tongue flicked black slime that sizzled where it fell. A single orb protruded from its skull just above the beak. Maggot-coloured tendrils hissed and waved where feathers or hair or scales should have been.

With blinding speed, Red plunged at Blue's spindly legs to topple it closer to the thrashing mouths that slavered in anticipation. At the last instant, Blue sprang into the air with the help of tiny wings that opened on its back. The crowd roared in surprise and surged closer to the action.

Red's headlong rush sent it crashing into the retaining wall and it lurched about, dazed from the impact. Blue raised a delicate leg over Red and matched its opponent's movements so that they seemed to perform a macabre mating dance. An instant later, Blue dropped onto Red's back and powerful arms locked around the crested head.

Red gouged and tore, ripping chunks of flesh from the thing that tormented it. Beak and tendrils whipped back and forth at the flashing mouths, and black threads of liquid spurted into the throng. The mindless frenzy in the ring was pierced by shrieks of agony as the spittle seared the exposed flesh of unlucky spectators. With one last surge of strength, Red lay broken in the dirt, its body convulsing in death. Blue swayed above its prey, spouting ichor from its wounds, then began pecking at the open, lolling mouths.

Occupied as it was, a beast handler had no difficulty releasing a much larger crossbow barb with precision into Blue's eye. It slowly toppled to the gore-strewn ground. Workers rushed in, some struggling to remove the dead bodies and others attempting to clean the ring.

Jon stared at the blank parchment beneath his hand, stylus frozen in mid-air. Nausea roiled in his guts. His mind flashed to the dock bullies raining blows on him as he lay helpless in the dirt, their taunts of 'cripple toy' ringing in his ears. His uncle had never, ever touched him, and Uncle Kory had not been born a cripple. But the bully boys didn't care much for explanations; all they saw was someone they could make suffer. Someone they could terrify until he heaved up his meagre breakfast, then laugh as they sauntered away. These creatures in the fight ring were as helpless as he had been; they, too, had been forced into something in which they wanted no part.

Compelled by a dark fascination, his eyes

moved of their own accord back to the ring, back to the dark smudges off to one side. *This can't be right.* Anger overcame the sick feeling in his stomach. The creatures had been ugly and vicious and he certainly would never want to encounter them in their own territory high on the northern plateau wastes, but they had their own lives to live and far more noble ways to die. To be forced to kill each other for entertainment's sake was just wrong. To no longer have control over one's fate, to be vulnerable before something more powerful, to feel the deep frustration and humiliation of helplessness...

He tore his gaze from the carnage to where the Members of Council sat along with their Advisors and a retinue of clerks and runners. They were here to witness the first of these events and some had actually watched the battles, but most were far more interested in the results at the betting windows. Their runners scurried back and forth with demands for information. The Council would receive a part of the proceeds. But what remained unclear to Jon and, he suspected, to the majority of the population of Alba was exactly how big that part was. 'To cover costs and provide funds for essential projects' Jon had been told as he was brusquely ushered from the choice vantage point where the Members sat. He wondered what that lot would consider essential— something to do with exotic foods and fine silks most likely.

In the crowd, Jon spotted Vern Hanking from the docks, and there was Delilah from the candle shop. People he knew, people he liked, people who

11

had been transformed before his eyes into part of a shrieking mob intent on blood.

The sharp crack of the stylus snapping in two between his taut fingers jolted him back to his duty, and to the black ink that dripped down his fingers and soaked the parchment. Damn!

He found another stylus at the bottom of his ratty canvas supply bag and while the crowd wended its way out through the doors of the arena, he wrote a few sketchy notes finishing with 'and they shoved the poor creatures into the ring and prodded them to attack each other.' Sighing, he knew he would have to rewrite more than that last bit.

When the throng finally thinned, Jon gathered his writing tools and trudged back to the Apprentice Quarters and to his worktable, giving the dining hall a wide berth. The sour queasiness in his stomach confirmed that food was not an option.

***

"Oh, Jon. I heard."

It took a moment for the voice to penetrate Jon's concentration and another moment for his eyes to focus on his friend, like a sleeping man waking from a bad dream.

He waved at the sheaf of paper in front of him. "I'm almost finished and I sure could use a distraction." Beneath the worktable, he unclenched the fist that his hand had formed of its own will.

Shondral nodded. "I'll meet you by the willow."

She turned away rather more quickly than usual but not before Jon saw the dismay in her eyes. He

12

must look as bad as he felt.

Jon stood to stretch the kinks from his cramped muscles. He made his way to the front desk and handed his report to the Duty Clerk without slowing his stride. He refused to meet the man's inquiring eyes; it would surely mean yet another barrage of questions about the already famous 'event.'

A loud cough brought him up short. Jon sighed, slowly turned around, and paced back to the Clerk. He knew what the man wanted to hear. "It was a very successful event for the Council. The tally was not yet complete when I left but one of the runners was carrying a large satchel," Jon spread his arms wide to demonstrate its size, "and had four large guards accompanying him." The Clerk raised impressed eyebrows. "The crowd loved it." That was the hardest part for Jon to admit and his voice betrayed his disgust.

"Mr. Montrai," the Clerk shook an index finger at him, "is it not your duty to portray events accurately and without prejudice? Is it not your goal to become an Historian?"

Jon stood with his head bowed so that the Clerk could not see the anger smouldering in his eyes. "Yes, sir. I'll try harder, sir."

The Clerk studied him for a moment longer. "You know, we had three other Apprentices recording the event. And, of course, a senior Historian." Jon had suspected as much. It would be unthinkable for the School to rely on just one Apprentice to cover such an important event. "So, as you see, I have other reports for comparison and will be able to determine just how much harder you'll have to try." He picked up Jon's report and dismissed him with a wave of his hand.

Shondral was in the School's garden when he arrived, standing with her back to him. Her fiery hair tumbled to her waist like tiny waves in a crimson sunset, contrasting yet somehow blending with the willow fronds that swayed around her. The unruly mane usually demanded its freedom, but today, Shondral had managed an uneasy truce with a leather thong binding it at the nape of her neck. She was tall and slender, and Jon's throat constricted as she turned towards him.

Flashing a bright smile, Shondral took his hand. "Let's hike to the meadow. I've a flask and some food."

Jon nodded, unable to speak just yet. He didn't want to vent the annoyance that the Duty Clerk had provoked at his one and only friend.

They turned and walked silently side by side. He loved that he didn't feel pressured to engage in small talk, or in any kind of talk at all. Shondral was that kind of friend. They were soon beyond the town limits and Jon breathed the sweet forest air deep into his lungs, purging the foul stench of the arena from them.

Cool shadows reached halfway across the meadow. They wandered to the far side where the sun's gentle warmth had dried the ground. They sat on a patch of pale grass and shared the bread and cheese, washing it down with the golden wine so popular at this time of year. But even its mellow glow could not ease Jon's troubled heart.

"I just don't understand it." Jon picked up a

stone beside him and lobbed it at a dead branch a dozen feet away. "How can people do things like that? First, you have the trainers—more like henchmen if you ask me—forcing innocent animals to destroy each other. Then you have the so-called civilised people of Alba loving every minute of it. And to top it off, the Council makes piles of money. It makes me sick."

Jon targeted the branch with increasing force, dislodging a piece of bark. As though that were the impetus to voice his suspicion, he continued.

"This is part of a pattern, I'm sure of it." His black eyes were intense. The School had pounded the skills of logical thinking into his brain; it made for logical writing, they claimed. But, away from the School, Jon disdained the practical, step-by-step way of thinking (he thought of it as plodding) and preferred taking a larger view of things, as though from a great height. "First there was the time that entire farm commune disappeared. You remember. It was the big estate north of here. They figured over two hundred people vanished. Two years and not one of them has been found." Jon picked up a long, narrow stone and scratched a line in the dirt beside him.

Shondral nodded and drew her shawl a little tighter around her shoulders. She had listened to many of Jon's theories and she knew how his mind worked; he would worry the bits and pieces into a picture that made sense to him. It was his strength and his obsession. Frustrating as it was for him, Jon needed the world to make sense. Wordlessly, she passed him the flask.

15

"And then we started hearing stories, suppressed mind you, about peculiar ailments that attacked only children." He scratched a second line parallel to the first. "And, I don't know... at first, they seemed to be unrelated incidents but I can't help but string them together with this latest insanity. Something is just not right." He scratched a third line representing the event.

Any talk of the disappearances or the illnesses had been discouraged at the School—odd, considering that it was part of the School's job to keep track of things like that. Jon had spent considerable time searching through the records, but had been unable to find other examples even remotely resembling these two. The town's long history was a quiet, predictable stream of harmless activities. Now there were three, three among thousands. He sighed. It was a stretch, even for him, to think that three were significant. But he did. They were just so different from everything else. For him, they stood out like a bright beacon.

Jon didn't think he was smarter than everyone else. On the contrary, some of his teachers and fellow students made it a point to remind him how much harder he had to work because he hadn't had the advantage of formal schooling when he was young. He hadn't had the discipline to be a proper scholar, they would say. But maybe that's exactly what let him see things in a different way. He trusted his instincts far more than he trusted any kind of 'proper scholar' methods. They had saved him from beatings and worse by the ever-present bully boys. Being small and alone, his quick thinking was the only real weapon he had had to defend himself. And when his instincts prodded him to look at something, he looked at it.

While Jon went over these incidents in greater and greater detail, trying to find some thread that held them together, Shondral's thoughts strayed to her beloved hamlet. An old memory, clear and sharp, came unbidden to her mind. The day had been so lovely that she and her father had only to look at each other before strolling to the edge of the clearing and onto the path through the sun-dappled forest. She could not have been more than five or six at the time and had to stretch her still-growing legs to keep up with her father's longer stride. She had made a game of jumping into the exact place where his boot had formed its impression in the soft earth. So engrossed was she that when he stopped, she bumped into him. Laughing, he lifted her up in his great strong arms and hugged her. Looking over his shoulder, Shondral drew in a sharp breath. He placed her back on her feet and, hand in hand, they stood on a rocky outcropping that overlooked a mountain valley. A broad slope of forest swept away before them. Interspersed here and there like randomly scattered jewels were crystal lakes reflecting the azure of the sky. In the distance, the foothills of the Sgeir Range rose in lavender and indigo undulations to the brilliance of the icy peaks that pierced the firmament. Everything turned blurry and she blinked away the moisture that had gathered in her eyes. Something became very clear to her in that moment; she loved the world that she lived in. But it was more than that; she loved everything about it. She felt drawn to protect it like a mother cared for her child, even though she was still a child herself.

Shondral breathed deeply of the sweet forest scent surrounding her and Jon. It was that exact scent that had triggered her long-ago memory. How wonderful that our senses could bring back such pleasant thoughts. She knew herself well enough to realise that this reverie was a direct defence against what she had heard about the event.

A group of boys in the dining hall had recounted the gruesome details to each other in voices loud enough to carry throughout the room. She had left the remains of her lunch untouched and hid her revulsion of what she couldn't help but overhear behind a sudden flurry of activity as she returned her tray and dishes to the cleaning racks. It wouldn't do to have them notice her distress; they would make a point of repeating the worst parts over and over again whenever she was nearby. She had learned in the first few months at the School that some boys chose tormenting others as their greatest form of entertainment. If she pretended disinterest, they usually left her alone.

She shared Jon's revulsion. It was murder, plain and simple. And, to her way of thinking, to enjoy the meaningless death of a fellow creature was more than cruel—it bordered on evil. It baffled her that evil existed at all and infuriated her that it could be disguised and sold as entertainment. She shuddered in the warm breeze. This was not the first time she had known evil.

Jon's voice was a soft rumble in the

background. It must have somehow been the memory of that day with her father coupled with Jon's suspicions and her brother's more recent trouble that sparked Shondral's intuitive leap since without any warning or conscious thought she came to a grim realisation of her own.

Jon stood, startling Shondral from her trepidation. "Maybe this morning got the better of me," Jon admitted. "Any pattern to this is probably in my own head." He threw another rock at the battered branch. *It would be just like me to dream this whole thing up.* When he did his homework, he had a tendency to embellish the ordinary incidents of the day, sometimes to his detriment (his teacher's sense of humour was sorely limited). He really had to learn to stifle himself.

Shondral had not yet spoken. *She thinks I've finally outdone myself.* Resigned, he turned to accept the gentle ribbing he expected. Her face was colourless. Alarmed, he knelt beside her. "What is it, Shonny?"

She looked into Jon's worried eyes and tried to smile. Jon's frown deepened. "I'm just a little tired, that's all." She tried another, more successful grin. "I mean, your theories are actually starting to make sense to me." She turned away from his scrutiny.

Jon was certain that something was very wrong. Shondral never tried to hide her thoughts from him; good thing, too, because she was terrible at it. What could be so awful that she couldn't speak of it? What had he said that had caused this reaction? "Are you sure you're all right?" He put his hand on her shoulder. The tension there surprised him and he

19

began kneading the tight muscles. "I hope you know that you can tell me anything."

She did not reply for a few minutes and leaned into the gentle massage. "I know I can, Jon, but this is about my brother and I think I'll save it for another day. You have enough of a puzzle to sort out as it is. Did you try to relate these three incidents? What were they? Oh, yes, the disappearing commune, the weird illnesses, and now the event to unusual weather conditions?"

Jon eyed her carefully. She would tell him what troubled her when she was ready and the transparent ploy to get him talking was perhaps to give herself some time. He immediately launched into detailed speculation concerning probabilities and possibilities while Shondral nodded and uh-hummed in all the right places. He would not forget her strange reaction and would definitely bring it up again.

It was getting late when they returned to the School, unaware of the dark figure that watched them from the shadows.

Jon was not surprised to see his report on the event strewn on his desk with the Duty Clerk's rude demands for a rewrite. As he performed the task, the distress that had overwhelmed him that morning came back with a vengeance. How could people, his fellow townsmen, people he thought he understood, support such a thing? How could they howl with glee at such useless violence and death? He had seen his share of violence but that was usually nothing more than a drunken tavern brawl or a theft gone bad. The people at the event were neither drunk nor stealing anything. How could otherwise normal, sane, respectable citizens build themselves into a frenzy of bloodlust and gambling? It seemed his whole day was plagued with questions.

His revision done, he bound back his straight black hair in its usual tail, placed the report carefully on the Duty Clerk's desk, and strode out without a backward glance though he could feel the Clerk's eyes boring into his back. He needed to find Shondral.

Her friends had not seen her and that meant she was in the Library, her favourite haunt. She was partially hidden behind a stack of books in a far corner of the study lounge. She flashed a smile at his approach and continued to pore over the musty volume in front of her. Leaning over her shoulder, Jon read the title: *Tales to Frighten Children.* His guffaw brought sharp hisses from the other patrons.

Jon dragged a chair a little closer and sat, craning his neck to see what could possibly have inspired Shondral to read such a book. She was hastily scrawling a piece of verse on a well-used corner of parchment. It read:

Tis truly a wondrous thing
ye have wrought,
and with aught
but kindlin' from the hearth!
Twas not near the wonders
told of by the elders.

"This is all I could find in this Ord-forsaken place," Shondral muttered.

Jon did not think he had been meant to hear

21

that. In fact, he wondered if she knew he was there at all, so intense was her concentration. But even more unnerving was that Shondral, who had praised the resources of the Library to the point of veneration, who had spent hour upon hour in this very place—for her to curse it struck Jon deeper than anything else she could have said. Whatever was wrong was very wrong indeed.

"Come on," he whispered, "you need some rest."

Shondral rose as if in a daze and followed him out of the building. She rubbed her strained eyes. "You're right." She put a hand up before Jon could ask her anything. "I promise I'll tell you everything, but not right now. Anyway, this has turned out to be a dead end." She stuffed the verse she had copied into a pocket of her tunic and turned towards the girls' dormitory. "See you tomorrow, Jon."

Jon watched her walk away, his concern a sharp ache in his chest.

***

The day was warm and clear. *Perfect.* Jon fairly burst with his idea.

He found her at breakfast with three fellow students and noted sourly that one was Raj. Jon did not trust his too smooth, too smart, too perfect ways.

"Grrrr," Shondral teased. "You look like you ought to start the day over again."

Jon realised he had let his opinion of Raj take over his face and put on an apologetic smile. "Just thinking. Good morning, everyone. Mind if I join you?"

Raj stood. "Not at all, we were just leaving. See you later, Shondral." Jon tried not to see the way he squeezed her shoulder.

Abruptly, he remembered his plan. "What do you say to things arcane, to mystic visions, to sorcerous divinations?" He wove his hands in a complex pattern, gradually moving towards Shondral's hot buttered scone. "Want to visit the gypsies?" The biscuit vanished up a loose sleeve.

Shondral put on a suitably amazed expression. "I can leave first thing after lunch." She glanced at the butter stain spreading through his sleeve. "If it's not spirited away, that is."

It was a wonderful day for a stroll. Jon and Shondral chatted about the weather, about their studies, and about the flowers and shrubs that they passed along the way. They wondered about the goods and amusements the gypsies would have concocted for this season. They discussed their least favourite teachers and which students would likely be made full Historians this year. Shondral read a few paragraphs from a letter she had received from her family that morning and Jon said that they really should visit his dad and his Uncle Kory the next time they were free.

This visit to the gypsy camp was a perfect distraction. It would give his thoughts time to settle and to perhaps coalesce into something that made sense. It would give Shondral time to clarify what was on her mind and turn to him for help. He wanted that chance to help; he wanted to be the one she trusted.

They heard it long before they saw it: gypsy

children shrieked at play, gypsy mothers screamed at gypsy children, and gypsy men bellowed and laughed over it all. With all the commotion, they did not hear the approach of the sullen, dark-haired boy who appeared on the path before them.

"Greetings, sir, ma'am."

Jon inclined his head. "And greetings to you as well." It never hurt to be polite. "Would you be so kind as to take us to your wise woman?" he asked.

Shondral clapped her hands together. Her eyes shone.

The boy studied them through unreadable eyes for several moments, then gestured for them to follow.

Jon and Shondral passed between two of the dozen or so garishly painted wagons, and in the middle of the protective ring they formed, children dashed about, dogs yapping at their heels. The women sat off to one side busy at a variety of tasks. Some wound coarse wool on rickety spindles and some pounded grain in wide shallow bowls, while others stirred what looked like thick mud. Regardless of what their hands were doing, their mouths all did the same thing: talk-talk-talk at great speed and at high volume. Jon marvelled at how they could possibly understand each other. He smirked. Or maybe they couldn't.

On the other side of the clearing, a group of girls was intent on hurling knives at a circle of wood. One of them, no more than seven or eight years old, leaned casually against the target, knives whizzing by her head. She met Jon's open-mouthed stare and winked saucily at him.

24

Shondral tugged at his arm; their guide had disappeared around a corner.

A short distance from the caravan stood a solitary wagon, dingy brown, with stars and crescent moons scratched into its surface. With a curt nod of his head, the boy left them.

Shondral shrugged, climbed the two steps at the back of the wagon, and knocked on the small door.

"Come in, come in. And, mind, wipe your feet."

They looked at each other, grinned, and did as they were told.

The wagon seemed much larger on the inside. Its walls, except for two grimy windows, were covered with shelves that overflowed with coloured bottles and dusty books. Three over-stuffed armchairs squatted around a low table.

"Sit, sit."

They searched the gloom at the far end. An ancient woman, short and portly, fussed over a small stove. A scarf of indeterminate fabric held her silver hair back from her face.

Jon cleared his throat.

The woman held up her hand as he opened his mouth. "Tell me nothing," she wheezed as she shuffled towards them, "the leaves speak first." She handed them two steaming cups and bustled about, dusting this and that while they sipped the pungent tea.

"Empty? Good. Turn the cup into the saucer. Quickly, now." She thumped into the remaining chair and peered through clear grey eyes at the soggy leaves.

"You," she looked at Jon, "believe your friend. And you, girl," she poked a stubby finger at Shondral, "go to the Mountains."

As the crone spoke, Shondral was astonished at the vivid picture of a mountain range that flashed in her mind. All she could tell for certain was that it was not the familiar Sgeir Range north of her village. In the foreground, her brother stood with his legs apart, hands on his hips. Milo had a broad smile on his face, something she had not seen for a very long time. "You can fix it, Shonny," he said.

The old woman heaved herself to her feet. "Leave me now."

Shondral could not move. She desperately needed to recapture that vision of a happy, sane Milo.

"What kind of reading is that?" Jon spluttered, unaware of Shondral's anxiety. "You've told us nothing! We want to learn something new!"

"You will, you will." She sounded annoyed. "Go, so that you may reach the town before dark." Abruptly, she leaned down and took Shondral's chin in her ancient hand; their eyes met. "And leave soon." She clamped her toothless gums together and would say no more.

Frustrated, Jon asked, "Well, how much do we owe you?"

Her face broke into a broad grin, transforming it into a roadmap of delicate lines. "Owe me? Owe me? That's rich!" Chuckling to herself, she picked up cups and saucers and left them staring at her empty chair.

Jon and Shondral left the wagon and plodded

down the trail, more confused than ever. Jon had secretly hoped for some simple answer, something that would explain everything, some vile plan that he could expose through his writing and become a hero. He should know better than that by now: nothing was ever easy. And the odds of him ever becoming a hero were roughly zero.

He knew exactly what his father would say, as he had so many times when Jon was a child. He would shake his head over the fishing net he was mending and tell his over-imaginative son that if he did not keep his mind on what he was doing, he would end up like one of the villains he made up: quite dead. His mother never said things like that. She liked his stories, and would laugh when he told her tales about the curious customers that had come into their small fish shop that day. Her warm embrace and the smell of the sea in her hair washed over him. Even after five years, it was as vivid as yesterday and he missed her with a familiar sadness. And Uncle Kory—he was Jon's greatest ally and had taught him practically everything he knew that was worth knowing. Jon really must remember to visit soon.

Shondral gripped his arm. Twilight was upon them.

"There's something in the brush behind us. On the left." Her whisper was much too loud in the stillness of the wood.

Jon turned and looked back. "Probably just some animal foraging for its dinner."

A twig snapped simultaneously with a muttered curse. The brush exploded and a knife embedded itself in the turf at Jon's feet.

"Run!" Jon shouted. He wheeled and grabbed Shondral's arm. They sprinted along the path, fear propelling them forward. Jon's shoulder blades were rigid with tension expecting the knife to thud into his back at every step. They raced over a low hill and reached the outskirts of town before he spared the energy to glance over his shoulder. No one was in sight. They slowed to a walk and took in great gulps of the early evening air. He led them up a narrow side street.

"This isn't the way," Shondral gasped, trying to catch her breath.

He pulled her into the cover of a doorway, thinking furiously. "I don't get it. Why would anyone attack us? Even gypsies? Anyone can tell we don't have any money." He pulled at his patched tunic. "It doesn't make sense."

"No, it doesn't make sense. And what also doesn't make sense is what happened at the gypsy camp." Shondral hesitated a moment, then forged on. "Did you by any chance see anything unusual while the wise woman spoke?"

Jon looked at her, puzzled, and shook his head.

"Well, it was probably nothing, but I thought I saw the clearest picture of mountains and..."

"We'll talk about it later," Jon interrupted, "when I'm sure we're safe." He stole a quick glance down the street.

They stayed out of sight. Jon knew all the back alleys and hiding places in Alba and guided them to a spot where, from their crouch, they could see the Apprentice Quarters as well as the buildings on cither side. Their searching eyes detected nothing in the inky shadows and, feeling a little foolish, they rose to cross the street.

A shadow of movement beside the doors to the residence immobilised them. They heard a soft cough and saw the movement repeated. The dorm was being watched! It was only the watcher's momentary distraction with coughing that had kept Jon and Shondral from being seen. Luck remained with them when a few minutes later a group of noisy students approached the residence and covered any sound of their rapid retreat from the area.

Several blocks away, they stopped to consider their situation. "Someone tried to kill us and we're being watched. But why?" Jon chewed on a ragged thumbnail.

"I'm afraid to think this," Shondral gazed back in the direction of the woods and the gypsy camp. "I don't know if there was something in that tea, or if my imagination is getting as bad as yours." She gently squeezed his hand. Jon knew that she liked his stories, but teased him about his effortless exaggerations. "I think I have to get my brother and go to the Mountains that I saw. And for some reason, someone might be trying to prevent it."

Jon stared at her. She could be wrong, and, in fact, was most likely wrong. Or she could be right. He couldn't think why anyone would want to prevent them from doing anything. Time to think about that later; time to be safe now. Nothing was more important to him than Shondral's safety. The realisation stunned him.

"What is it, Jon?"

Jon gave his head a quick shake and focused his mind on what had to be done. With an urgency that surprised Shondral, he convinced her that they should return to the dormitory, gather a few supplies, and leave Alba. Tonight.

After a very slow and careful study of the backside of the building, they entered through a defunct service door overgrown with prickly bushes and not watched as far as they could tell. Inside at last, they went first to Shondral's room. She stifled a yelp of surprise and turned to Jon, a heated rebuke on her lips. With a sick feeling in the pit of her stomach, she felt the flint and steel being crushed into her palm. She would have lit the lamp by the door as she always did when she came into her room. Horrified that she had nearly given them away, Shondral buried herself in a frenzy of packing with the meagre help of the streetlamp outside her window. They repeated the task in Jon's room and slipped out the same way they had entered.

The night enfolded them as they began their journey to Shondral's home in the Kobaska Hills.

Chapter 2

The Council Chamber was different than Valney remembered from his first days as a Town Advisor; it was dimmer, and a faint odour of decay lingered. A lot of things were different than he remembered—the taxes, the lotteries, that appalling event—and they were just the obvious ones. He knew about many other 'different' things' and he knew exactly when they had started. But without solid proof of wrongdoing, he was afraid to speak of his suspicion. Even if he found proof, how would it be considered wrongdoing when the majority of the people in this very room had agreed to the changes? They were not going to listen to his arguments about right and wrong, about where they must draw the line; they were too blinded by the wealth that these new and dubious measures had brought to them.

Besides, he had his family to think about. What would happen to them if he spoke out and was labelled a malcontent?

Even as he consoled himself for his inaction, the source of his suspicion entered the room to take her seat among the most influential Advisors.

She was a striking woman. Not beautiful in any conventional way and certainly not someone you would want to hold or caress. She was more like a force of nature: dangerous and unknown. Her face was carved from ice, her hair a raven thundercloud, her parted lips a bottomless crevasse, and eyes—eyes like twin glacial lakes, murderously cold.

Malissa. Her name squeezed his heart.

31

As those eyes swept the room, Valney prayed she could not read minds as well as she could manipulate them. He suspected that very bad things happened to anyone who crossed her.

The gavel sounded as the Council Triad entered the Chamber and the Town Advisors rose to their feet in the customary tribute to Alba's elected leaders. The agreement of these three men created town policy. They had power, surely, but it was the Town Advisors who brought the issues and proposals to their attention. The more support an Advisor had, the more likely the Council Triad would accept whatever was tabled.

Valney noted that Council Triad Member Nedral slumped low in his seat and stared at the table in front of him; perhaps he was ill. Bevann and Mahler on either side appeared not to notice their ailing comrade.

The Speaker's voice cut through Valney's thoughts; the meeting had begun. The usual requests for funding and a petty grievance between two groups of local fishermen were dealt with in short order. Everyone in the room, Valney included, was anxious for the report on the event.

Valney had been one of the Advisors requested to attend and report back to Council. He could not completely disguise the horror he had felt watching those beasts tear each other apart, but he had been even more shocked by the spectators' reaction. They had loved it. And, yes, they had spent a lot of money.

"Our preliminary calculations show a very handsome profit," announced the Speaker.

Spontaneous applause erupted in the Chamber and Malissa smoothly acknowledged the accolade.

"We expect larger dividends next month," the Speaker continued, "as word of this entertainment opportunity brings more customers into our town. Most of the rooms in the local inns are even now spoken for."

Even though he knew it was futile, Valney had hoped that these events would be cancelled. As the Candle Makers' representative, he just did not have the kind of influence he needed to stop them. To be more precise, he did not have the funds he needed to influence. He knew that was how someone like Malissa gained support. Her schemes, however suspect and unsavoury, brought more income into the town and that meant more money for the Council Triad and for many of the Advisors. It had changed them.

His conscience, troublesome thing that it was, would not let Valney ignore what he knew to be wrong. He had a duty not only to himself but also to his membership. Regardless of the consequences, he must tell the Council Triad what he really thought. He cleared his throat and raised a hand; the Speaker acknowledged his request to speak. Valney took a deep breath to begin just as Malissa's glare pinned him to his chair. A light sheen of sweat sprang out on his forehead, and his eyes bulged as he struggled to breathe. Alarmed, the man seated next to him pounded him on the back, then held a tumbler of water for Valney to sip. He managed a few swallows and sagged back in relief when the constriction in his chest released its killing grip.

Malissa lips twitched in satisfaction and returned her attention to the proceedings. Valney's moment of resolve crumbled to dust and he waved aside the chance to address the Council.

Was it his imagination or did he see a look of sympathy and understanding from Ojal? Had Ojal had the same thing happen to him? Valney grew quietly furious. Malissa was not only tainting the Council and Advisors with her poison words, she was using some kind of witchery to silence dissenters. If he could prove it and gather support from others that she had inflicted, Valney stood an excellent chance of having her dismissed not only from her position as an Advisor but also from the town itself. Alba did not tolerate the black arts.

The last item on the agenda was a new issue. "The Shipmasters' League objects to the increase in port taxes. The League claims that the levy is far higher than at other ports, and that it will boycott Alba if the tax is not lowered immediately."

Before any muttering sounded sympathetic to the League, Malissa's low, silky voice cut through.

"I will deal with the League. Shipmaster Oprum dines with me this evening and I will convince him that our request is not only necessary but equitable."

There was no doubt in the room that she would.

Long after the meeting had adjourned, Valney sat in the darkened Chamber considering how he might start his campaign to end Malissa's control. First he could warn Captain Oprum; it was a small deed but it would start him on the road to bringing down that woman. He stood, straightened his jacket, and emerged into the bright sunlight. Blinded as he was, he never saw his assailant or the dagger that slipped between his ribs.

***

Malissa entered her town house and discarded the guise of elegant poise she assumed for the benefit of outsiders.

How she abhorred the Council meetings! Yet today she had sensed that toad Valney's feeble attempt at self-righteousness and so perhaps it had not been a complete waste of time. At any rate, she would not have to suffer those inferiors for much longer. She smiled. Prag's sharp hiss brought him to her attention.

"It works?" Her inflection was more statement than question. After all, he had been commanded to make it work and her minions knew better than to disappoint her.

"Oh, yes, Mistress. Very well." Prag seemed confident.

"Show me."

He guided her to a door with a small peephole that he uncovered. Malissa gazed in at the wretch on the floor.

"It took three weeks to arrive at this condition," Prag informed her. The boy was about eighteen years old and had been strong and healthy at the beginning of the experiment. The gradual poisoning had slackened his muscles and consumed body mass so that he now looked like an old man. He convulsed every few seconds and had bitten his tongue so badly that it bled freely. His eyes were rolled back into his head as he writhed and flailed

35

about the padded room.

"And the antidote?"

At Prag's nod, a white-smocked attendant let himself in through one of the padded panels in the room. He timed the injection between convulsions. The results were immediate; the youth's breathing calmed and he slept peacefully.

"He'll wake in an hour with nothing more than a mild headache."

Prag knew she was pleased—after all, he was still alive.

Malissa proceeded to her study and summoned her head guardsman. In a few moments Sim stood in the antechamber and at her nod entered the sumptuous room. She allowed very few into these quarters, for it was here that she flaunted her power and fortune. Rich velvet hangings covered two walls, soft leather chairs sat around a desk with exquisite etching inlaid with the finest gold, and crystal cases protected precious gems from across Méadhon.

One corner was graced with an urn that measured nearly six feet tall. She had commissioned it from the elusive Horgants who dwelled beyond the Mjorn Mountains. They had been reluctant at first; she was, however, very persuasive. She caressed its smooth lines and idly followed one of the thousand figures painted on its surface as it danced a pagan rite of sacrifice.

Sim, too, represented success. He would die before betraying her, she had seen to that.

"Report."

He stood silently for a few heartbeats. "We lost

36

them."

Malissa showed no reaction.

"They left town and travel north-east, in the direction of the girl's home. My trackers pursue." Sim knew he would be punished; he had failed. "The Advisor at the Chamber was dispatched," he hastened to add.

"I know you did your best, Sim. We shall find them." She offered him a glass of wine and he accepted as he had to. He drained it in one gulp and was dead before her smile could terrify him.

Her rage somewhat mollified, Malissa proceeded to her dressing room. Mustn't keep the Captain waiting.

***

Captain Jeorg Oprum loved the sea. He came from a long line of Shipmasters and could imagine doing nothing else. He was not a tall man, but broad and sturdy, with a body used to working hard. The sun and wind had beaten his skin to a brown parchment that made him look older than his thirty-two years. Fine lines radiated from the outside corners of his brown eyes to burrow in the thick, sun-bleached hair at his temples.

Malissa descended the stairs to the foyer and welcomed her guest with a dazzling smile. Her dress matched her eyes and was cut to reveal the gentle swell of her breasts. "Captain! I'm so glad you could join me." She extended a delicate hand in his direction.

"My lady." He bowed over her hand. Jeorg had accepted her invitation, as he was obliged to. One did not refuse a powerful Town Advisor. He

37

expected to be bribed outrageously and looked forward to saying no to her face.

Slipping her arm in his, she led him to the intimate dining alcove especially prepared for tonight's guest.

They sampled delicacies from the plains, enjoyed his favourite fish, savoured desserts to feast the eye as well as the palate, and sipped vintage wines. Malissa was well versed in any number of topics and the entire evening was quite pleasant. She did not broach the topic of the port taxes or offer him any sort of deal and, because of this distraction or because of the skill of her staff, Jeorg did not notice that his dessert wine was served from a different decanter.

Jeorg returned to his ship, sated and puzzled by the evening. He had been certain that Malissa would attempt to buy his acquiescence to the tax. She must be trying to soften him up before striking. He knew she would strike, it was simply a matter of when.

The sun had barely cleared the horizon when excruciating pressure crushed his chest. His cabin boy was on the other side of a thin wall but he might as well have been on the other side of Alba. Jeorg could not cry out, could not make any sound at all. His body convulsed in a spasm that knotted his muscles in a massive contraction. He tasted warm blood in his mouth.

It was over as suddenly as it had started. He rolled to his side to keep from choking and gulped air into his oxygen-starved lungs. His entire body throbbed with each heartbeat and the bedding was damp with sweat. He pushed himself onto one elbow and reached for the tumbler of water on a nearby shelf to rinse out his mouth. His strength gradually returned and he washed and dressed. He did not waste the ship doctor's time with this strange malady.

There was no smile of welcome this time. Malissa was ready to talk business and Jeorg suspected his life would be part of the deal.

She led him to a door and directed him to look in through the small peephole. A pitiful human being lay curled in his own excrement and vomit, gnawing the sores on his arms. His bones protruded beneath blue-veined flesh and he gripped tufts of hair in his crippled hands.

"The attacks become worse. Breathing becomes even more difficult as the throat swells. Some of our subjects have broken limbs as they thrash about." Her cold, clinical voice explained his fate. "Depending on the strength of the administered dose, the victim dies anywhere from a few days to several months, no longer able to think coherently or to look after himself in any way. It is quite painful, I'm told." She turned her back on him and entered a small office.

Bile stinging his throat, he followed her.

"Sit," she commanded. "Sign." The papers for a formal agreement lay open at the signature page.

Jeorg knew that his life was being traded for this woman's insane lust for money and power. He met her triumphant glare, gathered the papers, and tore the agreement in two. He lay the pieces side by side and stalked out.

"You will sign it!" The razor edge of her anger

knifed into his back.

***

"I go to the estate." Malissa's voice was soft and very deep for a woman. She never had to raise it, though; these were her creatures and she had given them superior hearing, among other things.

Her estate was an hour's ride north and east of the town, snugly situated in a nest of low hills. Guard towers that were concealed with natural growth squatted on the apex of each hill. The valley itself was broad, mostly flat, and consisted of three hundred acres of prime farmland. The River Quiem, which found its beginnings high in the Mjorn Mountains, briefly touched the eastern perimeter of her property on its way to Alba and to the Sea of Orchès.

Her pride was fierce and hot as the carriage emerged between two of the hills to reveal her handiwork. On the left was the vineyard to make the wine that was her preferred method of administering the poison. She relished the knowledge that her victims quite enjoyed a vintage that would soon give them such excruciating pain. On the right side were the fields of Kammerle and nulKammerle—poison and antidote side by side.

But her greatest accomplishments lay straight ahead in the cluster of buildings and corrals. This was where she truly exercised her power, where she bent and twisted her subjects to her will.

Her servants hurried the carriage to one of the smaller, windowless structures. Malissa stepped down and strode towards the low door. It opened as she approached and she stepped inside. The putrid

40

stench of rotted flesh hung heavy and thick and caressed her nostrils; there was almost no light. She peered into one of the many cages that lined three walls of the building. The caretaker joined her and they gazed in at his Mistress' most recent creation.

It crouched in a far corner and was invisible to the untrained eye. Its black orbs did not glitter and when its lips curled back in warning, the obsidian of its pointed teeth was like shadow on shadow. The nostrils were wide and twitched at the fresh meat within reach. But its instincts and cunning, and what remained of its human intelligence, told it that here stood a darker, more powerful beast. It waited.

Malissa reached into a pocket of her cloak and brought out a small bundle. She untied it and shoved strips of material between the bars of the cage.

"Ah, my pretty one," she hissed, "I do have fresh meat for you. Come. Smell your dinner."

Its eyes never left hers, never blinked. It would do as she commanded. All her creatures did.

The Laracyl girl would be her darling's dinner, and her equally nosy companion would be its after-dinner treat. She paused; Sim's trackers were looking for the pair as well. She summoned a brief spurt of power to her mind, ignoring the lance of pain that accompanied it. What did a few seconds of pain matter when she could make the world do anything she wanted? She formed her command into a dagger of thought and sent it into the mind of the black creature. It reeled with the impact, then sprang for the bars, arms outstretched and claws intent on gouging its tormentor. Malissa laughed.

41

"My, my. You are ready to hunt. And now you also know of those incompetent trackers. Make certain they suffer." She turned to the caretaker. "Take it beyond the third hill. Point it north-east."

Malissa left the building, crossed the yard, and entered the manor where she relaxed while at the estate. With a cursory glance at the servants scuttling about to bring her food and drink, she sat at the table. The Council Triad ate from her hand and the Shipmasters' League would soon follow. All was as it should be except for that idiot child. She snarled. She hated anything not in her control and the compulsive attachment she had to Milo was not her choice. They were connected in some way that she could not understand. Milo had something she needed, he must. She would find out what it was. At least she could make him suffer even more than the occasional times she chose to enter his dreams and torment him—his sister and her friend would die a most unpleasant death.

Inspired, she had a fresh child brought to her; it would become her newest masterpiece.

***

Endel Laurs had been the ship's doctor for five years. He knew Jeorg Oprum was a strong man and he very seldom treated him with more than a bandage or two. In fact, Jeorg had not been bedridden since childhood. To have him horizontal on the examination table was unprecedented.

Endel thumped his patient's chest a second time. "Aye. It's as hollow as yer head."

Jeorg swung his foot at the doctor's posterior. He was familiar with how Endel's sense of humour

42

came out when something eluded him; it may not help him solve the problem, it just made the frustration more bearable.

"So, Doc, what do we do now?"

Endel removed his spectacles and placed them carefully on his desk. He contemplated them for a moment. Then he took a pristine handkerchief from his vest pocket and meticulously cleaned the lenses. He peered through them and held them up to the light coming in through the porthole. Satisfied, he perched them on his nose and fussed with the arms.

"You're stalling, Doc."

"I know, I know. Give a man a minute to think." Something was nagging at the back of his mind. He slowly coaxed the idea into the light where he could see it. And quickly pushed it back where the silly story belonged.

"If only you could get a sample of either the poison or the antidote from... that vile creature," Endel could not bring himself to say her name, "I would be able to deduce its nature."

Jeorg ground his teeth. He had already sent his best men to reconnoitre her town house and her farming estate. Guards were everywhere and well-armed, and from all reports, had an uncanny ability to see in the dark and to hear the quietest of his men. It had been only good luck that no one had been hurt. It would take far too many men to get past her defences; it would take an army.

"You know I can't sign the contract, Endel." Jeorg did not have to explain himself. "Is there something, anything that you can think of to do?" He studied his ship's doctor for several moments.

43

"So there is... but it's even more dangerous than trying to steal from that woman." He waited patiently, knowing Endel would tell him.

"I wouldn't say it was dangerous, exactly," Endel began, "but it's just a story, a myth, probably an invention." Jeorg's gaze left no doubt that he should continue. A pained expression crossed Endel's face; he sighed, and went on.

"The tale describes miraculous healing abilities. The world was younger then and it may be that the people were more gullible. It may be that they believed what they wanted to believe, true or not." His voice held more than a trace of cynicism; Endel did not hold with charlatans who took advantage of their patients and he did not hold with patients who could be talked into feeling well when they were not feeling well at all. Far be it for him to discount the power of the mind to help heal the body (and to help hurt it in the first place) but miracle healing was just too much for his scientific mind. If these healing abilities were even true, there had to be some other explanation.

"These so-called Healers of the Caves," Endel continued, "were said to live beside the sea in monstrous caves where they grew unique types of fungi and other plants which were used to make the elixirs that cured, according to the story, everything." He sat back in the worn swivel chair, fingers linked behind his head. Jeorg would make up his own mind about what to believe and what not to believe.

The silence lengthened while Jeorg considered the tale, his tanned brow furrowed in thought. "I've sailed around the entire Sea and there is only one set of large caves near the water, and they are a good three hundred feet up the Mjorn Cliffs. So how could their patients get in and out? Even for a healthy person, it's a tough climb." Jeorg rose and paced back and forth beside the examination bed.

"Perhaps the world was shaped differently then," Endel postulated, adjusting his spectacles. "Perhaps there are other entrances from the top or through the back. I can't tell you. The story doesn't say anything more specific about where they are, let alone about how to get in. I can hardly believe that I remembered any details at all." Endel fervently wished he had kept the whole thing buried in his mind because he recognised the look that came over Jeorg's face, he had seen it many times, right before the *Pride* sailed on one of Jeorg's hunches. Many of them had turned out, but failure this time could mean Jeorg's life.

"Hoy, Steven," Jeorg bellowed. His cabin boy poked his head in the door. "Tell the crew we sail on the morning tide."

"Aye, Captain." He dashed off to the first mate.

Doctor and Captain looked at each other. "A slim chance is better than none at all," Jeorg said.

Endel nodded, but he did not like the odds, not at all.

***

The attack that night was worse. Endel had instructed Steven precisely: send for him first, then loosen the Captain's clothing, move the furniture so he would not bump into it, and put the round stick sideways in his mouth. And above all, do it quietly.

45

The Doctor had explained it all very carefully.

None of it prepared Steven for the sight of his Captain writhing helplessly on the floor. It paralysed him. This was the man who had caught him lifting the Doc's money pouch and had punished him by making him work on the ship. The work was hard and, at first, Steven had been sorely tempted to sneak away and return to his life. But return to what kind of life? A doubtless short-lived one of petty theft. No, Steven knew a good thing when he saw it, and Captain Oprum had given it to him. This couldn't be the same man who thrashed like a beached fish and drooled on the floor.

The first spray of blood from the Captain's bitten tongue snapped Steven into action. He waited for the brief respite between convulsions and gently pried Captain Oprum's mouth open enough to insert the wooden wedge. All the while, he yelled at the top of his lungs for the Doctor. A passing sailor heard his shouts and ran to fetch Endel.

The entire crew knows by now, Endel thought, as he raced to the Captain's cabin. He would deal with that later. Steven skulked to one side with such distress on his face that Endel bit back his reprimand. He would deal with him later, too.

With dawn imminent, Captain Jeorg Oprum called his men together. He studied their faces, faces he knew well. Faces filled with uncertainty.

"Men," he began. He told them about Malissa's control of the Council Triad and how she was positioning herself to take control of the League. He told them about her treachery, about how she had poisoned him. He told them about the scouts he had

46

dispatched to her house and farm. He told them about Endel's tale. Then he told them about the Mjorn Cliffs and how he planned to scale them and search the caves. His voice grew stronger with the telling, his back straighter.

"This is not a voyage for profit. Any man is welcome to stay in port and await the *Pride's* return."

Many of the crew had sailed with Jeorg for a number of years and remembered well some of the 'not-for-profit' voyages, which had turned into very lucrative trips indeed. They knew that the Captain couldn't always promise a bulging purse at the end of a sail, but they were willing to take the risk. Besides, the stories of their adventures were much in demand when they returned to port, and that was always good for an evening or two of free ale.

Three of the newer members of the crew broke off from the main group and whispered together for a moment. One of them was prodded forward as spokesperson. He stood with his legs apart, perfectly balanced. "Captain, sir".

Jeorg remembered this recruit. Harron was his name and he was a good man; he worked hard. His opinion would be listened to.

"You know I mean you well, but I got me a family to feed. And there's the *Sea Wench* over yonder looking for a few men." He shrugged his shoulders and went below to gather his gear. His two companions followed suit.

"Anyone else?" Jeorg needed to know now; he had to be sure he had enough men. No one moved. He nodded to the first mate. A quick flurry of commands sent the crew readying the ship to sail. The seasoned sailors worked smoothly together and easily filled the gap left by the three who had disembarked.

Steven remained close by. Jeorg was grateful for his vigilance; he did not want to lacerate his tongue again. He winced as he remembered Endel's ministrations.

At daybreak, the *Pride* weighed anchor and slipped out of the harbour. Jeorg kept the departure as quiet as possible. Let Malissa think, at least for a few hours, that he could do nothing but bow to her will.

Jeorg looked back as the *Pride* rounded the peninsula of land protecting Alba's harbour. He loved the way the wide streets followed the half-moon shape of the harbour, each successive street paralleling the first up the gentle slope of the land. It reminded him of well-coiled rope. The largest dock, its timbers of burnished hardwood, was centred on the wide boulevard that split the town in two. Towering oaks lined the avenue leading to the grandeur of the Council Chamber, whose marble pillars glowed amber in the early morning light and gracefully announced the seat of government. A little lower and to the left, were the Library and the sprawling School complex. Along the waterfront, shafts of blue-grey smoke stood straight and tall, punctuating the market. The pastel shades and ruddy-tiled roofs of the homes of the fishermen and the craftsmen, the teachers and the merchants, and the myriad others that made this town unique, completed the gem that was Alba.

Although the dark cloud of blackmail now marred its beauty, Jeorg considered it a temporary setback. He refused to let the designs of one Advisor destroy him or this place. He gave the command to raise sail. The *Pride* gathered speed.

The voyage was uneventful, the Sea being gentle this early in the summer. Three days saw them within sight of the towering Mjorn Cliffs and even from a distance, Jeorg could pick out the black holes gouged into the face of the rock. He studied the sheerness of the Cliffs and shuddered as he contemplated his fate if an attack should come upon him during the climb. He searched for some indication of where the Cliffs became the Mountains, but they merged seamlessly and soared to such a height that they pierced a stray wisp of cloud. So approaching the caves from behind by climbing over the top was out of the question. Perhaps tunnelling through the entire base of the mountain? That was stupid. The only way to the caves was the slow, dangerous ascent, inch by inch, up the sheer cliffs that loomed closer with every breath. He would simply not have an attack.

It was approaching dusk when the *Pride* anchored a safe distance from the base of the Mjorn Cliffs. Jeorg and Aird, the first mate, assembled what they would need for the climb and for the search for something, anything, that might at least slow down the insidious poison that coursed through Jeorg's body. In a perverse way, Jeorg hoped for another attack that night; it might prevent one from occurring during the climb the following day.

Endel found them later that evening in the Captain's cabin. Jeorg and Aird were going over the equipment for the climb. There was new rope, slings, karabiners, and pitons—plenty for one more climber. Jeorg glanced up from his work.

"I'm coming with you." Endel put more finality in his voice than he had intended, but his mind was made up. If there was any chance at all of finding something useful, he had to be there. He was the only one who could handle the delicate fungi or whatever unusual plants they might find. After all, finding anyone in these caves, let alone a healer, was ridiculous at best. "I've climbed a little and, as you know Jeorg, I'm a very careful man." Endel stood with his legs apart, feet firmly planted, arms folded across his chest, daring Jeorg to deny him.

Never taking his eyes from Endel, Jeorg addressed the first mate. "What do you think, Aird, can you handle two amateurs?"

Aird had been with the *Pride* more than eight years and had earned his position over and over with the quickness and accuracy of his decisions. He was a strong man and taller than most of the crew yet carried himself lightly, like a dancer. Whenever he was on leave, Aird returned to his beloved home east of the Mjorn Mountains. He had been climbing up and down the Dreven Plateau cliffs all his life and though they were not quite as high as the ones he would face at dawn, he had experience.

Aird pointed to a crossbeam towards the back of the cabin. "Doctor, please lift your body so we can see your face over the beam."

Without hesitation, Endel placed a chair beneath the beam in question, stepped up onto it, took the beam in a firm grip, and swung his legs free of the chair. With a strength that no Doctor needed, his eyes met Aird's two dozen times over the top of the beam. He was breathing deeply and evenly when he rejoined them on the deck, a light sheen of perspiration on his forehead and a slight fogging on his glasses.

"You've been doing more than thumping chests," Jeorg laughed. "I'd be glad to have you with us. We leave at first light."

***

The dinghy splashed into the water as dawn caressed the tall masts of the ship. Jeorg, Endel, and Aird descended the ladder to the boat where two crewmen waited. Their climbing and camping gear was neatly stowed in the bow of the boat. Within minutes, they were rowed to a more or less flat boulder from which they would begin their ascent. They donned climbing harnesses and waited patiently while Aird triple-checked everything.

Jeorg watched the crewmen return to the ship and find a spot along the rail. The entire complement stood on the deck or hung from the rigging to watch. Many had voiced the fact that it was their job to take the physical risks, not the Captain's. Couldn't they bring whatever was up there down to him? Jeorg had not been the only one to wonder what would happen should another attack occur during the climb. No time for misgivings now.

Three of the twenty cave entrances large

enough for them to stand in were directly above them. With nothing to guide them to the correct cave, if there even was a correct cave, they chose to head for this grouping.

"I lead," directed Aird, "the Captain next, then you, Doctor." It was not a request. Aird made a brief sign of good fortune to Ord and turned his tall frame to face the rock wall.

From a distance, the cliff had appeared sheer but now that they clung to its surface, they found any number of good hand- and footholds. Aird led them step by careful step towards their goal. He estimated a distance of one hundred and twenty feet to the lip of the first cave. Alone, he would have found the climb invigorating. But with two of the *Pride*'s valuable Officers in his care, he would use all his experience to get them safely there and back again.

Aird came to a narrow ledge that would give them a brief respite and called to Jeorg and Endel to tell them of his discovery. Looking down as he was, he did not see the first gull swoop at his head. A man of lesser nerve would surely have flailed about, losing his balance. Aird thanked the gods that it was he the birds had chosen to buffet. Further along the ledge, it seemed, also afforded good nesting for the sea birds. Aird edged sideways away from the nests, but not before he had been thoroughly squawked at. Fortunately, they did not get close enough to peck him with their pointed beaks and were content to leave a sentry hovering nearby when he had put sufficient distance between himself and their hatchlings.

Jeorg took the moment's delay to slow his breathing and to gaze out at the sea. The *Pride*'s sails gleamed like a bright flower in a bed of emerald green. Three white gulls circled lazily above the main mast, their feathers dazzling his eyes when they banked. He sighed, and turned back to the hard grey surface that awaited him.

Below, Endel kept his eyes straight ahead, studying the rock wall with grim intensity. He knew that if he looked down, however briefly, he would be lost. He steeled his mind away from such thoughts and placed one hand carefully in a wedge, then one foot on the jutting rock he had spied. "This is to save Jeorg's life," he whispered over and over. Somehow, he would make it to the caves and would never let his companions know what it had cost him to climb so high with the sea and the rocks below beckoning him at every step.

When all three were on the lip of the nearest cave, Aird waved to the ship in a pre-arranged signal. The crew would know they had arrived safely and would watch the entrance for five days before launching a rescue mission. The first mate had given them more than enough tasks to keep them busy. The ship would gleam from stem to stern.

Endel did not turn to look at the view that Aird and Jeorg admired, and moved resolutely away from the edge. In the shadows of the cave, he drew a shaking hand across his damp brow and wiped the condensation from his glasses. He took several deep breaths and managed to get his water flask open and drink from it. Somewhat composed, he feigned great interest in the rock formations of the cave.

Aird coiled their climbing rope and secured it to the outside of his pack while Jeorg extracted a storm lantern and struck a spark to the wick. A few steps past the entrance, the ceiling soared beyond the reach of the lantern's glow. They heard the lonely echo of water dripping into water from somewhere up ahead. On impulse, Jeorg chose to keep the left side of the cave wall within reach. He now led the tiny expedition.

The floor was nearly smooth as if from long use and it sloped gently downward. The soft leather of their boots made no sound. They walked for several minutes before the ceiling curved down to become the back wall. Reflective minerals threw pinpricks of light at them like distant stars on a clear night. They passed beneath the low archway of a tunnel that disappeared in a sharp curve immediately ahead.

"Let me go first." Aird's voice reverberated off the walls.

Jeorg shook his head and led on. "You take the rear." This was the first time Jeorg had used the *Pride* and its crew for his own sake and it made him uncomfortable. If there was any danger ahead, it was for him to face.

The air seemed to grow brighter. It was also getting warmer. The tunnel straightened and Jeorg stopped so suddenly that Endel stumbled into him.

"What...?" Endel's question was answered before he finished asking it. They heard Aird's breath suck in as he, too, feasted his eyes on the spectacle before them.

54

Stalactites joined stalagmites in thin-waisted pillars, randomly yet perfectly placed about what could only be described as a cathedral. A soft ivory light came from everywhere. Jeorg's eyes ascended to the domed ceiling and he marvelled at the delicate firebirds playing in the air currents.

"It is pretty, isn't it." The strange voice shattered the moment like a hammer blow. As one, they spun to face the speaker, daggers drawn.

"Gentlemen, gentlemen, I could not possibly be a threat to you." His breath wheezed in what sounded like a chuckle.

Jeorg stared at the figure in front of them. The creature's eyes softly glowed creating odd shadows on its face and it took a moment for Jeorg to distinguish its features. It looked surprisingly human. He examined the rest of the creature and discovered why they had not seen it when they had entered the cavern. It looked exactly like a boulder from the neck down. Jeorg only guessed it had a neck; he could not readily identify where the head stopped and the rounded shoulders began. A voluminous robe the colour of the cavern walls fell to the floor in soft folds.

"I am your guide," the creature stated clearly. "All your questions will be answered. Please follow me." And with a piercing glance at Jeorg, added, "and I am human like you." He turned in a swirl of fabric and stepped into the tunnel that gaped behind him.

With a signal of 'stay alert' at Endel and Aird, Jeorg crossed the inky portal that had swallowed the strange human. This could be what they had come looking for or, more likely, it could be a trap. Either way, Jeorg had to know. They would follow.

Their guide mumbled to himself as he trudged along, but Jeorg could not understand anything he said and was forced to content himself with studying their escort as best he could. The face, he remembered from that brief glance, was clean-shaven and topped by snowy white hair that floated down past his shoulders. He carried himself erect, though any more of his body was completely hidden by the robe. His feet protruded occasionally and Jeorg saw ordinary feet in loose-fitting sandals.

They walked a long while through many tunnels, some with rough-hewn steps that joined caverns even larger than the first one at the cliff wall. The journey took them ever deeper into the Mjorn Mountains.

"Good, nearly there. See?" Their guide hurried, shuffling his sandaled feet.

Jeorg peered ahead and saw nothing but rock walls. Suddenly, the tunnel doubled-back on itself and they had arrived. Once again, Endel stumbled into him.

The panorama before them made no sense. How could there be fields and forests in the bowels of a mountain? How could there be children playing in the sunlight? Sunlight?

Their guide had come back and was tugging on Jeorg's sleeve. "Come. Dinner is ready."

Chapter 3

Their head-long flight from Alba had slowed to a brisk jog, deteriorated to a fast walk, and now they foundered along. They had bolted like a pair of scared rabbits at the first sign of trouble—trouble that was probably all in Jon's head. *It would be just like me to exaggerate this whole thing.* He knew that he tended to paint everything with bright colours, providing such wonderful contrast to the dark purposes that made a story so much better. But then they *did* have a knife thrown at them and someone *was* watching their dormitory. And Shondral *did* have some sort of vision at the gypsy camp. He didn't like it, any of it.

Shondral tripped and clutched at his arm. Jon felt a hot flash of anger, and was immediately ashamed. This was his idea after all, and who could ever be ready to run and walk and stagger all night long? Ord's pre-dawn glow lightened the sky; he willed the great star to rise over the horizon. They would stop and rest for a while when there was enough light to get a better look at their surroundings.

They were some yards past the ancient riabad tree when it registered on his brain. "There." He turned and pointed. They swam through the waist-high ferns and grasses that covered the forest floor wherever a tree had not staked its claim. Jon circled the riabad and spotted a thinning in the dense foliage. On hands and knees, he gingerly pried some of the branches apart and Shondral slipped through.

After a furtive glance around, he crawled in after her.

Sucking a finger where a thorn had punctured the skin, he surveyed what he knew they would find: a ring of open space around the ancient trunk. The ground was covered with years of accumulated needles making a springy, though somewhat prickly, bed. The entry he had forced closed in upon itself as the tree sought its natural shape. Jon caught a glimpse of the flattened grass where they had knelt at the opening. Too tired to do anything about it, he convinced himself that it, too, would spring back.

Shondral spread their blankets and was asleep before her head touched the ground. Jon sprawled beside her, his back to the outer wall. He breathed the sweet smell of her hair and fell slept as he exhaled.

***

Jon woke with the distinct sensation that he was being watched. Panic tightened his gut and jerked his mind to wakefulness. He opened his eyes the barest slit. Murky gloom blurred any details. His heart thudded in his chest; it would give him away to whoever or whatever was there with him.

"Are you awake?" Shondral whispered.

Shondral's voice brought reality crashing back into place. "What time is it?" he mumbled, turning on his side. He needed a moment to recover from his disorientation.

"Don't know. I've only just woke, myself." She peered at the wall of their shelter. "It's hard to tell from in here."

Jon stretched and winced as every muscle in his body clamoured for attention. Miserable, he sat up to massage his abused feet. He caught himself sinking into a morose, self-pitying state of mind and mentally kicked himself. That was the last thing they needed. He forced his attention to more practical things.

"We'll travel under cover of darkness until we're on the other side of the lake." Jon did not know if they were being pursued but it would be senseless to take unnecessary risks.

As they shared a meal of bread and dried fruit, Shondral put her hand lightly on Jon's arm and looked into his eyes. "Maybe someone thinks we're from a rich family just disguised to look poor, or maybe that gypsy woman has given us delusions of high adventure, or maybe we secretly want to create our very own event for the Book." Even a single line in the Master Historian Book was a thing to be coveted. It was where only the very best reports from each year were lovingly transcribed by only the very best scribes. To have a story in the Book was every Historian's dream.

"Or maybe our beloved fellow Apprentices are playing a huge practical joke on us," Jon joined in, "or maybe we've just made this whole thing up so we can go for a great long hike and camp in luxury." He gazed wide-eyed around their primitive shelter. "Or maybe..." He faltered as her grip on his arm tightened. She had not been trying to cheer him up.

"Because if none of these are true," Shondral's eyes bored into his, "the possibilities are very

59

scary." She had had a little time to think before Jon woke; things might not be quite as unlikely as she had first thought.

"We've come to someone's attention, that's certain," she continued. "One day we're talking about patterns you've seen. The next, we visit a gypsy and are ambushed on the way home, and then we find our dorm is watched. Now we're running. I'm trying very hard to understand this."

He shrugged. "We don't know who's chasing us or what they want. And I, for one, am not inclined to confront him or her or them until we do. They might not even be chasing the right people."

There was less light now than when they woke. While they rolled blankets and prepared to continue on their journey, Jon asked the question he had been avoiding. "Those scary possibilities, Shondral, what scary possibilities?"

"It's just a wild idea, concocted out of my overheated brain last night." Jon did not like the sound of that. Shondral had very good ideas.

"It's just that the timing is so weird." Shondral had set the pieces of Jon's dilemma side by side with her brother's. The connection was terrifyingly easy. "Two years ago Milo made this... this thing. Two years ago, this pattern of yours began."

"What thing?" Jon asked. From the look on Shondral's face, he wondered if he really wanted to know. *But how bad could it be?* He took her hand in his.

Shondral gazed at his fingers entwined with hers. There was nothing for it; she had to tell him. It could be critical. It could be related to what was

60

happening to them. "I've told you about my brother," she began, "but I know I never told you this story. I wanted you to meet Milo face to face, to form your own opinion of him."

Jon urged her on with a gentle squeeze.

"Just over two years ago, there was another," she hesitated, "incident in Morbella. The village elders dismissed it as a prank, just something to get attention; he was only thirteen at the time. But Milo insists that it's true and I can't help but believe him. He's my brother and I know him. He couldn't have invented something like this." Her voice strengthened as her resolve grew to tell Jon everything.

"It was early spring, about this time of the year. He was carving a doll—a gift for one of the girls in the village. Annie, I think her name was. He was completely in love with her." She smiled. "His work is really quite lifelike and he would go up into the hills whenever he was making something special; he claimed that he needed the peace and quiet to concentrate. Anyway, he was putting the finishing touches on the carving when he heard noises down the hillside from where he was working. He crawled over to investigate and saw Annie with his best friend. The girl must have sensed she was being watched and opened her eyes to give Milo a sneering leer before she turned her full attention back to her latest conquest."

Jon had the sinking sensation that Shondral had not understood his puzzle. How could this little love story, mildly tragic though it was, possibly relate to communes gone missing, weird illnesses, and that barbaric event? But Shondral was obviously distressed, so he decided to wait until later to lecture her on the finer points of listening.

"He was hurt and furious," Shondral continued, "and in his anger, he somehow crushed the carving to dust with his bare hands. He said that all of a sudden, his head felt as though hot pins were trying to get out and he had to wipe away tears of pain in order to see the horror of what was happening in front of him." She looked Jon straight in the eyes. "The pile of wood dust that had been his carving began to reform itself and to grow larger," she paused, "and came to life.

"It didn't speak to him before it disappeared into the woods, but it glared at him. Milo saw his own rage and betrayal of a moment before reflected back at him, and he saw intelligence and cunning." She bit her lower lip. "He wakes up at night screaming, covered in sweat. He says the creature that he made torments him in his sleep. We've tried everything to help him; the villagers think he's mad."

Jon was speechless. Should he laugh? Should he congratulate her? Should he suggest ways to make it a better story? Or should he be somewhat miffed that she had so completely ignored his own anxiety? No. Shondral was not like that. It was a wild tale, as wild as any that he had heard, but he believed that Shondral believed. The gnawing feeling that something was wrong would not go away. He struggled to bring Milo's story into that reality. He struggled—and failed. But what he did know with utter certainty was that he would help his friend understand what had happened to her brother. "Shondral, we'll figure it out, whatever it is."

Even in the dim light, Jon could not mistake the look of relief on Shondral's face. Without thinking, he pressed her hand to his lips. Their eyes met for a brief moment, dark and wide. *Slow down, boy.* "We have to get moving," he mumbled, and turned to push aside the thick screen of riabad branches.

Jon motioned for Shondral to remain within the secrecy of the riabad while he crept out to scrutinise the trail. He studied the path ahead of them and back the way they had come, and he studied the forest floor for a fifty-foot radius around their shelter. There was just enough light for him to be fairly certain that nothing had come near since their arrival that morning.

Shondral considered their plight while she waited for Jon to return. Maybe Jon could be practical when he needed to be. She looked around their little enclosure. Yes, he definitely had a practical side. Jon's stories of his childhood on the docks should have given her enough clues to have realised this, but they had simply never found themselves in a situation where his survival skills were needed. She hoped they would be enough to get them to her brother.

She and Jon had known each other for three years, since their Apprenticeship began. Their backgrounds were so different: he, from the busy port town of Alba; and she, from one of the tiny hamlets in the Kobaska Hills. Until now, she had never thought much about how they liked the same things and shared the same dreams. He could easily slide away from the friendship that had grown between them. She was taking a terrible risk. Could he open his mind to what screamed of fabrication? The only thing she had found that even remotely resembled what had happened to her brother was that little snippet of verse. She reached into her pocket and felt it there where she had stuffed it two nights ago. Scant proof that Milo was not the first to have done such a thing.

But there was something else that bothered her, she could tell by the tension in her shoulder blades. It was not the long hike to her home that troubled her; after all, she had made the trip several times before, and it was not the ongoing mystery of what had happened to Milo. This was a new sense of unease that had begun sometime during last night's blind run. At first, she had dismissed it as residue from the terror of their ambush and the discovery of watchers at their dormitory. The unease, however, had not abated after the day's rest. Irritated with herself, she shrugged it off once again. All they could do right now was to reach Morbella as quickly as possible.

She knew that Jon had not believed a word of Milo's story. It did not really surprise her; it sounded unbelievable even to her. What did surprise her was Jon's instant and total support. He was a true friend, and maybe more than a friend. The thought both warmed and alarmed her. Did she even think of Jon romantically? Her thoughts were much too muddled to consider this new wrinkle. It would have to wait.

At Jon's soft call, she emerged from the riabad's closeness and they continued up the darkening trail.

The familiar pine and spruce trees soon lost all definition but for the jagged outline of their top boughs against the deep purple of the sky. A light breeze stirred their travel cloaks as they paused for a sip of water and, for a moment, they breathed the cool, fragrant air of the forest. They continued on, the fleeting moment of peace dissipating into the night.

The protective screen of tall trees gave way to lower shrubs that were in turn replaced by tall grasses. The trail relentlessly curved toward the solitary bridge that spanned the broad, frigid waters of the River Quiem. The Western Bridge gave access to the flat and easily travelled road that connected Alba to Mriss and other locations inland. Although the river was the more direct route to the port-town, it descended a series of unnavigable steps on its way to the Sea. It could be crossed at two fords, but only when it had not rained for weeks; that particular circumstance would not likely occur until late summer. The road that went from Alba to Ked would take them too far out of their way. Notwithstanding all the good reasons in the world, Jon fervently wished they could be spared the exposed bridge crossing—it was the perfect place for a trap.

He led Shondral off the path to where they could see the lanterns at either end of the wooden structure. Dimly visible on the far side of the river was the stone building that housed the watchman who would emerge from his warm refuge, lantern in hand, and collect the crossing toll from them. All the while, Jon and Shondral would be visible to anyone within two hundred yards.

Their eyes strained to penetrate the inky shadows. The low hanging boughs made it impossible to see any distance into the forest. An attack could come from behind any one of a hundred trees on either bank.

Jon racked his brain for a way around their predicament. Traffic was non-existent at this time of night and they could not afford the time to wait for a group of travellers to use as cover. Perhaps instead of crossing over the river, they could cross *on* the river.

Shondral listened to his idea, excited at first, and then frowned. "If they're watching from the forest, they could see us in the water as easily as on the bridge. We'd sail right into their arms and even the watchman would hear nothing."

Shondral proposed an idea of her own.

Risky, but they would try it. They backtracked then cut cross-country to intersect the road beyond a curve that hid the bridge from view. Within the cover of the trees, they fashioned crude disguises— a little mud here and there to darken faces and hands, some padding on Jon's shoulders, and a bundle for Shondral to carry. With the dark night and a little luck, they would pass for a broad-shouldered farmer, somewhat stooped from labouring in the fields, with his wife and child on their way home. Hoods up, they stepped onto the road.

Jon supported Shondral with a hand under her elbow; in the other hand he carried their packs. He prayed the clothing stuffed in his tunic would not loosen. He flinched when their boots struck the wooden planks of the bridge, incredibly loud after their silent padding along the forest trail. If anyone were watching, they would surely investigate.

A yellow rectangle of light briefly framed the watchman as he came out to perform his duties. Jon waved amiably at him. On a lonely night like this, he would want to chat. Jon resolved to talk a little— it would seem odd not to—then plead the little one's health in the night air and that they could reach shelter within the hour if they did not tarry long. He whispered his intention to Shondral who merely raised the blanket a little higher over her 'little one's' face.

"Hoy, watchman, not much traffic tonight!" Jon's voice sounded as unnatural as his footfalls. But why would a bridge sentry think anything was awry? His livelihood depended on travellers using the bridge.

The watchman waited in the lamplight for them. "Hoy, travellers," he hailed them, "you be on the road late. Bandits and other unsavoury sorts ha' been seen hereabouts."

"Aye, watchman," Jon was at the edge of the lamp's glow but Shondral remained beyond the circle of light. "We tarried overlong at the wife's family, what with doting over the little one and catchin' up on the news..." He lifted his eyes skyward in the universal sign of patient suffering.

67

The watchman nodded in sympathy. He peered through the gloom at Shondral. "The wee one sleeps?"

Shondral continued to rock back and forth soothing the child. "Only just," she whispered. "She's had a busy visit, poor thing."

He turned back to Jon. "There be the small matter of the toll, sir, for you and your family."

Jon paled beneath the grime on his face. He could not recall if he had his pouch handy and he was reluctant to fumble about and possibly dislodge his 'shoulders.'

"Here, my husband." Shondral extended a closed fist towards him, eyes downcast.

The watchman satisfied himself that they had given him the correct amount, then offered the comfort of his fire for a brief respite and perhaps a cup of something to keep the night's chill at bay.

"We thank you for your kindness, but I fear to be on the road any longer than the hour to reach the first farmhouse in our Group." Jon counted on the difficulty of the watchman knowing every family in the large Groups. The greater number of people not only provided the various talents required for survival but also a certain amount of anonymity.

"You'd best be off, then." The watchman's disappointment was clear in his rough voice. He shuffled to the little building with its inviting glow and disappeared inside.

Jon and Shondral hurried along the road a short distance before melting back into the forest. They stopped to brush the dirt from their hands and faces, and to repack their things for the night's walk.

Jon gave her a quick hug. "Thanks for your quick thinking with the money. You're a marvel, you are. Have you ever considered the theatre?"

Shondral chuckled under her breath. "We do make a good team, don't we?"

Jon liked the sound of that very much.

Still too close to the bridge for comfort, they spared no more time to enjoy the success of their ploy and continued on at a brisk pace. The terrain sloped gently and in the distance they could see the inviting glimmer of the first homesteads. The flat, workable land suitable for farming gave little cover and they decided to forego rest stops; they must reach the next bridge at Lake Thungal by dawn.

The level path and their youthful resilience gave them the stamina to reach their goal with time to spare. Jon hunkered down, easing his back and legs. "The Eastern Bridge gets busy at daylight. We'll cross then."

***

It moved out in gradually widening circles, tireless in its mission. It picked up their scent with ease. Though more than half a day old, it was fresh to a creature designed for superior hunting and killing skills. Sure of its direction, it advanced with great speed.

***

They rested in the stunted wood that ran along the top of the ravine. From this vantage point, they commanded a view of the bridge, the river, and the road in either direction. Shondral knew that if they stood and moved a few steps away from the trees, they would see Lake Thungal and the town. With a minimum of discussion, they decided to have a look.

The River Quiem spilled into Lake Thungal a long stone's throw downstream and, at their conjunction, was Mriss. The opalescence of pre-dawn caressed the town in a hazy light so that it seemed to float above the surface of the Lake. The dwellings were stacked like many-coloured pancakes and garnished the lake like a water lily unfolding its petals.

Jon sighed.

"It does that to me too," Shondral said. "Every time." She went on to explain that the beautiful design was not for aesthetic reasons but rather to make the best use of the precious barbar foundation resting on the lakebed. The colossal barbar trees were as close to rock as a living thing could be. To fell one took many days' labour with tools edged in glittering diamond. It was then rolled to the river and, supported by dozens of air-filled bladders, the barbar floated. Jagged hooks on the ends of wrist-thick rope were wedged into splits in the bark and with the help of the River's current, four barges managed to cajole and guide this single tree downstream to Mriss. The log was then manoeuvred into position, rope looped around it every few feet, and lowered to the Lake's shallow bottom. Young swimmers descended to the barbar with planks of wood specially treated to survive in the water. They secured one end to the barbar and the other end to a previously deployed barbar. When several such planks were in place, the structure formed an extremely solid surface upon which the substructure of Mriss could be constructed. A few easily retractable bridges connected the town to the shore. The people of Mriss were safe from any land dweller, human or beast.

Reluctantly, Jon and Shondral turned away from the spectacle and crawled back into the undergrowth. As they waited for the traffic on the bridge to thicken, Shondral told Jon of her growing sense of unease, of her certainty that they had fooled no one but the watchman, and that they were being followed regardless of their cleverness. She had no facts to explain it, but something was not right.

"It's just the stress of this whole weird thing, Shonny. And you're worried about Milo." Jon had begun to feel exhilarated by their flight; it had become a grand adventure. But he would remain extra vigilant, just in case. Even as he scanned the countryside, Shondral gripped his arm, terror in her eyes.

She sprang to her feet and plunged down the hillside. "Come on!" she screamed. Panic squeezed Shondral's heart; she forced her legs to move faster as Jon caught up with her. They burst onto the road and raced for the bridge. A startled duck resting on the bank screamed loudly at their impudence and encouraged the rest of its flock to do the same. The ruckus spread like wildfire.

The keenest farmers already guided their livestock and laden wagons across the bridge. Jon and Shondral pushed past horses and cattle and sheep and goats, wreaking havoc among them. The farmhands tried in vain to calm their beasts and flung angry curses at the two youths.

The bridge's watchman had a glint of laughter in his eyes as he took Jon's money and surveyed the chaos around him. "Good entertainment on a fine morning, this." He winked at Shondral, then hurried to collect the toll from the next, less-than-happy customer.

Gasping for breath, Jon turned and stared at the area where they had broken cover. A black head swayed back and forth sniffing the air, then it was gone. "Your special sense," Jon managed, his eyes locked on the spot where the thing had vanished, "I don't for the life of me know how it works, but I'm very glad it does."

They rested on a convenient boulder by the roadside. Jon unslung the water flask from his pack. Shondral's hand trembled as she brought it to her lips and most of it dribbled down her chin. With the cleanest part of his sleeve, Jon gently wiped her face. She did not seem to notice.

"We must travel as fast and as far as we can while it remains trapped on the other side," Shondral said in a low voice, her eyes unfocused. Neither of them voiced the possibility that it might be able to swim. Shondral untied her money pouch from where she had concealed it around her waist and handed it to him. "You're the best haggler between us. Buy us some horses and whatever supplies we need. I think I'll just sit here for a minute."

He weighed the pouch in his hand; realisation dawned on him. "Shondral!" he exclaimed. "I can't let you do this! This is everything you have!" He lowered his voice, "And what are you doing carrying this much money, anyway?" Dazed, he saw his friend throwing away her dreams. Her family would never be able to earn enough to allow her to return to the School, at least not in the next year.

"I thought we might need it and we can re-sell the horses later. Anyway, it won't matter if we can't outrun that, that...," her already pale face blanched, "whatever that is."

The truth of what she said broke through his dismay. He squared his shoulders, put on his best smile, and strolled towards the ever-growing crowd on its way to market. In short order, he convinced a horse trader of the advantages of selling his poor beasts and tack now rather than risking no sale at all, what with the stiff competition and all at the market proper. Surely, his valuable time would be better spent returning to his farm, and with money in his pocket. Pointing out any real flaws, and some imaginary ones, Jon brought the price down to a more reasonable level even though the horse trader must have somehow known he was in a hurry and took unfair advantage. Perhaps to make up for this, the trader helped Jon to saddle the horses and, noticing that Jon did not have much experience with horses, gave him a few welcome tips on their proper care and feeding. After thanking him, Jon procured bread, apples, a wheel of yellow cheese, and oats from another of the passing farmers.

He led the horses to where Shondral sat. Her face was less pale and she rose on steady legs at Jon's approach. They stuffed the food in their packs, mounted their transportation, and continued north and east towards Shondral's home.

***

Malissa's assassin watched its quarry slip away. Unable to feel frustration, or much of anything at all for that matter, it began to search for suitable wood from which it could construct a small raft. Clutching the bundle effortlessly in long black arms, it slunk around a bend, safe from prying eyes. Before the burning orb in the sky reached its zenith, a crude raft was launched upstream so that its passenger merely guided it across the current. It leapt into the shallows; only the deep water was deadly.

No one paid the least attention to the child's raft that floated under the Eastern Bridge a few moments later.

***

Neither Jon nor Shondral had much riding experience and for most of the morning, they tried to find more comfortable positions in their saddles. However painful, they rode steadily and stopped only to let the horses drink from the streams that sometimes skirted the road and to let them sample the succulent spring grasses that flourished on the muddy banks. Jon and Shondral took advantage of these short breaks to stretch cramped muscles and relieve abused posteriors.

If they maintained this pace, allowing their mounts to rest periodically, Shondral estimated they would reach Camelia by noon the following day. After that, it was only another three hours to Morbella. Grimly determined, they continued with visions of a hot soak at the end of their journey.

Fortunately, the road was well maintained by the farmers and townspeople. They used it regularly for visiting family and friends, and for taking produce and livestock to market. Ked in the north and Mriss in the south competed for the farmers' and hunters' money. During the harvest festivals, these communities outshone even the bustling port-town of Alba with music and dancing, plays and juggling acts, and, of course, copious quantities of food and drink.

Shondral had never been permitted to attend; her mother stood firm declaring that she was too young, that she would get robbed or hurt or worse. It was no place for an unaccompanied young lady. "That's it!" Shondral exclaimed.

"That's what?" Jon wondered.

"You could take me. She wouldn't have any worries then," she bit her lip, eyeing Jon's disreputable-looking garb, "or not as many."

Perplexed, Jon waited for her to explain what she was on about.

With growing excitement, Shondral told him about the harvest festivals and how she was never allowed to go and how if he took her, she would finally get to see what all the fuss was about.

She wants me to take her to a party? "Sure. Whenever you want," Jon agreed.

Shondral laughed in delight, her face radiant in the clear spring sunshine.

Her joy did strange things to Jon's insides, like something warm and golden was coursing through him. Basking in the glow of her pleasure, he reached over to touch the fiery hair flowing down her back. Overbalancing, he barely caught himself, one hand on the pommel and the other scrabbling for purchase on his horse's belly.

Shondral's flicker of worry transformed into a strangled giggle and then outright laughter. His upside-down face turned crimson and she laughed all the harder.

He awkwardly righted himself and gave her his best indignant glare. But her laughter was contagious and he could not resist joining in. *Gods, I'm in love with her.* He busied himself re-tying his dishevelled hair, hoping that his flushed face masked his expression.

Close to midday, they reached what the locals called the main fork in the road, which branched north-west to Ked and north-east to the Kobaska Hills. In reality, it wasn't so much a fork as that the main road continued on level and clear, and their route sort of angled off into the woods and became immediately more rugged. They would have to keep their horses to a walk, for fear of damaging a leg. Jon thought again about the hot bath at the end of their journey and added a large meal to the list.

They met fewer and fewer travellers as the day progressed and by late afternoon they were alone. Shondral had said little since the last break and now she looked at Jon with renewed urgency. "Do you think the horses are fit enough to travel through the night?"

"They can handle it," he answered, "but I'm not sure *I* can." He grimaced, shifting his weight yet again. "But I will." By the tone of her voice, he

knew she must sense something and he was not ever going to ignore her instincts.

He studied the gap between the trees that was laughingly called a road. Some while back it had narrowed even more so that they now rode in single file with Shondral in the lead, her hair a warm beacon in the growing gloom. The way was clear, though, and their horses were fine. He was glad he had spent a little extra money on oats; there was no time, now, to allow them to graze.

Dusk was punctuated by the harsh cries of predatory birds, their uncanny vision seeking out small rodents and snakes. An occasional howl in the distance sent chills down Jon's spine and he drew his cloak tightly around his body and raised the hood. He tried humming a cheery tune to keep his mind off what lurked beyond his vision but even that small vibration jarred his aching body.

His nerves were wearing thin from the interminable ride and he hurt in places he did not know that he could hurt. The minuscule relief during their earlier respites had lost any merit long ago. In fact, he began to dread dismounting because then he would only have to climb back on again.

The temperature began to drop and the upper boughs of the trees creaked ominously. He scanned the narrow strip of sky visible between the towering trees and saw the stars disappearing one by one. The night sunk deeper in gloom and the oppression of the impending storm snuffed out the scurry and rustle of the woodland creatures.

Even though he expected it, the first cold slap of rain was the final insult. At least the horses did not seem to mind the rain; he guessed it cooled them. But neither he nor Shondral had the wherewithal to walk beside them and soothe them during a storm. When the first flash of lightning struck, Jon's mount bounced sideways then surged headlong in a panicked gallop. Jon frantically pulled on the reins but he could not even slow the spooked mare. A quick glance when the next blaze lit the path showed Shondral's mount gaining ground ahead of him and her back bent low over her horse's neck.

He wrapped the reins tighter around his fists and shoved his face into his horse's mane. His legs ached and everything inside him felt like it had been jarred loose and scrambled. It was all he could do to hold on.

He forced his head up at another of the incessant flashes—it was not as bright. As it faded, he saw Shondral's mount hurdle a fallen branch in the path, and watched in dream-like horror as she was thrown into the cruel arms of the forest.

A cry ripped from his throat, so fierce that it broke through the mindless terror of his frothing animal and the horse slowed. Jon leapt down before it had come to a complete stop and charged through the brush. He frantically called her name, not feeling the thorns that tore at him. A distant bolt of lightning briefly revealed a pale shape, then it was gone. He locked the position in his mind and cut through the distance like a madman.

Shondral lay unmoving with her back to him. The throw had wedged her between the broad trunk of a tree and a moss-covered boulder. The pale shape he had seen was her hand flung out behind her. Weak with fear, he knelt beside her head and, bending close, he heard her softly gasp. She was alive. In some remote place in his mind, he tasted the salty tears that mingled with the rain on his face.

With a cold efficiency he did not know he had, he checked her for signs of broken bones. His inexperienced hands finding none, he gently raised her leg that was closest to the ground and stuffed his cloak beneath it. Rushing back around, he lifted her just enough to slide her out from between the tree and the rock.

Jon laid her on the soggy, uneven ground only now seeing the blood matting her hair. He tore a sleeve from his shirt, stanched the wound, and bound it as best he could. He scrambled back to the trail willing his horse to be there. Despair gripped his heart: the flash of lightning that had helped him to find Shondral had also lost him his mare.

He returned to Shondral and cradled her in his arms. He would carry her to Camelia; it could not be far after their headlong flight.

The night stretched endlessly. The footing was treacherous on the muddy path and each step sent pinpricks of pain shooting up his legs. Shondral struggled feebly in his leaden arms and he almost lost his hold on her. Enraged at his weakness, he shook his head and took a deep breath, opening his mouth wide to catch the few drops of water that dripped from the boughs above his head.

A movement on the trail ahead jarred him to uncanny clarity. His leg muscles knotted in agony as he lowered Shondral to the side of the path and with as much stealth as he could muster, he approached the direction of the motion.

Cold dread descended upon him: what if this was a ploy to make him leave Shondral alone, unprotected, while he sought invisible attackers? Torn by indecision, he threw himself forward.

The newly frightened mare backed a few paces. His voice no more than a croaking whisper, Jon soothed the creature with nonsense mumbling and approached her one slow, shaky step at a time. She remained wary at first, then nuzzled his palm searching for oats. Still mumbling words of comfort, Jon gathered up the reins and led her back to where Shondral lay.

He draped Shondral's limp form across the horse's neck and climbed into the saddle behind her. Jon gathered her in his arms and used his knees to prod the horse to a slow walk.

After what seemed liked hours, the mare turned abruptly from the path and Jon imagined he saw a laneway; he no longer trusted his exhausted brain to distinguish between dream and reality. His horse, however, needed no encouragement to proceed into the illusory yard, the scent of hay an irresistible lure.

A light sprang from somewhere as other animals snuffled and called to the stranger in their midst. A man in a nightshirt flung open the door of a modest cottage, a woman peering around him. He squinted for a moment into the darkness then rushed out in his slippers to take Shondral from Jon's arms. Jon simply sat there and watched him carry her away.

"Come, boy," the woman called from the doorway, "tend to your horse." She pointed vaguely behind the house, turned, and hurried after the man.

Jon did as he was told and guided the mare towards a bulky outbuilding that had to be the barn. He absently noted that dawn was imminent.

"Lightning," he murmured, "that's what I'll call you." He stroked the exhausted mare and eased the saddle from her back. He found food and water and, after a cursory brushing, turned towards the barn door and recognised Shondral's horse two stalls down. These people, whoever they were, had had a busy night. He secured the door and limped, head down, to the house.

The man who had lifted Shondral from his arms nearly bowled him over in the doorway. Muttering an apology, he continued in haste across the yard. Jon poked his head inside and was momentarily dazzled by the light.

"Fetch the hot water from the stove," the woman commanded.

Jon let his eyes adjust for a moment before going any further into the house. Shondral lay on a cot before the fireplace and the woman was hunched over her. He took a step towards them then remembered the woman's request. Jon examined the room that extended the entire length of the cottage and spied a wood stove on the opposite wall. He shuffled over and, using the heavy gloves that hung nearby, carried the steaming kettle to the woman's side and set it down on the stone floor. She ladled a little into the bowl she had in her hand and pungent odours filled the air.

The darkness had obscured the rents in Shondral's clothing. She had hurtled through the thorny brush that lined the path and though it had diminished the force of her landing and perhaps even saved her life, it had exacted a price. The woman had removed Shondral's boots and cloak, and had cut open one pant leg. Jon gasped at the lacerations and ugly bruises.

"These are not deep or infected." The woman's diagnosis offered no comfort at the sight of her torn body. "But be careful not to move her head." She handed him a knife. He took a deep breath to steady his nerves and began slicing Shondral's other pant leg.

They worked silently until the woman was satisfied that all the wounds had been cleaned and protected. While she covered Shondral in soft linen and placed a light blanket over her, Jon banked the fire.

"We can do no more for her until Wil gets back with our healer." She drew him over to the table. "Now, young man, we shall have a look at you."

Jon suffered her ministrations in a daze, vaguely noticing how her eyes sparkled in the firelight and that she was older than her voice had led him to believe. She handed him a cup of steaming broth and watched while he drank it down. It relieved the emptiness in his stomach and radiated well-being down his arms and legs. He felt knots of tension unravel. She looked intently at his eyes and refilled the cup.

"Ma'am!" With a jolt, he realised he did not know her name. "Please forgive my manners." She smiled, now looking much younger than her silver hair implied. "My name is Jon Montrai and my companion..."

"Yes, yes, the young Laracyl girl," she interrupted. "We in the hills come to know each other." She cast a worried glance in Shondral's direction.

Jon learned that his benefactors were Wil and Myrna Thornberry, retired from Dryx herding. The Dryx, he knew from Shondral, were the mainstay of the Hills. Highly valued for their rich milk, they were no less valued for their fine, dense wool. Now, the Thornberrys were sought for the medicinal herbs that Wil grew and for the exquisite Dryxal blankets that Myrna wove. She told him about the herbs in the broth that he drank and about the herbs she had used on Shondral's injuries.

Shondral had told him about the closeness of the communities and how they looked after each other. This elderly couple would care for Shondral as though she was their own daughter.

Footsteps crossing the yard brought conversation to a halt. Wil and another man bustled through the door and the tall, thin stranger strode immediately to Shondral's cot.

Wil placed a reassuring hand on Jon's shoulder. "Don't fret, lad," he murmured. "Our young Elios is the finest healer there is."

The three fell silent, not wishing to disturb Elios' work. He called for hot water, which Myrna had foreseen. From his pouch, he extracted a delicate blade with which he deftly trimmed the blood-crusted hair from Shondral's head wound. He probed and prodded her scalp. Satisfied, he cleaned and dressed the gash.

When he joined them at last, he asked Jon for details of the accident. The Thornberrys listened with equal parts of concern and compassion.

"The blow was not severe, but coupled with the pain of her abrasions, the fright of such an accident, and the distance you had to travel to bring her here, she may remain unconscious for a while yet. When she wakes, give her some of your wonderful broth, Myrna; she will have the worst headache of her life." His gaze met Jon's. "We are indebted to you." He rose, bowed briefly, and left them.

Myrna busied herself in the kitchen portion of the great room and had breakfast in front of them before Ord had risen much further. There was early fruit grown in nearby fields, a steaming stack of what looked like bread, and more of Myrna's hot broth. Jon observed that his hosts poured some type of yellow syrup on their bread. He ventured to try some. It was like drops of sweet light expanding to fill his senses. When he reluctantly swallowed, he found their amused expressions on him.

"First taste of Dryxal cream, eh boy? I gather you like it." Wil clapped him on the back, immediately regretting it as Jon struggled not to wince through his smile.

Between mouthfuls, his host told him of the Dryx, the animal that thrived only in the Kobaska Hills. "They graze on the sweetest clover, high in the meadows. Them what know say that the conditions in our Hills are repeated nowhere else on all of Méadhon." He glanced at his wife for confirmation.

"That's true," she said, "and it is from the wool of the Dryx that we make yarn light as down and warm as a summer day." Myrna looked toward Shondral's sleeping form. "Our young lass is wrapped in the very best Méadhon has to offer."

With a guilty start, Jon realised that he had not thought of Shondral for some time. His appetite vanished. Heedless of the Thornberrys' counsel and of his own common sense, he appointed himself to watch over her and positioned an armchair to one side of the hearth. The fire lulled him and the soft cushions embraced his aching body, and he soon succumbed to his own exhaustion.

***

Shondral sipped from the cup that Myrna held to her lips, and listened to the older woman's soothing voice as she related all that had happened. It was this low murmur that roused Jon from dreams of futile escape; he could never quite see who or what hunted him, only that it was relentless and steadily gained on him.

Shondral wavered in and out of focus as though she was part of his dreamscape. He savagely rubbed his eyes with the heels of his hands and pushed himself out of his chair to kneel by her side.

"Shondral." No sound came out, only the shape of her name on his lips. She smiled at him—not a laughing smile this time but a smile that caused those strange and wonderful things to happen to his stomach again.

Myrna insinuated the cup of broth between them and Shondral dutifully drank the remainder of the now cool liquid. Her blinks grew slower until her eyes refused to stay open, and she sank into a deep, restful sleep. Jon tenderly arrayed the Dryxal blanket over her.

Wil gestured him to the door. "We'll look after you now." Without further explanation, he descended the steps, crossed the yard, and headed cross-country on a much-used path. Jon looked at Myrna who only smiled encouragement and turned back to her work. Resigned to the obligations of a guest, Jon stuffed his feet into his boots and limped after his host.

Jon clenched his teeth; the exertion of the previous night had taken its toll. His shoulders and arms throbbed with each heartbeat, his back ached, and his legs twinged with every step. To help take his mind off his misery, he hailed Wil who had stopped to admire a cluster of fuchsia Lady's Slippers.

"Just look at them, Jon. A true marvel. So delicate and so strong." Wil sighed contentedly and continued along the path which had grown wide enough for Jon to walk beside him.

"Your wife tells me that you're an expert in herb lore."

Wil's face broke into a wide smile. "Want to get me talkin', eh?" He took a deep breath, and proceeded to astound Jon with a profuse and detailed knowledge of dozens of herbs that he used in medicinal compounds.

He explained the properties of aloe and camphor, burnet and germander; the benefits of horehound; and the best growing condition for lamb's ears, southernwood, and tansy.

"I'll tell you about the other eight hundred or so on our way home." He shot a sideways glance at Jon and stifled a chortle at the astonishment on his face. Quite pleased with himself, Wil was almost disappointed that they had arrived.

Jon's attention had been wholly taken with absorbing Wil's words and putting one foot in front of the other. Now that they had stopped, he could spare a little energy for his surroundings. The hamlet of Camelia rose before him, built into the gentle curve of a low hill. Wil followed his gaze. "This way, everyone has a view," he chuckled, and led Jon along a well-trimmed hedge and into a squat building.

Heat and steam overwhelmed Jon (and what was that awful smell!). His senses reeled and he staggered into the wall beside him. He had read about hot springs at the School and Shondral had mentioned them once or twice, but that in no way prepared him for this onslaught on his senses.

Wil disappeared around a corner. Jon cast a yearning glance towards the door and fresh air, and stumbled after him. He entered a larger chamber and the air cleared somewhat but swirls of hot mist still obscured his vision so that he could not make out any details.

"Ho, Jon," Wil's voice called from somewhere to his left. "Over here."

He groped his way toward the sound. Forms gradually emerged and he recognised Wil's broad shoulders among them.

"Gentlemen," he was saying, "allow me to introduce you to young Jon Montrai from Alba." The gathered men murmured greetings. "Through great difficulty and self-sacrifice, he brought a wounded Morbellan girl to my door just before dawn this morning."

Jon attempted to retreat into the mist, only to back into more men who had collected behind him.

Wil had an audience and was thoroughly enjoying himself. He related a colourful, and occasionally embellished, version of what had happened and ended with seeking their permission for Jon to bathe. A low rumble of assent reverberated in the hollow chamber and the men dispersed as silently as they had arrived.

"I knew they would agree. We haven't had a good adventure in a long while." Wil guided him to a small room and showed him where to put his clothes.

Overcoming strangeness, which he seemed to be doing a lot lately, Jon mustered. "What happens now?" Wil guffawed. Jon guessed he did that a lot.

"Why, we shall set the healing waters of the earth to your sore and abused body. Just leave your clothes and boots here." He pointed to a shelf. When they were ready, he escorted Jon to the edge of a pool and descended a series of broad steps. "It's a little warm at first."

Eyeing the thick tendrils of steam rising off the water, Jon was not so sure. But was this not, after all, one of the things that he had promised himself at the end of their interminable ride? He put his right foot in the water. His toes curled involuntarily; he was being boiled alive! Mercifully, it lasted only a few seconds then receded to merely very, very hot.

Step by slow step, he immersed himself to the waist and followed Wil's back through a low tunnel. The cloying odour grew more potent and Jon breathed through his mouth. He reached out to steady himself on the uneven floor and touched warm rock. The tunnel continued for some dozen feet before it opened into a natural cave.

Lamps had been placed around the roughly oval cavern and the yellow light danced on glistening walls. Steam swirled in occasional wisps and, to Jon's immense relief, the smell became more tolerable.

Crude benches had been carved into the rock just above the water level and as he watched, a young boy scrambled up to sit there, legs dangling. Men stood near or sat on these benches relaxing or chatting, and off to one side, a small group copied the movements of a wiry youth who stood facing them. It resembled a slow dance.

The young man detached himself from the others and came over to them. Introduced as Jikal, he greeted Mr. Thornberry and was delighted to meet Jon. Wil's tale had already spread throughout the complex. It became apparent that Jon was to join what at closer inspection was a drill on muscle limbering exercises. Why had Thornberry inflicted this on him? He sought out his host's face but saw only the ever-present smile.

Under Jikal's watchful eye, Jon leaned facing a smoother section of wall and slowly stretched one leg out behind him. As he fully expected, his muscles screamed at this affront, but once he relaxed it again, the pain was gone. Incredulous, he stretched the other leg; his good fortune held. It's the third wonder today, he marvelled: first, the Dryxal cream, then Shondral's face, and now this.

Wil surreptitiously watched his young charge and was quite pleased at the amazement on Jon's face. He turned to old Jake to discuss the trouble he was having with his basil.

Jon's arms were next. He grasped his hands behind his back and raised them ever so slightly. His tormented shoulders threatened to separate from the rest of his body but when he lowered his hands again, they felt wonderful. Next, Jikal supported him as be bent his knee while he kept his upper leg perpendicular to the floor. The muscles of his thigh strained to accommodate this new abuse. When he lowered his foot, the aching knot was released into the healing waters.

Jikal demonstrated back movements and Jon's attention was completely absorbed; he wanted to remember every step. Jikal seemed pleased with his rapt student and spent much time going over the stretches.

"How does the water influence the effect of the motions?" Jon asked, hoping it was not rude to do so. Jikal spoke in a low voice so as not to disturb the others. The waters, he explained, bubbled out of the earth here in Camelia and in several other places along the hills that stretched to the Sgeir Range in the north. Jon nodded; he had studied Méadhon's geography.

"There are minerals dissolved in the water," Jikal continued, "which help to re-balance the body. Stretching weary muscles while in the water enhances the absorption. Both are useful separately, but more powerful together."

"The smell," Jon began, making a face.

Jikal smiled. "You get used to it. It is from one of the minerals that has other properties besides healing."

Jon laughed aloud. He felt wonderful. Jikal's eyes danced, proud of his work.

"Come, lad," Wil called, "Myrna's dinner is not to be kept waiting."

Profusely thanking Jikal, Jon waded with a new spring in his step to Wil's side. "I lost all track of time," Jon apologised. "It was so interesting that I just didn't think..."

The big man clapped him on the back, noting that there was no wince this time. "No need for that, boy, no need at all."

They showered and dried themselves vigorously with rough towels. Jon reached for his shirt and trousers, and grimaced at the thought of the mud-encrusted material against his tingling skin. He exclaimed in surprise as he shook out clean and mended clothes. Grateful to bursting, he threaded his way back through the corridors on Wil's heels and out into the sunshine.

Myrna met them at the door with her index finger across her lips to warn them that Shondral slept once again. After a second excellent meal, full of taste surprises and doubtless quite nourishing, Jon was ushered into their bedroom, no arguments. He undressed and blissfully lay between the sheets. Two breaths later, he was oblivious to the world.

***

This time, it was his stomach that woke him. Enticing aromas drifted into his refreshed mind. Gazing about the room before committing himself to full consciousness, he was mildly surprised to see that it was still daylight, though the soft glow said Ord was low in the west.

The broad bed and much of the furniture in the room was simple yet elegant with easy curves rounding the corners. The wood was the colour of warm, golden honey and the indigo coverlet reminded him of Alba's harbour at dusk.

He began to doze again when the sound of Shondral's laughter had him sitting bolt upright. He hurriedly dressed, dragged a comb through his straight black hair, and hastily tied it back. More or less presentable, he joined the others.

Shondral wore a long blue gown gathered at the waist by a narrow copper belt and her red hair had been artfully combed to hide the bandage behind her ear. Their eyes locked and her smile hurt his throat as she came to stand in front of him. Raising her hands to his face, she gently brought his lips to hers in a kiss that made the rest of the room disappear. He gathered her in his arms and held her close, losing himself in her.

Myrna discreetly cleared her throat. "Let us celebrate your recovered good health before dinner cools." Shondral and Jon joined the Thornberrys at their table, the four of them together for the first time.

They chatted about this season's herds and how Camelia, Morbella, and Jemma contributed such valuable goods to the southern towns. They talked about the splendid dishes Myrna had created, seasoned just right with fresh herbs from Wil's greenhouse garden.

"You could probably use some fresh air," Myrna suggested once the table was cleared. "After all," she good-naturedly poked Jon on her way out the door, "you've been horizontal in there for a full day."

His jaw dropped. Before he could sputter inanities, Shondral spoke up. "It would certainly do me some good." She gathered her cloak and arm in arm with Myrna left the men to decide what they would do.

Wil shook his head. "That woman," he chortled, and followed his wife's silver head out the door. Jon swallowed his embarrassment, and caught up with them at the end of the yard.

They strolled in the mild dusk, wending their way to the heart of Camelia. Wil and Myrna greeted what must have been the entire population of the hamlet taking the evening air. It was a daily social activity where events of greater and lesser importance were discussed, where young men and women tried not to notice each other, and where children and dogs played and tussled with each other entertaining everybody.

The square at the centre of town was the favourite gathering place. During the day, it bustled with commerce but come dinnertime most of the shops closed their doors. The few that remained open tantalised the Camelians with spicy drinks and sweet delicacies to treat themselves with after a hard day's work.

Lanterns hung from strategically placed posts that also supported planters filled to overflowing with fragrant white blossoms so tiny that Jon could not make out their exact shape. In the centre of the square, a mosaic of stonework surrounded a superbly detailed sculpture of a Dryx. The statue stood four feet high at the shoulder and the long neck extended gracefully in an outward arc. The large brown eyes looked down at Jon along a delicate snout and the lipless mouth seemed to smile. A pair of backward-curving horns crowned its head. Except for its lustrous eyes, the entire Dryx was snowy white.

A commotion on the far side of the square interrupted Jon's study of the archaic lettering at the base of the statue. People rushed over, anticipating a surprise entertainment. Hand in hand, Jon and Shondral circled the crowd to get a better view.

A wave of tense silence washed over the populace at the sight of the cage. The people of the Hills did not kill predators; they knew the importance of maintaining the balance between predator and prey. Instead, they enticed unwelcome animals into wooden crates positioned around the grazing Dryx and released them once the herd had moved on. The herdsmen had laboured hard to bring the cumbersome thing down from the meadows.

"We didn't know what to do with it," a spokesman was saying as he wiped the sweat from his brow. "We feared to let it loose."

Shondral gripped Jon's arm painfully. He turned to her. Whatever he was going to say died on his lips. Shondral's face was a mask of terror, a shaking arm pointed at the cage. Then he felt it too: a loathing so complete it froze his heart. His eyes desperately searched the cage but he could detect nothing in the dim light.

It sensed them, though. Hissing, it uncurled and placed its hands on the bars that contained it. Until now, it had served no purpose to expend the energy to escape and it still digested the witless creature that it had found in the cage. But with its quarry twenty paces away, it snapped the thick bars as though they were twigs and launched itself from the cage.

Jon lunged sideways, putting himself between Shondral and this demon of impossible strength. It covered the distance before anyone else in the square could react and bounded to Jon's shoulders. Its hands reached for Shondral's throat as it crushed Jon's head between its knees. Blind with pain and unable to move, Jon saw distorted images of people gaping in horror.

A shriek from hell split the night. The demon's vice-like grip on Jon's head loosened abruptly and its body thumped to the stone paving, a dagger embedded in the back of its head. Jon fell to his knees, retching.

Someone approached. Belatedly, Jon groped for his knife and lurched to his feet. He must protect

95

Shondral. Staggering, he felt her hands steady him. Relief that she was uninjured lent him strength and he crouched to defend her.

She stepped around him and fiercely hugged the slight stranger. Over the top of her head, the stranger looked up. Jon gaped. He looked into Shondral's face, but on a boy. He knew that the old, tormented eyes must belong to Milo.

Chapter 4

The people in the square ceased all activity to stare at the three strangers.

"Please bear with them, gentlemen," their guide whispered. "They have never seen outside folk. They're just curious."

One little girl boldly stepped into place beside Endel. She raised her hand to touch him, daring herself all the way. Startled, Endel jerked his hand away from the contact. The girl tensed for an instant, ready to flee. Seeing the innocent cause of his flinch, he laughed warmly and took her small hand in his. A shy smile lit her face.

"My name's Lara," she said. "Where do you come from?"

"Lara. What a pretty name," Endel said. "I'm Doctor Laurs. Aren't we lucky to have names that fit together so well: Lara, Laurs." She giggled. "As to where I'm from, well..." Perplexed, Endel wondered how much she knew of the world above ground. He was rescued from the lengthening silence by the arrival of a welcoming group. Lara scurried back to her admiring friends.

"Welcome to Uamh, Captain Oprum." An elderly man took Jeorg's hand in both of his. "And this must be Doctor Laurs. We have long hoped a physician would visit with us." He repeated the encompassing handshake. "And Aird, our brother of the Plateau." He placed his wrinkled hands on Aird's shoulders and they touched foreheads in the traditional salutation of the nomads. Aird blinked in surprise; he had leaned forward without thinking.

97

The old man proceeded to introduce the people with him, oblivious of his guests' shock that he knew their names and more. "This is Bruaich, who heads our education system." A comely, middle-aged woman stepped forward. "And Féadan, in charge of research." A short man beside Bruaich nodded his head. "Géodha, who looks after our agriculture." A lovely young woman smiled at them. "And I am Maol, our healer." He gestured at the happy, flushed faces of the people in the square. "And I must say that I am very good at my job." He chuckled to himself; the others in the welcoming party smiled at their leader's obvious pleasure in himself.

Maol looked about for a moment seeming to gather himself. "Oh, yes. I forget. You must be thirsty and hungry after that long hike through the caves, not to mention that ghastly climb." He turned and gestured for them to follow. "Come. You can freshen up, then we'll speak of your purpose here."

Jeorg stood motionless, trying to grasp what was happening around him. He had too many questions screaming in his head. As much as he had seen of the world, this defied all understanding. These people shouldn't be here, they shouldn't be able to live in the middle of a mountain, they shouldn't be able to know his name. He wondered if he had suffered another attack from Malissa's poison, fallen on the slippery cavern floor, and was hallucinating in an unconscious stupor.

A soft voice at his side interrupted his feverish thoughts. "This is real, Captain Oprum, as real as Alba." The one introduced as Géodha stood beside him. "Forgive Maol. He also forgets how unusual Uamh is."

Hallucination or not, Jeorg, Endel, and Aird followed her lithe figure into a large domed structure at the far end of the square. She led them down a hallway and into a bright, airy room.

"This is yours for the duration of your visit with us," Géodha told them in a voice warm with welcome. "Please join us at the end of the hallway when you are ready." She smiled and left them.

Jeorg closed the door and examined their surroundings. Along one wall were three substantial beds separated by thin screens and assorted plants. A long gown similar to the ones the adults of Uamh wore was neatly laid out across the end of each. The table on the opposite wall held basins of steaming water lightly scented with an unfamiliar, fragrant herb. Directly across from the door was a window that spanned from ceiling to floor and almost as wide. It looked out over a lush flower garden framed by a copse of trees. Whatever these people were, they knew how to treat a guest.

Jeorg cleared his throat. "I know what you both are thinking, especially you Endel. You want to rush in and learn everything this Maol healer person can tell you so that you can rush back to Alba and show those Academy colleagues of yours that, just as you suspected, there is more to learn than they thought possible. It would vindicate your choice of becoming a ship's doctor." Endel looked abashed. "And you, Aird. How Maol knew the Dreven Plateau nomad greeting is beyond me and I know it makes you suspicious. But, both of you," he looked from one to the other, "until we know more, stay pleasant but on guard. Although they seem peaceful and you can hardly contain yourself to learn more, Endel, we will take no risks. In the meantime, I suggest we find out all we can. And keep your daggers strapped to your leg." He pointed meaningfully at Endel's blade sheath lying on the table.

After receiving acknowledging nods from both his officers, Jeorg gestured to the wash basins and they proceeded to strip out of their soiled clothes. Once they had refreshed themselves, they chose clean clothing from their packs, preferring the familiar style of trousers and tunics to the gowns. Unused to such long, draping material, Jeorg feared it would hamper their movements.

They joined Maol and the others in a large circular room at the centre of the dome. The ceiling rose high overhead and was punctuated in a dozen places by arched windows that filled the room with light. Several other doorways like the one through which they had entered opened into the room.

Their hosts sipped from tall glasses and mingled near a table arrayed with bread, fruit, and cheese. The educator woman, Bruaich, noticed them first. "Join us! Eat! Drink!"

No wasted words there, Jeorg thought. Her tone was friendly, though, and they approached the table. Jeorg noted that Aird scanned the room, and he silently gave thanks that his first mate was along. If anything was amiss, Aird would find it.

"We would like to thank you for your hospitality," Jeorg said as he neared the group of

Uamhans, "and hope that we may have the opportunity to offer you a similar welcome in Alba." As he spoke he watched their faces. Féadan, in particular, seemed quite upset. Géodha, on the other hand, looked fretful while Maol and Bruaich shared a knowing glance. All was not as idyllic as it seemed.

Maol ran a long-fingered hand brusquely over his balding pate. "Perhaps you would like to try some of the breads we make. Our fields are on the other side of the trees you can see from your room. The grain is quite tasty. Doctor, you must try some." Maol succeeded in bringing a tenuous welcoming mood back to the group. He guided Endel to the table, describing the foodstuffs and their nutritional value in the detail that only a practitioner would appreciate.

Féadan appeared at Jeorg's side to help him select from the foreign foods. As their hands were side by side choosing fruit from a large crystal bowl, Jeorg remarked on the sharp contrast between his own nut-brown skin and Féadan's milky white complexion.

"Just one of the many differences that I am certain we will discover," Féadan said. "I have often speculated what Ord's light can do, but I must confess that this is one aspect I had not considered." He chuckled low in his throat and his dark eyes sparkled.

When they were seated and had eaten a little, Bruaich stood and walked to one side so that everyone could see her. Her dark hair was styled in an intricate braid that began at her temples and capped her head in concentric circles.

"As an educator of Uamh, I teach the young ones to read and write. I also tell them of the world outside Uamh and why Uamhans remain here." She paced as she spoke, her hands clasped at her waist. "But before any of that, I tell them about Lifefire, for it is the sole reason we survive. We have learned much about its nature and how it can be used to sustain us." She paused to gather her thoughts. "And now I will tell you about Lifefire, Captain, because we desperately need your help."

Jeorg Oprum was a brave man. He had shown great courage and leadership as the *Pride's* Captain and, as the spokesperson for the Shipmasters' League, he had often championed innovation. He had sailed to exotic ports and done things most men only dreamed of doing. He had helped others in far worse shape than the people of Uamh. The odd thing was that these people appeared to be in far *better shape* than most. What could cause despair in a people that appeared as safe and prosperous and healthy as these Uamhans? What could be wrong? Bruaich's words sent a tendril of fear coiling through him.

She was speaking again. "Lifefire is the stuff from which all things are made. The fungi that Maol uses, the fruit trees Géodha grows, the water we drink, the land we stand on, the clouds in your sky, and you and me. We believe that even Ord and the other stars in the heavens and the worlds that must surely circle those other stars are all from Lifefire.

"The Source of Lifefire remains a matter for speculation among our philosophers but what is generally accepted is that all Lifefire originated from the same Source." She sipped from her glass to moisten her throat, and tucked a stray wisp of hair behind her ear. "Lifefire can be manipulated to a degree. Maol uses it to create medicines. Géodha uses it to enhance the nutritional value and variety of our food. Féadan uses it to improve a wide variety of things, including our own human bodies. It is truly powerful, even magical at times," she locked eyes with each of their guests, "and it can be truly dangerous."

No one had eaten since Bruaich began. Even the Uamhans, who must know this intimately, ignored their plates. Jeorg tried to understand the ramifications of what this woman was saying even as his mind balked at the very idea of Lifefire. It sounded like some kind of charlatan's trick, and he was not a little insulted that these people would think so little of his intelligence. Magic, indeed.

Endel broke the silence this time. "As a physician, I am quite used to postulating theories and establishing tests to prove or disprove them. I hope you will not take offence, but I for one would like to see what this Lifefire can do." He proceeded to vigorously clean his spectacles.

"Of course, Doctor. I would have been surprised if you had not asked for a demonstration." Bruaich closed her eyes for a moment. Through one of the many doors leading into the chamber stepped a young girl with a newly hatched chick cupped in her hands. She placed it on the table in front of

Féadan. It chirped and raised its open beak to the Researcher.

"I would normally let this chick grow at its own pace." His voice was low, not wishing to startle the young bird. "We endeavour to make any adjustments in harmony with what already is. This example is purely to give you an idea of what can be done."

He closed his dark eyes; his brow furrowed in concentration. There was a blur on the table in front of him and, where the chick had been, strutted a full-grown hen ready to hatch chicks of her own. It fluttered off the table and the young girl who had brought it in a moment ago gathered up her much larger charge and left the room.

Aird had watched through sceptical eyes. In fact, he had been looking at anything but Féadan and the bird. His sharp eyes detected no trickery.

Féadan took a long drink from his glass and when he looked at Jeorg, there was a weariness about him. "It does take some effort to wield Lifefire and one needs something, anything, to start with, be it a baby bird or this glass of water I'm holding." He drained the glass and refilled it from a pitcher near his elbow.

"Now that you have a certain amount of background, gentlemen," this time it was Maol who spoke, "we will answer the questions foremost on your minds." He chuckled, quite pleased with himself.

Jeorg raised his eyebrows and looked at the old healer in puzzlement.

Géodha stepped in. "You forget yourself, my dear friend." She placed a hand on Maol's shoulder and turned to the Officers of the *Pride*. "Please forgive him. His good nature is sometimes at the expense of others." She smiled fondly at the old man.

Maol sobered. "So sorry, gentlemen." He looked genuinely apologetic. "It has been so long that we of Uamh can read each other's conscious thoughts that I find it quite unusual that you cannot and did indeed amuse myself at your expense."

Ah, Jeorg thought. This is how they knew our names and how they had known to send a guide to meet us.

"Limited telepathy is one of a number of improvements we have made to ourselves," Féadan explained and, sensing their discomfort, hastily added, "and it is used strictly when mutual agreement exists." He pursed his lips. "Or when Maol forgets himself."

Endel slapped the table with an open hand. "Incredible! I must know everything!"

Maol found this hilarious and could not help but fill the dome with his guffaws. Géodha shrugged in exasperation and raised her eyes to the ceiling.

Calming himself but with lips still twitching with amusement, Maol looked directly at Endel. "And we will do everything in our power to cure your Captain."

Jeorg Oprum chose that timely moment to succumb to another attack.

When he woke, he lay on a bed in an unfamiliar room. The curtains were drawn, a boon for his aching head. His mouth was as dry as dust and he gingerly reached for the glass of water on the low table next to his bed.

"Let me help." The voice was so soft he barely heard it. A slight figure rose from a chair to his left. "I'm sorry if I startled you."

Jeorg shook his head and gasped as white pain lanced behind his eyes. A cool cloth was placed on his forehead.

"Please. Try not to move."

"You can count on it," he hissed through clenched teeth.

She brought a straw to his lips. "Maol said you should have a little to drink when you woke."

He sucked tentatively on the straw. When the pain did not worsen, he proceeded to drain the glass, and slept again.

It was still light the second time he woke. Feeling much better, he moved his head a little from side to side. *Yes, much better.* He spotted a washbasin and, next to it, a chair with a gown draped over it. He rolled onto his side and pushed himself up to a sitting position. In a few moments the room steadied and he made his careful way to the water. He was bringing the gown over his head when the door opened a crack.

"Good. Maol said you would be awake by now." Endel squinted into the room, one hand on the doorknob, the other balancing a tray. "He also said you would be hungry." He shouldered the door fully open and came in.

106

"Seems he's right on both counts." Jeorg smiled. "I will eat everything in sight while you tell me what has happened since our meeting with the Uamhans."

Endel nodded as he placed the tray on a side table by Jeorg's bed and dragged over the room's two chairs. "This place is incredible! The advances in medicine alone are staggering! I've been spending my time with Féadan and his team while they puzzled through the poison causing your attacks."

"Wait a minute," Jeorg interrupted, "how long have I been here?" He indicated the room they were in.

"Let's see," he frowned. "I make it just short of three days."

"Three days!" Anger clouded his face. "Why did I not awaken?"

Deep concern furrowed Endel's brow. "That was your worst attack, Jeorg, it lasted a full fifteen minutes longer than the previous ones. I decided as your physician to let them perform a few tests." He held up his hand before Jeorg could interrupt again. "Maol, Féadan, and I discussed your symptoms. They took a few samples of your blood and tissue and have worked steadily to identify the poison Malissa gave you. While you were sedated, your body recovered and you suffered no further attacks." His earlier excitement returned. "They found it, Jeorg, this morning! Féadan is preparing the antidote as we speak. Not some medication to take over and over, but a cure that destroys the agent she introduced into your body!" He grasped Jeorg's arm. "We did it! We beat her!"

His joy was contagious. Jeorg was beginning to believe in magic, just a little.

While they were still grinning at each other like school children in a candy shop, Féadan came to the door with another man Jeorg did not recognise. "Captain Oprum, I would like you to meet my assistant, Riab. He made the breakthrough in unravelling the nature of the poison."

Jeorg stood and approached the two Uamhans. He looked at Féadan. "How does one express thanks in Uahm?"

He puzzled over this a few moments. "Why, anyway we wish, I suppose." Jeorg extended his hand to the young man that had saved his life. In mid-motion, he stepped forward and embraced the Uamhan. He did not speak.

"Are you feeling quite well, Captain?" Féadan asked when the two men had separated. Jeorg nodded. "In that case..." He removed a vial from one of the pockets in his gown. "I'm afraid it doesn't taste very good."

Jeorg swallowed it in one gulp. "You're right," he confirmed, screwing up his face in disgust.

Endel could contain himself no longer and laughed at the sight of his Captain taking his medicine. If Maol had been there, Endel was certain he would have joined in.

***

Aird absorbed everything Géodha said. He was certain that the miracles the Uamhans had wrought with their crops could be applied to the small plots

108

of arable land on the Plateau. If his people could grow enough to eat and do it in one place, they would have the chance, at least, to develop new skills, to increase trade, to better their lives. They would not be forced to move from place to place, following the weather patterns, and staying just long enough to plant or to reap whatever harvest of grain they could before moving on. With luck, the barricades they had built a few months before would have kept the birds and other animals away from the tender shoots. But more times than he cared to remember, his tribe travelled great distances only to find dry, trampled earth. There would be no bread that winter.

Géodha pointed to plants with bright red leaves the size of his hand. "That is cumbas." She carefully plucked one of the leaves where stem met stalk. "We crush it for its juices." She tore off a strip and handed it to him. "Not only is it tasty, but it works to close wounds before much blood is lost."

He bit into the cumbas. Its delicate rose flavour filled his mouth. "How much do you need and how long does it last?" he asked. This, too, would be like a miracle to his people.

She knew he spoke about its healing properties and picked up a small rock at her feet. One side had an edge to it.

Aird took her hand. "Wait." He lifted his trouser leg and drew his blade. "Use this."

She showed no surprise. *Of course,* fumed Aird, *she reads my mind.* He reversed the knife so that the blade was extended instead of the handle. She looked more puzzled than guilty.

"What is it, Aird? What's the matter?" She searched his face, keeping a tight rein on her telepathy.

Aird studied her movements, her posture, her face for some sign of duplicity. She was simply not afraid of him. "Nothing," he muttered, and handed her the knife hilt first.

Géodha shrugged off his strange behaviour; they had much to learn about each other. "This will hurt a little." She held his hand and made a small incision in his index finger. Blood flowed for an instant, slowed, then stopped altogether. As he watched, the edges of the wound fused together leaving a pale scar.

"The scar will vanish in an hour or so." She beamed at him, proud of her creation.

Aird barely controlled the rage that welled up inside him. "Why have you not shared these miracles?" Géodha stared at him, not understanding.

"See my thoughts," he commanded her. Images flashed across his mind—images of hunters with their stomachs gashed open by the horns of some beast, of women bleeding to death in childbirth, of children fevered and puffy from the sting of an insect.

Géodha gasped and twisted the cumbas leaf in her hands until its red juices dripped to the ground. "We did not know..." she faltered, caught in Aird's nightmare. The impact of so much suffering buckled her knees and hot tears course down her cheeks.

Alarmed, Aird knelt in the dirt and offered the support of his arms. Could it be that the Uamhans

110

know nothing of pain and suffering? He felt shame at what he had done, but at the same time his resolve hardened to bring the salvation of Lifefire to his people.

At last she calmed and slumped against him. "How could this happen?" she whispered. "How could such a wondrous gift disappear?" She looked up at him, despair in her reddened eyes. "Lifefire is there for all. Why do you not use it?"

"We knew nothing of Lifefire before Bruaich spoke to us."

She drew a shuddering breath and gazed unseeing at the crushed cumbas leaf in her hands. "Bruaich and the others have long been convinced of this, but I just could not believe it."

Aird sought to console her somehow. He thought back to the educator's words. "Perhaps that is what Bruaich meant when she asked Captain Oprum for his help."

Géodha nodded and got to her feet. She brushed the dust from her gown and raised her eyes to his. "Let's find out."

They walked back through the fields to the dome where Aird and the others first met with the leaders of Uamh. He towered over the girl beside him and shortened his stride to match her pace. She kept her gaze down and he noticed how her long lashes made feathery shadows on her delicate cheekbones and he remembered the softness of her tawny hair as he had comforted her. The Uamhans did indeed have much to offer.

Endel's laughter drifted down the hallway. They headed toward the sound. With a jolt, Aird remembered Jeorg. He lengthened his stride, a surge of hope filling him, all else forgotten.

They entered the private room that Jeorg had been resting in. Aird strode to him and studied his face, oblivious of the others in the room. This was his brother of the Sea, loved and trusted, equal to his brothers of the Plateau. He had not realised how great his concern was until he felt the rush of relief at Jeorg's triumphant grin.

"I am well."

Aird let out a whoop startling the Uamhans and making Endel laugh all the louder. He lifted Jeorg off his feet in a most unceremonious bear hug.

"They will have to mend my ribs too," Jeorg gasped.

Aird set him back on his feet, his grin splitting his face in two.

Féadan and Riab were the next to be assaulted by Aird's exuberance. He shook their hands, bestowing praises and blessings on them and their children, and their children's children. His eyes met Endel's. Triumph flashed between them.

"Is the Captain well enough to continue our meeting?" Géodha's soft-spoken question dissipated the festive mood.

When Jeorg nodded, she continued. "Then I shall contact the others to meet in one hour." She turned to leave and looked back. "Captain. It is my turn to forget myself. I am most pleased to see you well." She forced a smile and left them, Féadan and Riab following in her wake.

Aird felt their eyes on him and he looked at his companions, regretting that their moment of celebration was so soon ended. "She was deeply disturbed by what my mind showed her of the death and suffering that exists and that could have been prevented. She thought that at least some of the benefits of Lifefire were known to us. And she doesn't know why it is unknown in the outside world." His voiced grew soft and dangerous. "Or why it is purposefully kept from the outside world."

Jeorg and Endel exchanged glances. "We don't have enough information yet to formulate any conclusions, let alone accusations," Jeorg said evenly. Aird had often spoken of the plight of his people and of his deep concern that the nomad population was steadily dwindling. These Uamhan medicines would be like a miracle. Jeorg also knew of his first mate's hot temper. "We must remain calm until we know more. We do not, I repeat, do not, want to anger these people."

Aird's rigid stance did not soften. Putting his hands on the tense shoulders, Jeorg forced Aird to look at him. Slowly, Aird's muscles relaxed, and he nodded his agreement. "We will find out the truth, Aird, I promise you."

An hour later, the seven were gathered. Géodha did not look up as her fellow Uamhans and the Officers of the *Pride* found their seats.

"Since our friends cannot see our thoughts," Bruaich began, "I will use words to the best of my ability to explain our great need.

"Our history dates back nearly two hundred generations. Some among us are assigned the task of maintaining chronicles so that we may see our growth and remember our accomplishments. The

113

chronicles are also used to outline anything else of importance. One such thing of great significance occurred some 3,000 years ago.

"The records describe a glow on the horizon that grew ever larger. As it expanded, terrible forces wrenched our beloved planet. Mountains were born and became infernos, flat lands were pushed up into the sky, and the farms in front of these caverns disappeared as the foothills plunged down a thousand feet and the Sea rushed in to obliterate all that was." Bruaich sighed into the silence. "Most of our people were lost then, and those that survived wished they, too, had been taken.

"They, who are our forefathers, were deep within the Mountains when the holocaust struck. The tons of rock over their heads that could have crushed them like so many insects instead spared their lives. They lived, and a fierce desire began to grow: a desire to master the forces that had destroyed all they knew. This desire founded Uamh and, as years passed, they created a new and better life for themselves and their children. This soon became more important than understanding and conquering the forces of nature." A faint smile curved her lips.

"No Uamhan has been face to face with outside folk since that time."

Jeorg had been patiently sitting through a history lesson he had studied as a youth. The Great Cataclysm, his teachers called it. The Uamhans were not the only Méadhonians to have survived and recorded how the world had been changed. Bruaich's last statement, however, jerked him back

114

to complete attention. They have survived 3,000 years in these caves; not survived, he corrected himself, flourished.

"This does not mean that we know nothing of the goings-on," Maol interjected, "or that some among us have not tried to reach you."

"True." Bruaich went on to explain that a number of expeditions had been attempted. Trees were felled for their wood and yards of material became sails. These and all the other necessities for constructing seaworthy craft were carried piece by piece to the cave entrance in the Mjorn Cliffs. There, the boats were assembled and lowered by a series of ropes and winches into the sea. They were eighteen feet long—the limit that could be safely lowered down the cliff face. They had little knowledge of how to test the vessels for seaworthiness or how to sail in anything but the softest of breezes. None returned. The people of Uamh forbade further launchings and chose to focus their energy on seeking alternative ways to contact the world outside.

"Thanks to Féadan's work, a few among us can project our consciousness into the outer world. We call them 'far-seekers.' It remains only a matter of time," Bruaich became animated for the first time in her discourse, "before we will be able to touch even the stars."

Jeorg and Aird had spent long nights gazing at the majesty of the heavens. In the comfort of trusted friendship, Aird had spoken of his people's belief that the stars were ancestral spirits weaving a pattern across the universe. When the pattern was complete, it would be the Face of God. Jeorg yearned to be a part of that unfolding pattern, voyaging among the endless stars and touching the universe.

"That is speculation," Féadan interjected, startling Jeorge from his reverie. "At least for now."

Bruaich knew she had strayed from the critical purpose of the meeting and muttered an apology.

Géodha cleared her throat and nodded at Bruaich. It was Géodha who next spoke. "Although we have only just begun to see the outside world through our far-seekers, we have learned of a threat that could destroy us all." She met Aird's gaze. "And I have just come to truly believe that knowledge of Lifefire has disappeared from the world above us. Only we Uamhans retain this knowledge that every Méadhonian has a right to know—that every Méadhonian must know—in order to defeat this evil."

Evil? Jeorg wondered. *What evil?*

Maol took up the tale. "The far-seekers number seven to date. Féadan moves slowly and carefully with manipulations made directly to Uamhans." The old healer ran his hand through his non-existent hair. "The first two began journeying four years ago and are the strongest. Féadan wisely insists that at least two minds project together, never alone. And with the new far-seekers, three or four accompany each other." He motioned for Féadan to elaborate.

"We still struggle to fully understand not only the actual process but also its limitations. We do know that the energy of one far-seeker can be sensed and directed by another far-seeker. They are

116

able to see, hear, and smell their surroundings and they can join energies, in fact, to strengthen each other and heighten sensory input. So far," he concluded, "they have travelled to the Kobaska Hills in the east and to the border of the Raylorn Fen in the south."

A young man joined them. "This is Roinn," Féadan introduced. "He is our senior far-seeker and will tell you what he has seen."

Roinn shuffled his feet, his head bowed. A thick mat of brown hair fell forward obscuring his features. He stuck his hands in his pockets, straightened his shoulders, and looked at his audience. The youthful face, just starting to beard, was a disconcerting contrast to eyes that had seen too much, too soon. Jeorg felt a moment of anger at innocence stripped before its time.

Roinn cleared his throat and began. He told them of a far-seeking journey two summers ago far across the land to the peaceful hamlets of the Kobaska Hills. He went there often: the land was beautiful and the people were much like Uamhans. On that trip, he felt a great wrenching of his spirit that he did not understand. His companion, Teber, had had to help him return to his body. No one else had felt this and so it remained a riddle.

Last summer, Roinn sensed other milder wrenchings and, this time, Teber felt them as well. Concerned, Féadan localised the disturbances and sent four far-seekers together to confirm the location and perhaps discover what they were and what caused them.

117

"We soared, though soaring isn't quite the right word, to the place Féadan showed us," Roinn continued. Bruaich stood and pointed to a wall map of Méadhon, to an area north-east of Alba. "We descended into a valley with fields of crops surrounding a group of buildings. We could see nothing unusual so I directed our flight inside one of the buildings." He squeezed his eyes shut. "We immediately sensed the wrenching again and, at that range, we knew that it was Lifefire being used. But it was all wrong. Something hated and hated. We fled as fast as we could."

Maol rose to comfort the boy and lead him to an empty chair.

"What is so traumatic about this," Féadan explained, his voice tight with emotion, "is that we thought Lifefire incapable of being misused. We were blinded by our traditions, by our naïveté. Our isolation had wrapped us in ignorant security." His face became a mask of fierce resolve. "But now we know better and we must act."

"The dilemma is far worse than it seems," Bruaich said. "Lifefire exists to be used, and we now know that it can be used to destroy as well as to create. However, unlike its creative side, the destructive aspect appears to be self-generating. In other words, once begun, it can eventually compel all Lifefire into its evil shape." Her voice filled with despair. "We don't understand why this is so."

The silence in the room grew heavy. Jeorg didn't pretend to understand either. But he knew that Malissa must be involved. To his surprise Aird leapt to his feet.

118

"We must not lose to that vile creature! We will return to Alba and crush her!" Aird strode to the map and jabbed a finger at the place Roinn and the others had found. "This place belongs to a so-called Town Advisor, Malissa. And you," he pointed to Féadan, "have already seen her handiwork and defeated it." He pointed to Jeorg. He glared at each of them in turn and returned to his seat having completed the longest speech of his life.

United by a common enemy, they laboured over strategy far into the night.

Chapter 5

Like many sizeable towns, Alba had its bad neighbourhood. What had begun as a jumble of shacks and lean-tos jammed between the harbour warehouses and the stone retaining wall that separated the dock area from the town proper, had mutated into a cesspool of thieves and murderers, drunks and drug-users, gamblers and perverts. Strange to think that it had been one of his regular haunts. As a young boy, this seamy side of town had fascinated him—it had been like prying up an old rotted log just to see what crawled and slithered beneath. Jon had wandered through the squalor not long ago, and although it remained much the same as in his youth, he had come to the awful realisation that it was not the sorry state of the depraved that darkened his spirit, but rather sight of the families that were forced to live there. They were the real tragedy. The women clutched their children, able to offer little comfort. The sunken, haunted eyes of those children had disturbed his sleep for weeks.

Similar features now stared back at him from Shondral's brother. But Milo's countenance could never be the result of mere physical abuse and deprivation; it was of an entirely different magnitude. His mouth was a tight slash, and the muscle along the right side of his jaw jumped every few seconds. Deep lines creased his pallid forehead and, as he dragged his fingers through ragged hair, his hand shook like an old man's. Purple blotches underscored his eyes, but it was the naked anguish in them that pummelled Jon's soul. Whatever had happened to Milo was beyond anything he could imagine.

The trance that seemed to possess him was shattered by the touch of cool hands on his forehead. Elios' mouth moved but Jon could hear nothing over the ringing in his ears. Strong hands helped him sit next to Shondral on a bench that had appeared. A cup of water was pressed to his lips and he automatically sipped from it.

Jon willed himself to look at the black body that still twitched in death. He vaguely noticed that Shondral stroked his hand and this distracted him for a moment. When he next looked up, the herdsmen were using wooden prods to shove the thing's carcass up a ramp and into the wrecked cage. Several women dragged steaming buckets to the stone paving where its body had lain and scrubbed at the stain. A putrid stench drifted to where he sat. He groaned and was hastily assisted to his feet and brought into fresher air.

After a few deep breaths, his head cleared and his hearing began to return. The square buzzed with speculation, and from the tone, not much of it was kind. In fact, some of it was downright ugly with accusations pointing directly at the Laracyl boy's appearance. Milo, it seemed, was a popular topic of discussion, especially when peculiar things happened. Jon knew from just that one long look that this was not the first time Milo had confronted something as unholy as that black beast.

Wil Thornberry stayed behind to see what would be decided about the night's trouble while Myrna gathered her charges and made a discreet exit from the square. The healer accompanied them to the cottage and examined Jon and Shondral more closely, then spoke quietly to Milo for a few moments.

"There's nothing wrong that a cup or two of your broth won't fix," Elios pronounced as he headed for the door. "What they all need," and he looked meaningfully at Milo, "is a good night's rest." He nodded farewell and quietly left.

They had just settled near the hearth with mugs of hot tea, delicately flavoured with soothing herbs, when Wil came in. "They're upset and scared, and so they've set sentries around the village," he reported, "but with you three out of sight, they're trying to convince themselves that the danger is over. More like they just don't want to believe what they saw with their own eyes." He sighed. "It's just as well I suppose. When that beast leaped to your shoulders, Jon, well I thought my own heart would stop beating right then and there." He shook his head. "It's no wonder they're afraid, but being afraid is no way to fix things. You've got to take it and shake it and..."

"Now, Wil," his wife interrupted. "I insist that we wait for the light of day to discuss what happened any further." She made eye contact with each of them lingering longest on her husband and, satisfied that she had their agreement, turned to Milo. "Now, tell us all the news from Morbella."

Glad of the distraction, Shondral and Milo eagerly caught up on family news, and with lively comments from their hosts, chatted about all manner of hamlet affairs. It was not too much later when Myrna insisted that Shondral get some rest. She reminded them that it had been less than two days since Wil had carried her into this very room, bleeding and unconscious.

Milo and Jon spread blankets on the floor between where Shondral lay by the hearth and the door to the cottage. They positioned their daggers within easy reach; the unspoken message was that the thing that had attacked them earlier that night might not have been alone.

"It was a lucky throw, you know," Milo confessed as they settled down for the night. "I haven't touched a knife since..." His voice trailed off and he turned to face to the wall.

Luck or not, Jon was glad to have him with them.

After breakfast the next morning, Shondral pronounced herself well enough to travel as far as Morbella; she left no room for argument. They had imposed on the Thornberrys' kindness and generosity long enough. Myrna made a fuss, all the while preparing a picnic lunch for them.

Wil had slipped out of the house before dawn to discover if the sentries had seen anything during the night. All was quiet and their best trackers had found no trace of any other strange animals.

When Wil returned in time for breakfast, he offered what words of caution he felt their young guests would heed; but what could ever prepare anyone for what was unknown? That beast was like nothing he had ever heard of and he knew in his gut that there was far more that troubled the threesome in his house than an unnatural beast.

The Thornberrys accepted that the trio had to rush off to solve the mystery that plagued them, as all young people must do. But they had enjoyed the company, and it was with melancholy that they bid them goodbye. Wil and Myrna watched from the porch until the dust had settled. With an arm around his wife's shoulder, Wil and Myrna turned and walked back into the cottage, silently lamenting the unfulfilled dream of children of their own.

Jon and Milo walked, leading Lightning. Shondral sat astride her horse, which was the only concession she would make to her fast-healing wounds. Jon pondered their discussion at the breakfast table. He had given a quick summary of the last few days and, with meaningful glances at Shondral, left out the gypsy augury and much of their own speculation. Instead, he elaborated on how they had fooled the watchman with their clever disguises and on his own prowess at haggling for the horses. He had admitted that perhaps the thing that had followed them was somehow connected to why he and Shondral had decided to visit Morbella and see Milo. He had then insisted that since the beast was dead and that according to Wil's own report there was absolutely no sign of another, they should be safe on the journey to Morbella.

Wil and Myrna had listened to his story, but Jon was fairly certain that they suspected that he glossed over and even omitted details. He feared that if they knew too much, it might endanger them. He hated deceiving the Thornberrys. He vowed that, when it was safe to do so, he would tell them the whole story.

With a start, he noticed that they had already travelled well beyond Camelia.

Shondral reached forward and patted the warm, silky neck of her horse. "I think it's time you had another name besides 'horse,' don't you?" That began a lively discussion of the merits of various names for her gelding. They finally decided on Midnight, after his glossy black coat. Not too original, they agreed, but the horse had made that long ride in the dark. It added another dimension of appropriateness to the name.

Jon hesitated to turn the conversation to darker topics, but he must start somewhere. "So, Milo," he began, "how did you end up at the right place at the right time?"

Being close-knit communities, the hamlets not only helped and protected each other, but they also heard each other's news and gossip almost as fast as it happened. Milo had had word of his sister's accident late on the same day it had happened and left for Camelia as soon as his chores were finished the next day. His parents had watched him leave, worry etched deep into their faces, but they knew that Shondral was well looked after and that Milo was more than capable of bringing her home. Milo had arrived just behind the herdsmen with the caged monstrosity.

"Just another bit of luck, Milo?" Jon teased.

"And I could use a whole lot more." Bitterness etched Milo's voice. He had forgotten how much he missed being with people—people who genuinely wanted to be with him. His friends had long ago stopped their casual drop-in visits that had been so welcome and avoided his gaze when he passed them on the street. He could not blame them. Even his parents had begun to look on him more as an invalid than as their normal, but very frightened, son.

Jon ached for the torment in Milo's voice and for the helplessness in Shondral's eyes as she watched her brother. But all the sympathy in the world would not help Milo one bit. What they needed was a plan of action, he told them. This unleashed a torent of ideas and they got down to business.

They went over every detail of what had happened and what they suspected, and it was sometime during that discussion that it dawned on Shondral that Milo's carving resembled not only the girl he had been infatuated with but also the woman Town Advisor, Malissa. She had seen the sketches her brother had drawn before beginning the actual carving and, yes, there were similarities.

"I was interested in her as one of the few women to ever be elected, so I asked around, an Apprentice doing her homework," Shondral explained. "No one knew much about her or where she came from, or even when she began to farm and, suddenly, she's the Crop Grower's Advisor to Council. I figured she bought her way in. Not a story to take to the Historian." Shondral and Jon exchanged sardonic smirks.

"Raj and his friends cover Council affairs," she continued. "He's told me how Malissa has them jumping. The event was her idea."

Jon could only shake his head. It was entirely possible that one Advisor or another manipulated the Council; he, among many others, had often suspected something of the sort. He had even fantasised about personally exposing the culprit and saving the people of the town from being abused by political machinations. Becoming a hero. Ha.

"Coincidence," Jon muttered. Although he was not denying that certain affairs were somewhat bizarre, he was far from ready to believe that Alba was run by an animated piece of wood. "The carving looked like the girl it was for, right? So maybe there are a lot of girls that look like that."

Shondral stared at him hard before painstakingly itemising the evidence once more.

Exasperated, Jon finally agreed that Malissa and Milo's carving might, just might, be somehow connected.

"I know better than to rush to Alba to face Malissa," Milo said. "If the carving even is her," he hastened to add at Jon's look of disbelief. He was certain that whatever or whoever tormented him could also easily do the things that Shondral and Jon had described, and it was the best lead yet. "But we'll need more than luck to destroy such a creature." A dark cloud seemed to lower over Milo's face and in a cold, analytical voice, he told them of his recurring nightmares. "There is no pattern to when they come, which is worse in a way. I never know if she's waiting for me. She attacks as soon as I fall asleep, and every time it's different, worse." The lines in his face deepened. "At first, I tried to stay awake. I'd work until dawn, then run to the lake for a swim. Once, I lasted nearly three days.

She was so furious." He grimaced. "I wish I had died." Shondral put a hand on his shoulder.

"I finally figured out that she couldn't actually hurt me. Not physically, anyway. So I tried to find out *how* she was doing this to me," he glared at them, "and to stop her any way I could."

His most recent plan had been to visit remote villages where rumour said he would find sorcerers and witches. He was willing to ask anyone and try anything. So far, these trips had ended in disappointment. The 'sorcerers' turned out to be frauds and the 'witches' crazy hags who conjured nothing but tall tales and vile tasting potions.

As Milo spoke, Jon's mind threw up a red flag. He followed it back to the obvious question. "Were any of the sorcerers in the Mjorn Mountains?" He and Shondral had concluded that since the mountains she had seen during the gypsy's reading were not the Sgeir Range, they must be the Mjorns.

Shondral clapped her hands together, startling Midnight. "Of course," she cooed as she soothed the gelding.

Milo watched the interchange, perplexed. Word from the distant Mjorns seldom reached the Hills and there were very few among the villagers who had ever attempted the long and hazardous trek. Of those few, only old Halam was still alive, and he was crazy.

Shondral squared her shoulders and once again described their visit to the gypsy soothsayer and the clear picture of mountains that had flashed in her mind. "If there is no one that can help you in the Sgeirs, there might be someone in the Mjorns. I know it's not much, but what else have we got to go on?"

Based mostly on feeling, intuition, and Shondral's vision, along with a smattering of guesses thrown in, they roughed out a plan that would take them through forbidding lands into the even more forbidding Mjorn Mountains.

***

Shondral knew that their parents would vehemently forbid such an expedition, even without informing them that they planned to enlist a crazy old man as their guide. She knew they would do everything to stop them. They would argue that not only would no help be found in the Mjorns, but that the three of them could also be hurt or even killed by bandits, or wild animals, or an avalanche, or who knew what else. They would fret, cajole, argue some more, and threaten some painful punishment if they were disobeyed. And watch like hawks so that sneaking away would be impossible.

So it was that they crept into Morbella under cover of darkness, acquired a horse for Milo and some supplies for their journey, leaving what Jon argued was far too generous an amount of money to pay for everything. Shondral also insisted on leaving a brief note for their parents, arguing that they might not send anyone after them if they were reassured that Jon had amazing tracking and survival skills. She invented a few more qualities about Jon's hunting expertise and mountain training and made no mention whatsoever of Halam. It likely wouldn't work, but she had to at least try to ease some of their worry.

As prepared as they could be, the three companions mounted their horses and rode into the night. They set up a crude camp several miles from the village and far enough off the trail to be undetected and, as they ate a cold supper, fleshed out their plan. They would travel south then west along the skirt of the Dreven Plateau cliffs. The land was relatively flat and they should make good time. When they reached the Mjorn foothills, they would ask the locals for clues to a more precise destination. But first, they would visit old Halam. Satisfied that they had done all they could do for one day, they curled up close together in their blankets and slept.

Halam's cottage was some distance from the village and it was mid-morning before Jon, Shondral, and Milo dismounted at the edge of the clearing that surrounded the dwelling and tethered their horses to a low branch. Warily, they approached the doorstep.

A figure burst from the shack in greasy brown trousers held up by frayed red suspenders. The unruly silver forest on his chest matched the taller but equally unruly forest on his head. He stood with his fists firmly planted on his hips and glared at them through bushy black eyebrows that quivered with indignation.

"I think we might be better off without him," Milo whispered, his eyes wide.

"What have we got to lose?" Shondral whispered back, and caught Jon's nod of agreement. Appearances, after all, could be deceiving. She hoped.

130

They had decided on the way that Shondral would speak; her soft voice might be more soothing, or at least not alarm him. "Halam?" she began. "We would like to talk to you about your journey to the Mjorn Mountains. We need to go there for help to defeat a great evil." She winced at how melodramatic she sounded.

Halam became perfectly still and stared at them for several long seconds. He broke into a wide smile, which was as disconcerting to them as his words. "Be welcome, Fire-Wielders," he boomed.

He ushered them onto the ramshackle porch and into the cosy refuge he had built for himself. Neat white cupboards lined the wall to the left and were filled with cooking utensils and dried goods. To the right, hundreds of leather-bound manuscripts were protected from dust and moisture inside glass-fronted cabinets. In between was a table with a scattering of mismatched chairs, a well-used rocker, a large bench piled with cushions, and an equally large dog sprawled upon a threadbare rug. All this they noticed only peripherally. What captured their attention was the back wall of the cottage that was not a wall at all: Halam overlooked a piece of paradise.

A dense hedge more than fifteen feet high provided a rich green backdrop for the garden that exploded with colour. Blossoms as large as a man's head grew from sturdy shrubs, and delicate bluebells wove intricate patterns along the feet of a thousand daffodils. To one side, a miniature waterfall cascaded into a pool filled to bursting with white and pink and yellow lilies.

131

Milo stepped to where a wall should be and gingerly extended his hand. With a small popping sound, his index finger went right through the invisible barrier. He jerked his hand back and stared at it: it was uninjured. He looked at the barrier and could find no mark where he had punctured the 'wall.'

Tearing his eyes away, Jon stared at the grizzled man beside them. Halam's bright eyes were barely visible, but Jon detected a glint of amusement in them and had to fight down a sudden urge to pin up his eyebrows so he could get a better look.

"You must promise me one thing:" Halam broke the garden's spell, "that you tell no one of this. And, yes, yes, I'll tell you all about the wall. Later."

Their host settled in the rocker by the fireplace, his feet propped on the dog's flank. He laced his fingers, rested them on his slightly protruding belly, and waited for them to speak.

Jon, Shondral, and Milo crowded on the bench, awkward and not a little uncomfortable. Impulsively, Jon decided that it could do no harm to trust this man—they had to trust someone—and if things didn't work out, who would believe a crazy man anyway? He recounted the entire incredible story to him. Halam closed his eyes while he listened and reached over now and again to pat the dog's huge mahogany head.

"And so we go to the Mjorns," Jon concluded. "Will you help us?"

Halam said nothing for a long time. He

preferred quiet and solitude. Morbella was too noisy, he had claimed one day in a loud, annoyed bellow, and had left there a good many years ago. He spent his days with his books and his gardens, and his nights contemplating the stars. He grew his own food and was quite content to limit his necessary visits to Morbella to once or twice a year and, at first, the people of the village worried that he might become ill or injure himself. But as the years went by, it became clear that Halam never suffered from common ailments as most folk did, which only added fuel to the rumours of his peculiarity. Halam was not a simple man, though he tried very hard to appear that way. And if the village folk thought he was strange, all the better—they would leave him alone.

And so it was with some dismay and not a little anger when, earlier, Halam had heard horses and light chatter invade his domain. He had watched the three of them step cautiously towards him. As sudden as a summer storm, he sensed power in them, especially in the girl, a power he had not felt for many years. Though the memory was faint, he had known that he would never forget the feeling— the spine tingling, hair-standing-up-on-the-back-of-your-neck feeling. And they wanted to know about the Mjorns; the long years of waiting were over.

Yes, he had travelled to the Mjorns and the memory of it flashed before him in uncanny detail...

***

Lost in a blinding snowstorm, frozen and weak from exposure, Halam stumbled into a secluded tropical valley. He was certain that he had died and gone to his just reward.

The enchantment had inexplicable vagaries though: he needed to eat, he needed to drink, and he needed to breathe exactly like he had to do when he was alive. He convinced himself that these were very small paradoxes and, after all, did not the ripe fruit hang within reach, and were not the nuts and berries everywhere, and was there not spring water to drink? He could be happy here.

He found a small lake in which to bathe and was doing just that when an angel appeared. What else could she be? She looked at him, said his name, and beckoned him to follow.

He rushed to dress, afraid he would lose sight of her in the dense foliage. But she waited for him. He followed her into the forest and they came upon a path from which he glimpsed a structure through the trees. Wonder filled him when he realised that it could be seen *above* the trees. He was awed. That must be where the gods lived.

The angel led him up the wide stairway of the temple and left him in the vast marble foyer. He humbly waited for a sign.

He heard shuffling footsteps and with his head bowed in reverence he could just make out a portly gentleman from the corner of his eye. Halam said nothing, secretly wondering why a god would choose to be elderly and a trifle on the stout side. It was not his place to question these things; after all, the gods could appear any way they wished.

"Halam," the god greeted him as he approached, and Halam looked up. "Call me Oriander."

Oriander waddled (Halam knew that was blasphemous) over to him and smiled broadly, displaying a picket-fence set of yellow teeth, another idiosyncrasy, Halam supposed.

"It's been forever since we've had company!" Oriander said as he pounded Halam on the back and led him further inside the magnificent edifice.

Now Halam had been a reasonably good man but he was fairly certain that there must have been others who had arrived before him. A seed of doubt began to grow.

Oriander jovially described Banifour, the valley they were in, and the Great Hall through which he piloted a gawking Halam.

Ribbons of light spun rainbows about the Hall and cradled chandeliers of fine crystal. The walls were hung with rich tapestries, and some depicted scenes he recognised: the bustling harbour at Alba, the town of Mriss suspended magically in mist rising from Lake Thungal, and the Lakes of the Claw as they must look from the clouds. There were other exotic scenes that fascinated Halam, but he thought they could not possibly be from anywhere on Méadhon—the light was wrong.

Halam's gaze was drawn to the inky blackness beyond the chandeliers. As his eyes adjusted, the sparkles of brilliance that had attracted his attention resolved into a perfect reproduction of the night sky above Méadhon. Mouth open, Halam forced his attention back to Oriander who had at last exhausted

135

his reservoir of patience, taken him by the arm, and propelled him forward.

Oriander was anxious to begin his work on the long-awaited pawn.

***

Jon had finished speaking many minutes ago. *The old man probably thinks we've come here on a dare or, worse, he's fallen asleep.* Anger and frustration boiled inside him. They *would* find out what was going on and they *would* stop Milo's torment with or without Halam's help.

Shondral had not bothered listening; she agreed that Halam should be told everything and she trusted Jon to recount their story. She needed the time to explore what was happening to her; its build-up had been so gradual that she was only just becoming aware of it. Something had been unravelling in her mind, had been coming apart and shedding layers of opacity at the same time. It was as if a blazing diamond was trapped inside a tiny box, which was in turn trapped inside a slightly larger box, which was in its turn trapped inside an even larger box—like those clever ornaments she had once seen at market. And the boxes were disintegrating one by one, from the outside in. The diamond, whatever it was, remained beyond her reach, tantalising her.

In retrospect, she knew exactly when it had begun: the day she and Jon were in the meadow, the day of the event. Although the pattern that Jon suspected had to be linked to Milo's incident, Shondral felt certain that it was part of a much larger pattern that was unfolding. She could not say what it was or how she knew it, but she knew it. Just as she knew that the demon Milo had killed was part of that pattern and as she knew that they had embarked on a path to much more than ridding Milo of his nightmares and Alba of a few unscrupulous officials.

Milo, too, was in turmoil and had been for two interminable years. He called it hate and horror and torture. It branded his soul and lured him to its perverse power. All he had to do was give himself up to it, follow it, become one with it, and his suffering would be over. He had been on the precipice any number of times and it was only his absolute belief that it was wrong that anchored him in the solitary battle he fought night after night. He brushed his hand against his sister's and felt Jon beside him. He rejoiced that he was no longer alone and felt guilty at the same time. What if this thing he had created could get into their minds too? What if, by being close to him, by helping him, they were further endangering themselves?

Gods, if only he could go back to that day on the hillside, if only he could change what had happened, if only he had not been so infatuated with Annie. How could he have been so blind? But to catch her with his best friend had been more than he could take. Rage had overwhelmed him and he had wanted badly to hurt something. In the sometimes-perverse way of the universe, the hurt had been twisted around and directed inward, and he inflicted upon himself a sharp, hot pain. He thought his head would explode. He could barely see through the sudden spurt of tears and it was only the cramping in his hands that made him look down at the pile of sawdust that had been his carving. When the dust slowly reassembled itself into a woman, he thought he must have suffered a brain injury and was imagining terrible things, but the pain was too real. And the hate that emanated from the woman that now stood before him was too focused. He had fallen to his knees, retching. If only he had known that the pain he had felt that day was nothing, a mere gentle prelude, in comparison with what she would mete out to him in his dreams, he would have done anything to stop her then and there.

Halam was far from asleep. His silent musing was necessary for him to recall from his memory the details of what he must do. Oriander had neglected to say that they would be so young and so green, or that they would take so long to get here. He was a few years past his prime, but an incidental like that would not stop him from returning to Banifour. He cleared his throat and looked up at the ceiling.

"We'll need a pack mule for extra food and other gear. Eich here will come with us. He has a keen nose for trouble," Halam slapped the great dog's flanks, "and he sure could use some exercise." Eich manoeuvred into a better position for the next love pat. "We leave at first light."

They blurted a dozen questions at him that he deftly averted. They had asked him for his help, hadn't they? They had work to do today and lots of time to talk once they were on the road. Time to explain everything, he lied. They resigned themselves to be patient but scarcely noticed it in the flurry of tasks their guide assigned them.

Halam handed Jon a pouch heavy with coin and sent him back to Morbella for supplies. With a hat pulled low over his eyes and a cloak that reached his knees, the townsfolk would think him a travelling prospector and be happy to take his money and quickly send him on his way. Meanwhile, Halam had Milo spread the contents of their satchels over the floor of his house and ruthlessly pared it down to the barest necessities.

"But I must bring these!" Shondral could not believe that one spare tunic was all she was allowed. "Some of us need a change of clothes more than once a month." She glanced at his grimy trousers.

Halam stood his ground. "These?" he pulled at the fabric. "They can be thrown in a stream, cleaned with a bit of sand, and dried inside of an hour. And they'll look as good as new." He studied the faded pants. "Well almost."

Milo retreated to the far end of the room and busied himself with another of the endless jobs that Halam had assigned them. He struggled to contain his amusement as the unlikely-looking pair glared at each other, hands on hips—his sister with her beautiful long hair and neat garments, and Halam with his ratty... everything.

"Let me put it to you this way:" Halam said, "if your horse carries clothes, he can't carry food."

Shondral chewed her bottom lip for a moment and shrugged her shoulders. "Better dirty and fed than clean and starving, I suppose." She had enjoyed their minor altercation; it felt good to argue over ordinary, everyday things.

"Smart girl," Halam said. "And for equally excellent reasons, we will apply this most splendid emollient to our gear." He rummaged through his shelves and produced a jar.

Milo wandered closer. "What is it?"

Halam answered by handing him the jar and pointing him and Shondral to the pile of gear. Noses crinkled, they kneaded the foul-smelling grease into the seams of their packs, boots, mitts, and cloaks.

Jon returned just as they thought they had finished this malodorous task. Of course, some of Jon's purchases had to be greased as well. With a sigh, Shondral and Milo stoically carried on with the work; no sense in anyone else getting their hands in such a state. Meanwhile, Halam and Jon bagged and labelled dried vegetables and fruit, some of which Jon did not recognise. At last, they stuffed the mountain of equipment and food into assorted pouches and packs duly assigned to animals and riders alike. The only one saved from this frenzy of work, and indeed from carrying more than a spiked collar, was Eich who had slept soundly through it all.

They ate a hearty meal and climbed into their sleeping sacks, and without further

thought to what lay ahead, dropped into an exhausted sleep.

With their heads on the floor and all pointed in the same direction, Eich had no trouble sweeping Jon, Shondral, and Milo awake with a long, slobbery kiss. They washed—perhaps a little more vigorously than usual—breakfasted, loaded the mule and horses, and were off as Ord peeked over the horizon.

That first day they would travel through familiar territory—familiar not because they had been there before but because they were still in the Kobaska Hills and the terrain remained much the same as near the villages. They would bear south and west along the ravine that separated the Hills from the Plateau. Halam claimed that the fissure could be crossed if you knew where to look, and would save several days' journey because then they could travel directly west along the top of the Dreven Plateau instead of angling south to where the ravine eventually petered out.

They rode in single file with Milo behind Halam, who had the mule tethered to the pommel of his saddle, followed by Shondral, with Jon bringing up the rear. This would prove to be their usual arrangement. Spread out as they were, they had to raise their voices to talk and, after several failed attempts at conversation, each was left with his own thoughts.

Jon had looked forward to having some time to ponder, but as he considered their circumstances, he discovered that it was not such a satisfying experience after all. Ever since this whole thing began, the questions far outnumbered the answers. His latest collection of unanswered questions concerned their new-found leader. Why had they so quickly entrusted their lives to him? How had he built that invisible wall and how had he created his marvellous back yard? Why did he leave his home to come with them in the first place? And why had he greeted them as Fire-Welders? Or was it Wielders? He had forgotten about that in their frenzy of preparation. They knew nothing about him except for the gossip of the hamlets. Jon's frustration was reaching combustion levels; he would have to have some explanations soon. The only trouble was that, lately, any explanations just seemed to open up a whole new batch of questions.

Tired from worrying at these riddles, Jon shunted them aside and resolved to instead study the terrain they travelled through. He quickly discovered that this was one of his better ideas. The rolling hills were wooded, iridescent with golden sunlight on tiny green buds. The forest floor was swept clean, anticipating the graceful ferns that would soon sway in the cool breezes. The strip of sunshine on either side of the path was riotous with spring flowers: brilliant orange leaves the shape of a lady's manicured fingernail, lavender blooms like minuscule crinolines, and blood-red spikes capped with delicate pink droplets. The entire collage floated above a dense ground cover saturated with clouds of tiny white stars. It soothed his soul.

Throughout the day, they stopped briefly to water the horses and grab snacks for themselves that they ate in the saddle. At last, Halam called a halt for the night beside a trickle of a stream. He once again assigned tasks and, before long, their camp was set and a pot of soup bubbled over a blazing fire.

Jon searched Shondral's face for signs of weariness. She smiled at him, tired and sore, but no more than they all were. They chatted about what was in the soup that Halam made and about the pleasant ride that day, if you ignored a little stiffness here and there. Jon stood and used a convenient tree to help him stretch his legs. The others watched in fascination for a moment. At Jon's sigh of relief, all three of his companions were soon demanding that he show them the movements and Jon found himself happily instructing them just as Jikal had shown him. They helped each other balance on one leg. Eich eagerly joined in this new game and did his best to topple his master to the ground. Halam grabbed at Jon for support and the pair of them performed a bumbling balancing dance with Eich doing a crazy circle race around them. Shondral and Milo laughed until tears leaked out of their eyes.

"You can never tell what that dog will do next," Halam muttered. "He's got a mind of his own and a warped sense of humour." Eich sat well beyond arm's reach, tongue lolling out, and with as much of a grin on his canine face as he could manage.

Supper and stretching finished, they rolled out ground sheets and sleeping sacks. *Now*, Jon thought, I'll ask him now. Even as he phrased the first question in his head, Halam spoke.

"There are some things you should know."

Eich lay just within the ring of firelight and his ears came to attention at his master's voice. Halam told them the remarkable story of Banifour...

***

Oriander led him beyond the Great Hall to a corridor with dozens of closed doors. There were no markings to hint at the wonders that must be behind them. They stopped in front of one, seemingly at random, and Oriander gestured for Halam to open it. Trembling with excitement, he pushed the handle and entered into a desert wasteland so vast that it could not possibly be contained within the Great Hall. Halam stood in the sand, jaw agape.

"It's always far more effective to show than to tell, don't you agree?"

Oriander conducted him back through the door and into the hallway, turned right, and opened a second door. The smoke and stench struck Halam full in the face, blinding him. He squinted through watering eyes and wished he had left them shut.

"The world can be violent without any help at all," Oriander chuckled.

Halam peered at his fate. The brink of the inferno stretched to either side of him. He followed the jagged line it made until, with a jolt, he saw that it met itself across the plumes of smoke to form a rough circle. Oriander's words penetrated his despair. He was looking at a volcano, not some form of Hades. Shuddering with relief, Halam exited once again into the cool, welcoming corridor.

Not knowing what to expect, the ordinary living quarters through the next door were at first threatening and unfamiliar to Halam.

"Make yourself comfortable. A drink?"

Halam nodded, grateful for something mundane. Settled in a comfortable armchair with the warmth of an excellent brandy coursing through him, Halam studied his host. At first glance, Oriander seemed an ordinary man with ordinary features. There was nothing about him that warranted particular notice until their eyes met. A sudden, ominous foreboding gripped Halam. He tried to turn his glance aside but could not look away. He commanded his lids to close, to blink; they defied him. He was drawn into twin pools of darkness.

In helpless outrage, Halam was forced to watch as his entire life was displayed and dissected for Oriander's close inspection. Halam cringed when secrets he had long since buried were scrutinised; his most private and intimate thoughts were laid bare. He screamed his fury and tore at the phantom raping his mind.

"You'll do," Oriander declared, "and in time you may attempt to have your revenge on me." The scorn in his voice was thick with malice.

Halam barely heard him over the thundering of his heart and the ragged gasps that hurt his lungs. He forced his breathing to slow. Revenge? It would take a thousand lifetimes to quench the fire of rage that burned in his breast. He bunched his muscles and strained to launch himself at the monster who had violated him.

Oriander's mouth twitched into a cynical smirk, savouring the torment. The raw emotion was delicious, and it was with some regret that he adjusted the memory of the probe in Halam's mind. He would remember his torment very well, but it would last only an instant and Halam would forever wonder why he felt so angry and frustrated a moment later. Halam may never fully remember what had been done to him. Pity.

"More brandy?" his congenial host asked. Shrugging off a bewildering surge of anger, Halam extended his glass; it was an excellent vintage and his throat had suddenly gone dry.

Oriander rang a delicate bell and soon three others joined them. Halam jolted to his feet. He recognised the woman who had summoned him at the lake. With her was a second woman who had to be Oriander's sister, so close was the resemblance, and another man with skin darker than any Halam had ever seen.

"May I present my fellow Guardians: the lovely Ushival, whom you have met, the equally lovely Aoineadh and, yes, she is my sister, and, in all his glorious ebony, Risto."

Halam bowed deeply to each as they were introduced and waited until they had seated themselves before returning to his own chair.

"And this, my dear comrades, is Halam, adventurer from the Kobaska Hills."

They told him their story, intertwining their voices as though speaking from one mind: in millennia past, when Méadhon was a fledgling world, they had come to celebrate its birth, for a planet that supported life in such abundance was a priceless discovery. Banifour and its Guardians protected this treasure against harm from both within and without. No, they were not the original Guardians, but they and others like them had been on Méadhon for thousands of years.

They told him of the wondrous power known as Lifefire. They spoke to him of its properties, of its uses, of its marvels. The 'rooms' Oriander had

146

shown him were samples of what it could do. It was how they ascertained the health of Méadhon and how they sustained themselves. Lifefire was birth, growth, and death in a continuing cycle. But it could be abused, and it was for this reason that they had interfered with Halam's life. They had foreseen a future on Méadhon that must be stopped, a future where the earth was scorched and blackened, bereft of life. It was their solemn task to prevent this, and they needed Halam's help.

Halam did not have to ponder his decision. He knew he would pledge his life to protect his home.

He woke outside his cottage in the Kobaska Hills with the knowledge of what he had to do: he would wait in readiness every day for three companions who spoke of evil destruction, and he would take them to Banifour.

***

Glowing embers were all that remained of their campfire; it had gone untended as Halam spoke. Jon was nearest the wood they had gathered earlier and stoked the fire. They did not offer comments or even bid each other goodnight; no one wanted to break the spell, even when Halam had suddenly stiffened and went silent for a few moments during the tale. The crackling of fresh fuel lulled them to sleep, their questions forgotten in visions of wonder and magic and an overwhelming desire to help save their world.

It was on this night that his nemesis chose to force another of her mind-breaking nightmares on Milo. "Malissa, no!" he cried.

147

"Ah, you finally know my name. Took you long enough." The sneer in her voice was a palpable thing.

He tried to shake himself awake but it was useless, as always; once she had her grip on him there was no escape. Darkness and loathing speared him with utter hopelessness. He lost all sensation: sight, touch, scent, sound—he could not scream his terror. As he suffocated in total deprivation, she gloated and crooned her empty promises of pleasure and power that could be his if he came to her. His weak but firm denial sent her into throes of rage and a promise of immediate punishment. This part changed; she relished variety. Red-hot knives made delicate incisions on his chest, just deep enough to draw blood, and moved simultaneously towards his face and groin. The intense agony shattered her grip on him.

Shondral protected his head while Jon and Halam gripped his arms and legs to keep him from rolling into the fire. Sobbing through clenched teeth, Milo let them know he was awake.

Halam prepared a fragrant broth over the rekindled fire. Cup in hand, Milo haltingly confirmed that her name was indeed Malissa, but she could easily be lying about that. He described what she had said and done. As he spoke, the sight of his twisted features and contorted body replayed themselves in Jon's mind. They had been powerless to stop it.

The combination of broth and fatigue soon calmed Milo and he slept undisturbed for the remainder of the night.

Light drizzle began sometime before dawn and continued throughout the morning. They were grateful for the water-repellent properties of the pungent grease they had applied to everything. Eich and the other animals were not so lucky, however; their coats were plastered to their bodies. Jon felt sorry for them but could not think of any way to help short of donating his own cloak. He squinted through the rain and it seemed to him that the water did not penetrate their fur after all but instead rolled off their backs as if they were ducks. Jon remarked on this to Halam.

"How would *you* like to be soaking wet all day?" Halam sniffed. "Of course they're waterproofed." He nudged his horse and trotted ahead.

Eich looked up at him and smirked. *I must be losing my mind*, Jon thought, not at all surprised.

Shondral dropped back beside him as the trail widened. "Now don't let that old goat get your goat," she teased. "He's just a little put out that you'd think he wouldn't look after the animals." She explained how the herdsmen had long ago learned to extract the oil from the Dryx's wool. When they sheared them in early summer, the wool was compressed between two oak trees that had been smoothed and fashioned into huge rollers that were made to spin towards each other. A fine mesh suspended below separated the oil from the wool and when it was added to a denser base of fat, it was transformed into a natural and most effective, though smelly, water repellent. It could be applied to fabric such as their cloaks, or to live animals by brushing it into their fur.

The ravine they sought began as a deep gorge hundreds of miles to the north where the Dreven Plateau met the Sgeir Range. Either the Plateau had risen or the land around it had dropped, and many suspected that the cataclysm that had changed the shoreline of the Sea of Orchès had also created this terrible gash in the earth. It isolated the nomads that dwelled on the Plateau and, even though it meant a life of hardship, they would choose no other life. It was the rare nomad who ventured forth from his home.

They sighted the canyon by mid-morning. Halam dismounted and gave his reins to Milo. He scuttled along the ridge, stopping every few minutes to peer down the embankment. "Here it is," Halam muttered to himself, and declared an early lunch.

After a cold meal of bread and dried fruit, Halam squinted at the sky and began the steep descent leading his horse and their pack mule. Milo, Shondral, and Jon followed suit and were soon warmed by their exertions. This side of the ravine was rocky and offered good purchase and they reached the bottom without incident. They rested briefly and after some thought Halam decided to tackle the other more difficult side before conditions worsened.

Halfway up, however, the drizzle turned into a hard rain. It quickly converted the narrow switchback trail into a river of mud and loose rock that grew more treacherous as boots and paws and hooves stirred the whole mess together. Jon sank into the treacherous sludge and his boots threatened to stay behind, swallowed in the mire that sucked at them. The sluggish pace, the leaden sky, and the annoying rain that revelled in finding its way down his neck gave the day truly dismal proportions. Jon raised a weary head from his tribulations to see how Shondral managed, and to perhaps commiserate.

His intention was distracted by something, no, by someone. By someone missing. Halam had vanished.

151

Chapter 6

A strong sense of determination united the Uamhan-Alban team as it wound its way back to the cave mouth and to the *Pride*.

Maol had insisted on coming and on bringing Riab with him. After all, he had argued, they were the best qualified to battle any other virulence that Malissa could concoct. He did not have to add that they could also be of assistance in the highly likely event that there were other, more battle-oriented injuries. Roinn and Teber, the two strongest far-seekers, were indispensable for the plan to work; and Géodha was needed for her intimate knowledge of all growing things and could be of assistance with healing—she had been Maol's apprentice for a short time.

Aird had left some time earlier with Riab and the young far-seekers. The Uamhans required no lanterns; it seemed that the glowing eyes of the old guide that had startled them in the cathedral were one of the Lifefire enhancements indispensable to cave dwellers. The possibilities awed Jeorg and, he admitted to himself, frightened him a little. When the advance team reached the cave entrance, Aird would signal the ship of their success and of the additional passengers. The crew would have to be told the truth about Lifefire at once and somehow be made to promise secrecy. They needed every advantage they could get, however small, until Malissa could be apprehended. She had had at least two years to hone her evil skills while the Uamhans could barely bring themselves to even think about

Lifefire in the way that Malissa used it. Notwithstanding the odds, Jeorg itched for a chance at retribution for what Malissa what she had done to him and, doubtless, to others.

Endel was oblivious to the trek; he and Maol were so engrossed in learning about each other's medical worlds that they had to be guided over debris on the trail by amused friends. There would be revolutionary treatments introduced to the world and much fuss over the myth come true.

Jeorg smiled to himself. It would be good to be on his ship again. In four days—had it been only four days! —the world as he had known it had completely changed. This amazing and overwhelming Lifefire would bring so many wonderful things to the people of Méadhon: new medical cures, new types of food, new abilities of the mind, new life spans. And new dreams. Lifefire could give Méadhonians the freedom to explore new possibilities in any number of disciplines; they would be able to devote the time normally spent simply surviving in pursuit of bigger and more profound goals. For Jeorg, that meant travelling beyond the edges of the continent. It meant seeing the whole of the world. It could even mean seeing more than that. He looked up at the rocky ceiling of the tunnel they were traversing but its ridges and reflected minerals did not register on his brain. His eyes were seeing far beyond the mountains; he was seeing the stars. His desire to be part of that exploration so consumed him that Jeorg could barely concentrate on the incredibly large stumbling block in the way. He shook his head. Self-discipline built from years at sea helped him to marshal his thoughts and he rallied, more motivated than ever, to rid Méadhon of its nemesis.

Géodha's trepidation had been escalating steadily since she embarked on the long march away from the warmth and safety of Uamh. It was making her head spin and she felt ill. She could barely believe that, of her own volition, she was about to expose herself to the vast openness without the Mountain over her head to protect her. It's not that she had never had the opportunity to trek to the cave entrances. Memories of her youth were marred with the coming-of-age ritual that her peers inflicted on themselves. She would never forget poor Maria. Like Géodha, Maria had hesitated to undertake the 'test' but she had gone. They had had to carry her back. Maol was so infuriated that he posted guards at the tunnels. Maria recovered, but the haunted look on her face was still clear in Géodha's mind. After that, Géodha invented any number of excuses to avoid the challenge, and her friends finally stopped harassing her. But she had never been accepted into their inner circle. Maybe that was why she had thrown herself into her studies and why she was such a staunch supporter of the far-seekers. She had convinced herself that there had to be other ways to learn of the outside world without relinquishing the Mountain that sheltered her from the endless abyss above her head.

The light grew more intense but was very similar to Uamh's; Géodha did not give it much thought. She walked behind Maol and Endel and concentrated on their backs, her footing, the problem of Malissa, anything but what she would soon have to face. She had had the foresight to bring something to soothe her nerves but wanted to wait until the last moment to administer it.

She never got the chance.

Maol and Endel stepped to either side to give her an unobstructed view. Her sense of perspective reeled and, at first, she could make no sense out of what she was seeing. A vast bowl of blue merged with a vast bowl of green and in the green bobbed a child's toy boat. The whole thing could easily have been a brilliant painting.

Aird was at her side. "This, too, is real," he said. He put a hand under her elbow to steady her; she had not realised she was swaying forward, toward the edge. He pointed to the toy boat. "I never realise how much I miss her until I see her again."

The tableau crashed into place. Géodha stared at the ship. The scurrying movement she had thought was a trick of the light resolved itself into men—sailors climbing in the rigging and rushing about on the deck.

Alarmed, Aird gripped her arm more tightly and turned her toward the cave. Her face had lost all colour and a sheen of perspiration covered it. It had never occurred to him that she would react like this; he had assumed that all Uamhans had trekked to the cave's mouth and cursed this oversight during the team's selection. "Endel." Maybe the Doctor had something to help her. But it was Riab who came to his call.

He placed a hand at her throat and felt her forehead, deep concern on his young face. "I thought she was handling it," he murmured as he poured a dark liquid onto a cloth and pressed it to the back of her neck. It smelled slightly of stale beer. The two men helped Géodha to sit and in a matter of seconds, her breathing was deep and regular and her cheeks back to their normal, healthy glow. Géodha and Riab looked at each other and she nodded.

"I'm fine now, Aird," Géodha said. "Confronting one's worst fear and finding it beautiful is somewhat... disorienting." She smiled at him. "I will not be caught off guard again, but I thank you for being there." She scanned her fellow Uamhans, especially Maol, but he was enjoying the view with the same exuberance as young Roinn and Teber. "I should have known that that old goat would have been here before."

Maol raised frosty eyebrows and turned to her with the hurt look of a chastised puppy. "Oh, don't play innocent with me," she teased and joined him, arm in arm, to gaze in wonder at the white gauzy puff of cloud that she had only read about in schoolbooks.

Three dinghies had been dispatched from the ship and awaited them at the bottom of the cliff. Aird had fashioned a harness to lower the non-climbing members of the expedition and soon, the Uamhans and a still-recovering Jeorg were at sea level and being rowed to the ship.

Endel buried his fear. Gritting his teeth and cursing his pride, he rapelled down the face of the Cliffs while Aird looked on.

Chapter 7

Malissa sat in the guard tower nearest the barracks. From here, she had an uninterrupted view of her domain. With the long tube Nedral of the Council Triad had given her, she could study battle practice in one field and the speed with which Kammerle was being harvested in another.

Also from her perch, she could reprimand any deviation from her commands simply by pointing. One of her death-birds would swoop down from its glide pattern high above the estate and descend unerringly to claw the object of her disapproval. She had had to experiment on dozens of creatures to perfect the venom so that the merest graze of talon or beak caused mind-numbing pain followed quickly by death. There was no defence. It was very effective as a disciplinary measure, but, sometimes, when she was bored, she would summon one for no reason at all. It kept everything running smoothly.

Her thoughts flicked to the poisoned wine that had made puppets of the Council and of other key people, but she was tired of this passive game. She ached for violence. She needed to crush something. The failure of her minion to obliterate those two Apprentices fuelled her anger. They suspected too much; they would not escape again.

Milo still eluded her. She snarled. She could sense his mind when he slept and knew that he heard her thoughts and felt her tortures, but she could not 'see' him. She did not know exactly where he was. Her experiments would be accelerated; she would try something new. Yes.

Satisfied, her attention was drawn back to the activity below. Her armies were nearing readiness and would attack simultaneously: Mriss, Ked, Alba, the hamlets—all would become her slaves. They would have no time to protect themselves, no chance to help each other. Only the young ones would be spared, ripe for her manipulations. She licked her lips in anticipation and summoned a death-bird to heighten her pleasure.

Chapter 8

The four-day voyage to Alba was spent in a frenzy of preparation for their confrontation with Malissa. En route, Roinn and Teber journeyed to her manor in Alba and to her farming estate, though they stayed well clear of any contact. The house was quiet but the farm was seething with activity. Barracks had been built and more were under construction. Hundreds of deformed shapes writhed over the fields like some wormy plague, while taller more man-like creatures drilled in precise formation within the capacious square formed by the buildings. It would have gone unnoticed from the ground because of the screening provided by the low hills but was plain to the reconnaissance of the far-seekers.

The news of Malissa's imminent mobilisation forced them to accelerate their plans. Time was no longer a consideration: they had none. They must strike at once with quick and deadly accuracy.

The *Pride* docked at the farthest pier, well away from the busy commercial district of Alba. The crew was given their customary shore leave and became the eyes and ears of the enterprise. They sat in the taverns to drink and carouse with their fellow sailors, all the while straining for some morsel of information that could help in some way. Jeorg allowed them one precious day and they reported two tales.

The first was about a peculiar illness that had struck several prominent citizens. As Jeorg suspected, Malissa had poisoned others besides himself. The second tale was far more curious. One of his crew had happened upon a hushed group gathered around a merchant from Mriss:

"A devil!" he exclaimed, and pounded his fist on the thick wooden table. "It was," he insisted, through the jeers of his audience.

"It'd be a new story, anyhow," bellowed a longshoreman with a long white scar marring his cheek from the outside corner of his eye to his chin. "Let 'im tell it." The room quieted; they loved a good story, the truth was irrelevant.

The merchant reached over to top up his defender's mug.

"Now then," he continued. "The people of the Hills are a backward but honest sort." *Often to my own personal profit*, he thought, as he ordered another round. Oiddel seldom missed an opportunity to make new friends.

"They trapped it in a wood crate with bars the size of my leg." He clambered onto a table to demonstrate its girth. "You could hardly see it, so black it was. And all slimy." He grimaced and wiped a hand down the front of his tunic. "Its red eyes scorched a man's soul, they did." He waited for the 'Oooohs' and 'Aaaahhs' to die. "Then it snapped the bars, easy as this." He viciously broke the slender piece of kindling he had been saving for that moment. The three sailors closest to him jumped back and Oiddel waited patiently while the taunts about their lack of backbone and comparisons to old ladies died down. When it was quiet again, all eyes were riveted on the merchant. Even the busy barmaids had stopped to listen.

161

"It screamed like a hundred women bein' flailed alive. Even busted the eardrums of some of them that was standing too close. Then it slithered out of the cage and stood on its two hind legs, smoke pourin' out of its nostrils." He paused for a long drink relishing the taut attention of his audience.

"It strutted about gouging great gashes in the cobbles. They say it wasn't no bigger than a young boy but must ha' weighed a thousand pounds. It opened leathery wings and, before anyone could so much as take a breath, it bounded fifty feet in the air, and dove straight at two youngsters. It knocked them to the ground and reached for their throats with six-inch claws." Gasps of horror filled the room. "But just then," Oiddel lowered his voice for effect, his audience craned forward to catch every word, "a stranger appeared out of nowhere. He drew a sword that flashed like great Ord and roared a challenge. The monster reared up from its helpless prey and charged. In one mighty motion, the brave champion threw the sword like a dagger. It flew straight and true," he paused for a few seconds, "into the beast's black heart."

The thick, smoky silence lasted a full three breaths before the mob howled its appreciation, whether they believed old Oiddel or not. The merchant was well pleased with his performance; he would make a few new friends tonight. And what are friends for if not to buy your wares?

***

Aird had sent three of his more discreet deckhands into Alba to find out more about this creature of the story, and about the people it had attacked. But it remained a mystery.

Jeorg had looked in the best of health until Géodha applied her unguents to his face and hands. He now appeared to be a truly sick man, wasted and pale. Aird and Riab accompanied Jeorg to meet with Malissa under the guise that their Captain needed help to walk. He was, after all, a victim of her insidious poison.

Malissa's features contorted into a feral grin as she looked upon her prey. Aird and Riab hid their faces in the hoods of the cloaks they wore while they studied the house: one with the shrewd awareness of a nomad and the other with the enhanced senses of a Uamhan. Malissa ignored them, intent on the signature Jeorg scrawled on the contract. A small man by her side placed a vial in her hand, which she exchanged for the signed document. She turned and left them. No one had spoken a word.

When they were several blocks away, they stopped to breathe the sweet night air wafting in from the Sea. "Most unusual," Riab began, then grunted as Aird elbowed him in the ribs. The Uamhan nodded belated understanding and they continued silently to the docks; it was unsafe to speak anywhere but on the ship.

When they had joined Endel, Géodha, Maol, Roinn, and Teber in the Captain's quarters, Riab began, "She, or perhaps 'it,' is most unusual. Although she is made of flesh and blood just as you and me, she has no," he groped for the right word, his expressive mouth pursed in concentration, "no spark. No soul. She's more like a yampré—cunning, driven, and intelligent, yet full of hate and at the same time incapable of compassion or love, or even of *thinking* of them.

"There were others in the house," Riab continued, "like her in some ways but not as much somehow, not as intense. Sort of watered down." He shrugged, unable to provide a clearer distinction.

They considered this discovery, each lost in their own thoughts. Géodha broke the silence. "In Uamh, we use Lifefire to enhance what is. Is it possible," she directed her question at Riab, "to alter what is into something totally different?"

One of Riab's apprentices had postulated the same preposterous idea. It had never been examined because it was such a blatant affront to nature. Somewhat naive thinking, Riab realised to his chagrin, especially when that naïveté could endanger them all. In the light of having seen Malissa herself and sensed the creatures that surrounded her, he forced himself to consider it. Vile and unspeakably cruel to the creature so used, but he had to reluctantly admit that it could be done. It would take a mind with intimate knowledge of Lifefire and no scruples whatsoever. He felt dirty thinking about it, and saying it aloud to the anxious faces around him made it worse.

"There's one piece missing, though, a very large piece," Riab chewed on a thumbnail, "and that is the origin of Malissa herself. She is capable of manipulating Lifefire, but who showed her? Could she have discovered this herself? Because, if not, we may have an even more powerful enemy."

Before Riab's ill-timed conjecture could erode what confidence they had, Jeorg took charge of the meeting. "We must be even more cautious." It was entirely possible that Malissa was a pawn in a much larger game. But if they waited to uncover plots within plots, all would be lost. "The Shipmasters' League deploys its men tonight. Aird will take command, with Roinn and Teber providing intelligence."

He turned to the healers. "Géodha, Maol, and Endel will set up a field hospital." Endel's sharp intake of breath was audible in the close quarters of Captain's cabin. Jeorg continued. "You will set up a few hundred yards this side of her estate. Right about here." He pointed to the location on the map laid out on the table in front of him. "When we return to the *Pride*, you will have a chance to study the plant samples that the men bring from her fields."

While the others busied themselves with final preparations, Jeorg crossed the room and put a hand on Endel's shoulder. "I know you want to be in the thick of it; I know that you usually are. I know this is the hardest thing I've ever asked of you, but if my guess is right, we are going to need every ounce of medical help you can give us." He looked into his friend's eyes and saw reluctant acceptance. That would have to be enough.

He raised his voice, "And I will pay another visit to Malissa and keep her occupied as long as I can." He glared around the room, daring anyone to defy him. No one did.

It was much later when Captain Jeorg Oprum

boldly approached Malissa's door for the second time that night. Her guards had been ordered, as usual, to prevent anyone from disturbing their mistress's rest. It would be far better to kill or to be killed than to risk disobedience. But Jeorg was ready for this. Six burly crewmen crept along the walls, three on either side of the entranceway. They quickly dispatched the two guards and disappeared into the night.

Roinn had pinpointed her lingering spirit for him and Jeorg flawlessly made his way to her chambers. She looks so innocent and ordinary, Jeorg thought, as he levelled the crossbow at her heart and prepared to wait until she woke.

The square of sky visible through the barred bedroom window began to lighten and still she had not moved. Excellent. The attack on her farm has begun and she is an hour's ride away.

***

Malissa's mind boiled with anger. That stupid boy had help! It had taken her greatest effort yet to pry it out of him, but pry it she did. He was with those two meddling brats. Her wrath shaped their fate: death-birds. She would return to her body and leave for the estate immediately.

Her eyes snapped open with the jolt of mind meeting body and focused on Jeorg Oprum. She had been so intent on her night's work that she had not sensed him. *I'm getting careless*, she cursed. It would never happen again.

She stretched seductively. "Good morning, Captain. How nice to see you again so soon." She artfully allowed a thin shoulder strap to fall,

166

revealing a beautifully formed breast.

His eyes never left hers.

"The contract," he commanded.

"We made a deal, Captain."

"Deal? That was blackmail and I will not sacrifice the League for one man."

"How very noble of you," she cooed. "Did I not tell you that the attacks will recur without periodic doses of the antidote? No? I must have forgotten."

"It seems that neither one of us is interested in keeping this deal." Jeorg waved the bow. "So why don't we discuss a small exchange? Your life for mine."

"Certainly," she agreed. "Now just put that away and I'll have a servant bring a vial of the actual cure, not just the temporary remedy." She leaned back into the mountain of pillows and stretched her arms over her head, caressing the curve of the headboard. With a casual stroke of her finger, she triggered the release mechanism of the paralytic agent.

Her gloating eyes registered on his brain and he vainly struggled to pull the hairpin trigger. "The paralysis is complete, Captain," she spat out the last word like she had tasted something foul. Two servants entered. "It was ridiculously simple to incapacitate you. All you had to do was breathe." Her inhuman laughter filled the room. "Take him to my carriage. We go to the estate."

They gingerly removed the crossbow from his unresponsive hands and carried him from the room. *If only I've given them enough time*, Jeorg thought bitterly.

***

Géodha, Maol, and Riab had given the attacking men as much protection as they could. Faces were darkened and scents disguised; jars of the cumbas leaf juice had been distributed. And though far from medicinal, powerful incendiary devices had been fashioned.

In teams of four or five, volunteer crewmen from nearly all the ships in port travelled to Malissa's estate and secreted themselves near their assigned targets, awaiting the signal.

Aird had not moved from his position atop the guard tower. Taking it had been a brief, vicious fight, and without surprise on their side, they would most certainly have lost men. Malissa's thugs were battle-trained and battle-ready.

Roinn and Teber sat slouched in a corner, their spirits roaming above the estate. They had reported that League men controlled the other towers and that the rest of the attack teams were in position. Aird marvelled yet again at this amazing ability—to soar high above the world, seeing it through the eyes of a bird. When this was over, he promised himself, he would approach Féadan. Perhaps he was not too old for a modification or two.

Aird gave the all-clear signal and, though he could see no movement, dozens of men approached the barracks. He heard the first shouts from Malissa's troops and within minutes the whole estate was awake, commands buffeting the pre-dawn air.

Roinn stirred and Aird immediately went over to gather the latest report. Teber remained aloft.

"The crops burn and so far our men keep the enemy away from the water tower. We have lost some ground, though, and are hard pressed. Some of the creatures are as big as Masodinya and others as tiny as my fist. They carry only crude weapons, though. Wooden lances sharpened to a point and knives fashioned with sticks and blades of rock."

"How many?" Aird asked.

"I couldn't see very well because of their colouring and their difference in sizes, but they cover the entire area," Roinn's lips tightened, "and more pour from the buildings."

Aird turned his face away from the Uamhan. Fear leapt into his heart. Had they thrown away the lives of their small force? They thought they had a fairly accurate estimate of enemy numbers and had planned accordingly. It was far too late to call for reinforcements. How had she kept them hidden from the Uamhans' senses? He would think about that later.

Aird turned to Riab, a plan forming as he spoke. "My friend, we go to heat things up a little." Aird left orders with his second in command, looked once more at the far-seekers, and, with a few of Géodha's surprises in his pack, descended into the darkness below. Riab followed, apprehension clear on his face.

They were camouflaged in dingy brown tunics and trousers, and dirt-coloured paste on their faces and hands. They half-ran, half-crawled to the cover of the nearest building. The first blush of Ord-rise was visible over the hills that surrounded the farm. The deep shadows would not conceal them much longer.

Men and brutes were fighting and dying a few yards beyond where Aird and Riab skulked. From their cover, they could clearly see the details of Malissa's handiwork. The revolting beast nearest them towered over the men who attacked it. It smelled of long dead remains and was covered with leaking sores. Its four tree-trunk arms ended in crude daggers that rotated continuously in tight circles. The fighting sailors could not get close enough for a strike. Unable to tear their eyes away, Aird and Riab watched as it cornered two of the men against a building and advanced on them, ripping and gouging. It did not stop until it had hacked through its victims and destroyed the wall behind them.

His gorge rising, Aird pulled Riab away. No one noticed their stealthy advance or saw the black objects they rolled into the midst of the command headquarters. Their mission accomplished, they spared no more time for secrecy and ran hard, away from the building. The thudding of their boots could not be heard above the din of battle, which was itself momentarily drowned out a few seconds later by a satisfying explosion.

Malissa's troops continued their fierce slaughter for several more minutes, and then a certain lethargy seemed to spread over them. They plodded around in circles before sinking to the ground, like a dog finding a comfortable spot.

The small force of attackers stood motionless, poised for action, unable to comprehend what was happening.

Aird surveyed the field, his brain denying the extent of their losses. His superior height allowed him to see far more than he wished. Rage replaced denial. He ordered the now placid creatures killed and methodically began to skewer them, one by one. His men watched, stricken in the aftermath of battle. He glared at them until they, too, took up the gruesome task.

A message runner found him covered in slime and blood, eyes gazing vacantly upon the carnage. "A carriage approaches," the breathless man reported.

Aird seemed not to notice him, and Riab gently shook his arm. "It could be Malissa." His voice was hoarse from the smoke. "Give the signal to retreat to the towers."

Like an automaton, Aird gave the signal, followed Riab, and made his lanky frame climb the guard tower. He had never dreamed it could be like this. The ashen faces of Roinn and Teber met him on the platform and he forgot his own aching soul to comfort the two boys with a hand on each of their shoulders.

The pounding of horses' hooves dispersed the fog from Aird's brain. "Are the crossbows in position?" he asked. Teber forced his eyes to focus on Aird and nodded.

"Roinn remains aloft," Teber whispered.

The nomad hoped with all his heart that it would soon be over.

The carriage came into view, slowing as it neared the gates. Roinn stiffened, his back arched, mouth agape. A hoarse cry ripped from his throat and his eyes rolled back into his skull. He crumpled to the wooden floorboards, his face a mask of death beneath the sweat-dampened locks of hair that stuck to his forehead.

"I shall do far worse to your precious Captain!" Harsh laughter assaulted their ears. A round object was flung from the coach and glittered as its slow spin reflected the morning light. The driver turned the carriage and whipped the horses to a gallop.

Aird scrambled from the tower and added his crossbow bolt to the others being fired as he raced after the disappearing carriage. The quarrel embedded itself into the wood beside the driver. He reloaded in an instant but the carriage was out of range. He stared at the cloud of dust moving steadily away from him.

Riab found what Malissa had thrown from the carriage and brought it to the nomad. But Aird already knew what it was—the Captain's League medallion.

The battle was lost after all.

***

The wounded and the dead were carried aboard the *Pride* in crates disguised as ship supplies—no sense in panicking the townsfolk.

In all the activity, Teber slipped quietly into the cabin that he and Roinn had shared. His grief overwhelmed him; he was more alone than any of the others could possibly imagine. Not only had Roinn been his best friend, but they had also shared the glory of far-seeking together. He sat on his bunk, and with his head in his hands, let the tears come.

Aird could not rest, and he occupied his mind with plotting Jeorg's rescue even though they had heard nothing yet from the trackers that pursued her carriage. Endel found him in the Captain's cabin later that night. He dropped into one of the guest chairs as Aird poured him a glass of whisky from the bottle he had been nursing.

Endel rubbed his red-rimmed eyes and sighed. "Thank all the gods we have the Uamhans with us. We'd have lost many more."

Aird acknowledged his comment with a weary nod. "Three hundred good men left the safety of their ships last night because we asked them to. One hundred and twenty-seven returned." He covered his eyes with a bandaged hand. "We thought it would be easy."

"Aye, and there's Jeorg missing." He extended his glass for a refill. "There's nothing we can do to bring back the men who died fighting those things. But think of what would have happened to the people of Alba. The women, the children. It would have been a complete slaughter." His mouth was tight with anger and he ignored the spectacles that slid to the end of his nose.

"I know you're right." Aird's dark eyes met his over the top of his glass. "It's the mindless cruelty, the cold-bloodedness that I keep seeing." He fingered Jeorg's cap on the desk between them. A moment later, he surged to his feet. "It's the waiting that gets to me." He pounded his fist into the cabin's main beam.

A breathless deckhand burst into the room. "We found her," he gasped.

"Sit, man," Endel's medical instincts took over, "before you fall and give me yet another wound to tend."

"She took us on a merry chase," he continued as soon as he had sat and caught his breath. "Up towards Mriss, then doubled back through a maze of farmers' tracks barely wide enough to handle her team of horses. We lost her for a bit there. I still haven't figured how she did that." He rubbed at his forehead. "Anyway," he quickly took up the tale again, "she's taken over the Council Chambers, sir. Booted everyone out."

"Did you see the Captain?" Aird asked.

He lowered his eyes. "Not exactly, sir." He brightened. "But a couple of her guards carried a chest into the building. I'd say it was big enough to hold a man."

"What's your name, son?" Aird felt the boy deserved some sort of reward.

The boy stood proudly. "It's Harval Greensmith, sir, ship's boy on the *Wench.*" He saluted smartly.

"I'll see you get a bonus, Harval." Aird returned his salute. "Dismissed."

So Malissa had decided to drop her flimsy pretence as Advisor and usurp the Council Chambers openly? What were her plans? They had destroyed her army of brutes. How else did she hope to take over the port? Aird was suddenly gripped by the horrible thought that this morning's carnage had only scratched the surface.

But first, they would rescue Jeorg. He would be well guarded, but perhaps a small, select band could

174

do it, especially if a well-timed and rather large distraction gave them cover.

Aird's thin smile told Endel all he needed to know. The *Pride's* first mate had a plan. Somehow, Endel knew he would not like it one bit.

Chapter 9

Eich, mud-spattered from paw to shoulder, growled deep in his chest. The fur on his neck bristled and he strove in vain for a way around the people and animals blocking his path.

Jon wiped the rain from his eyes, but the awful fact remained—Halam was gone. His mind raced. They could rush whatever had taken Halam and overwhelm it before it attacked someone else, or they could approach quietly and hope to surprise it, or they could lure it out and topple it off the narrow track and down the steep slope.

In Jon's moment of indecision, Milo turned to face his sister and, with his attention away from the canyon wall, did not see the swarthy arm that snatched him into the side of the cliff.

Jon and Shondral stood motionless for a moment. They had seen where Milo had disappeared but there didn't seem to be any opening. It looked like a solid wall. Jon slipped his dagger from its sheath and motioned for Shondral to fall back behind him. She squeezed between him and the cliff wall and Jon glimpsed her fear as their eyes briefly met. They inched forward, their backs hugging the cliff. The horses followed them up the worsening trail; Eich crouched at Jon's heels.

A muted din came from nowhere. Before he could discover its direction much less figure out what it was, Jon was jerked off his feet to land unceremoniously inside an aperture that blended so well with the cliff face that he had stepped right in front of it. Shondral was dragged in behind him.

Their eyes quickly adjusted to the dim light for it was a sombre day. The flickering shadows from two smoking torches camouflaged their captors who seemed to blend into the cave walls. Halam and Milo appeared to be alone in the centre of an open space.

"Who are you and why are you here?" a gruff voice barked.

With sound to help, Jon made out the glitter of eyes at the back of the cave.

"My dog, our horses," Halam demanded.

"They are taken care of," a second voice interrupted.

"Enough," the first voice snapped. "Answer my questions."

"We seek nothing on the Plateau and travel this route only because of our urgent need to reach the foothills of the Mjorns as quickly as possible." Halam did not fear the tribes of the Dreven Plateau but he knew that it would be well to proceed cautiously especially when they were outnumbered by at least three to one, not to mention that his side consisted of one man and three children.

The first man spoke again. "These are dangerous times to travel so unprotected. And with young ones." The rebuke was clear in his voice. "Do you not fear attack?"

Halam scoured his memory for something that would convince the nomads of the importance of their mission and that would perhaps even elicit their help. They were a spiritual people who worshipped benevolent gods and believed that their lives were guided by omens which manifested themselves in all manner of disguises. It was the function of their Shaman to interpret the meaning of these omens and, without question, the nomads obeyed the Shaman's illumination as divine.

"We have sensed a grave danger and go to pray for Méadhon's salvation," Halam lowered his head respectfully, "at the Shrine."

Deep silence charged the air for a handful of seconds before it erupted in muttered intonations and a frenzy of rapid hand motions. Jon could not make out what they said or did, but was stunned at their numbers: they were surrounded by no less than fifteen kidnappers. Any attempt to escape now would be suicidal. They would have to wait for a better opportunity. *If one ever comes*, the cynical part of his mind taunted him.

Halam continued. "I would speak with your holy one."

That clinched it. Orders were given and the flurry of activity that ensued included blindfolding them with rough cloth. The nomad who checked their bindings explained in a rough whisper that the Chieftain himself would sacrifice the entire guard if the system of tunnels and caves were revealed to outsiders.

Jon cursed himself; he had had his chance to do something, to try to save them, and he had wasted it. That was twice in just a few minutes. He promised himself that he would not throw away the next opportunity. He would ruthlessly quash the endless alternatives and arguments that his mind conjured. He had had enough with analysing every little thing; he would act first and think later.

Twisting and turning, up and down, the four companions stumbled along.

In more savage times, thieves and murderers had raided the nomad tribes, not for what little they had of material value, but for the women and children who could turn a handsome profit at the barbarous slave markets. The Shamans from all over the Plateau had gathered to decide the manner of retribution and, after many days of beseeching the gods, had emerged pale and exhausted. They decreed that since their wives and mothers and sisters and precious children must walk alone and in darkness, so, too, must the slavers who had taken them.

Every nomad on the Plateau able to travel to the ravine had helped in some way. The strong had dug and carried rock and buckets of dirt, the weak had supplied food and water. With bare hands, crude tools, and a burning desire for revenge, the nomads had carved an intricate and deadly maze within the very roots of the Plateau.

In five seasons, the Shamans' solution was in place.

Sharp-sighted youths were posted along the ridge where the evil ones could be seen ascending certain paths that were plainly the easiest to climb. When any were spotted, guards took up positions at the concealed cave entrances. Once caught, the slavers were bound, blindfolded, and brought deep within the maze where they were left to wander, alone and in darkness. Some found their way back to the wall, starving and quite mad, but most were never seen again. Rumour of the Plateau's

179

vengeance spread and, soon, only the ignorant or the very arrogant risked their wrath. Sentinels had remained vigilant along the rim for many years until the Shamans had decided that the greatest danger had passed and a skeleton patrol would suffice.

And now, quite suddenly, the full complement of guards had been summoned once again. This was surely a harbinger of great import.

Their nomad captors guided them through the convoluted labyrinth. Steps were negotiated and they had to crawl for short distances. Speaking was forbidden. After hours of this sightless, soundless, gruelling march, they scaled a crude ladder. The sense of space was immediate and the damp air that condensed on his exposed skin confirmed to Jon that they had emerged at last from the maze. They marched for another hour before their blindfolds were removed and they were herded into a crude hut. Bruised and scraped, they collapsed on the rush mats that covered the dirt floor.

As he rubbed an abused elbow, Halam's nose sent an urgent message to his stomach. He eagerly reached for the pot simmering on a brazier of hot coals and ladled out heaping bowls of stew for each of his charges.

When he had taken the edge off his hunger, Halam studied them. Milo was the only one whose age might qualify him as a child, but one look at him was enough to convince even the most unobservant that this was not the face of carefree innocence. He could imagine what Malissa's mind rape must be like, and that profoundly disturbed him. It seemed familiar to him in some way that he

180

could not quite grasp. The one thing that he could grasp was that he would do everything in his power to free the lad of his torment. The Guardians at Banifour had prepared him for the possible destruction of the land, but they had said nothing of the human casualties.

Halam turned his attention to Jon. Here was someone he understood. The flippancy and impatience smacked of his own youth; it had been exactly those qualities that had compelled him into any number of brash adventures. Growing up on the docks had given Jon a solid measure of acumen, although he seemed reluctant to act on his instincts, and a wiry strength hidden in his slight body. Halam knew he could rely on him regardless of the scepticism with which Jon viewed their quest.

Shondral was the mystery. The energy he had first sensed in her was somehow different from the energy at Banifour. But how could it be different? Were there aspects of Lifefire which even the Guardians did not understand? Was it even Lifefire? Halam sighed. Whatever it was, it was growing in her and, for now, he had to assume it was part of the Guardians' plan. To his perceptive eye, Shondral did not understand these inner changes and struggled to fathom what was happening to her. When he felt she was ready, he would take her aside and discuss it.

They finished the stew and mopped up the last of the juices with dark crusty bread. With help from a little of their drinking water, they removed the worst of the dirt and grime from their hands and faces. A bare moment later, they were summoned to appear before the clan Chieftain and his Shaman. They brushed crumbs and dried mud from their tunics, ran fingers through their hair in a futile effort to become presentable, and followed the broad back of the nomad who had fetched them.

Jon had never seen a nomad camp before, although he had read about them. From what he could see in the starlit night, there were numerous huts in no apparent pattern, each punctuated by a thin trail of smoke. As he had seen from their own hut, the basic circular shape was fashioned from flexible but sturdy biala poles which were then completely intertwined with tough plateau grass. A low door was covered with the skin of some animal and a smoke hole in the exact centre of the roof completed the nomad dwelling. Stacks of wood were piled beside each door as well as bladders of water and other items whose purposes Jon could only guess at. The camp was nothing like he had envisioned—so much for the accuracy of his schoolbooks. He was becoming convinced that you had to personally experience something before you knew it. What did that say about the integrity of the Historians? They could not possibly have been present at some of the occurrences they had written about. Did they simply imagine what might have happened? Did they make up stories just like he did? Jon quickly buried that line of thinking; he would drive himself crazy.

They rounded a bend in a narrow lane and before them stood the Chieftain's hut, although 'hut' was an understatement. It was twice the height of the others and covered ten or twelve times the surface area. An enormous, black-bearded guard stood on either side of the entrance and the silhouettes of other giants could be seen at intervals around the circumference of the hut. Jon's tired mind pulled together the strands of another observation: they had not seen one other person except for their guide and these sentries during the entire walk through the camp.

The guards stepped aside to let the little company through. Dozens of candles lit the interior. *Smart*, Jon thought, *blind your 'guests' while you get a good look at them*. When his eyes had adjusted, he looked into the solemn features of the tribe's Shaman. Although Shamans could be easily recognised by the long black robe they wore, their only sign of office, the man that faced Jon could have been covered in gaudy baubles or worn nothing at all. His eyes declared what he was far more effectively than anything he might have worn: timeless, ageless; clear and deep as the Sea; dark and fathomless as the night sky—they saw all, knew all. Jon stood motionless as the holy man stared at him. His chest hurt and he remembered to breathe. That slight conscious action broke the spell that held him and Jon turned his head away from the disconcerting contact. The Shaman moved his gaze to Shondral.

While he waited for the nomad's scrutiny to be completed, Jon peered about the antechamber. Heavy drapes surrounded them, muffling sound from within and without. The candles were set in wooden holders along the wall of drapes that separated them from the main chamber. They were

183

being examined or tested by the Shaman, Jon realised, before being admitted into the presence of the Chieftain.

The Shaman sighed, a sorrowful sigh. He opened his arms, palms forward, and brought them together in a thunderous clap. The drapes were drawn back to reveal a portentous gathering of no less than thirty Chieftains and Shamans. "This one," he laid a hand on Halam's shoulder, "has been to the Shrine. And these two have been touched by the Fire." He indicated Milo and Shondral. "The other," pointing to Jon, "is no threat. They travel together to the Shrine to seek guidance. These things I have seen." He touched his forehead with the tips of his fingers, glided to the far end of the room, and settled himself on a plush cushion.

Without further instructions, they remained standing while they were studied once again.

Halam knew that the leaders of the nomad tribes rarely gathered in person; it was unnecessary given the abilities of the Shamans. That they were here, now, in such numbers sent a cold tendril of alarm up his spine. He shifted from one foot to the other wondering how long they would be forced to stand still while they were gawked at.

An elderly woman noisily cleared her throat. "Where are our manners?" Sputtering, she shook a frail index finger around the room. She looked in the newcomers' general direction and smiled toothlessly. "Please, make yourselves comfortable." She flailed an arm at the youth behind her. "Boy, refreshments for our guests." Satisfied that all was well, she resettled herself and dozed off, snoring softly. Jon and Shondral shared a fleeting smile.

The tension of the moment eased. "My mother is a very wise woman." The man who had spoken rose from his nest of cushions. He was tall and dark like all the Drevenese and wore the braided beard that distinguished him as a Chieftain. He glanced at the young boy behind his mother who then soundlessly showed the foursome where to sit and served them a steaming drink. The Conclave continued its business as though they were not there.

"It knows we exist and will come again. How can it not? It needs to feed upon us." The Shaman, Coccin, was white lipped with anxiety.

It had been Coccin who had first tasted the threat to the Dreven Plateau and, indeed, to all of Méadhon. He had been fasting and keeping vigil with the stars in the barren tundra near the Sgeir Range. His mind soared above his beloved Plateau as it cleansed itself in the weightlessness of meditation. Open and vulnerable, he barely escaped the black wave of hate that scoured the land to the east and south. Torn between the need to get as far away as possible and the need to discover more, Coccin delicately approached the fringe of the being that raged in ever-widening circles. With its attention focused elsewhere, it did not detect his light touch.

His spirit had recoiled with such force that it was many hours before he could piece together what he had sensed. The creature he had touched was so distorted that he could not discern if it was even human. It craved power and fed like a raging fire consuming everything in its path. Even though it did not even know he was there, it sucked at him, draining his life. The deep-rooted instinct for self-preservation innate in all the People was what saved Coccin, but not before he had glimpsed the plan of total annihilation that drove the entity. And it had at its command a vast army of beasts.

His brother Shamans, scattered throughout the Plateau, heard Coccin's spirit cry out as it plummeted back to his body. It was their intervention and united strength that had saved him from becoming a soulless husk. They remained intertwined with Coccin long enough to learn the cause of his near demise, and immediately returned to their own bodies. Their Chieftains must learn of this threat at once. The members of the Conclave had ridden forth to gather here, the designated meeting place.

Nepeta, the Chieftain who had greeted the companions, stroked his braids. "I do not deny your words, Coccin. And your brothers speak with one voice. No one denies this." His fellow leaders rumbled assent.

"What is not clear is how we battle something which is not of flesh and blood." Nepeta folded his arms across his chest and took no part in the heated debate that ensued. He was in his seventh year as Chieftain of the Rhudha tribe and Protector of the tunnel mazes. His People numbered greater than fifteen hundred souls, triple the size of any other tribe. This gave him much power within the Conclave. It also gave him a heavy burden of responsibility for *all* the Drevenese, for any attack on the Plateau had to come from the cliffs and it would be him, Nepeta, who turned it aside. On the day that Coccin had discovered this new enemy, his own Shaman, Didyma, had burst into his private chamber and, without explanation, had demanded that the guard on the ravine be doubled. Nepeta buried his irritation as he recalled that rudeness, for tonight he fervently wished he knew nothing of his Shaman's reasons for acting so disrespectfully. The holy men insisted that the creature must have a body to survive; they simply had to find it and destroy it. Nepeta knew that he would be chosen to accomplish this impossible task. It must be done, but he was reluctant to send scouts beyond the Plateau. The world below was rife with unfamiliar danger, and the unknown could kill as quickly as a well-thrust dagger.

"She seeks me." Milo had to shout to be heard over the din. Every eye in the room swung to his face. Even Nepeta's old mother started awake.

"Silence!" Nepeta was incensed that a child would presume such importance. He glared at the insolent boy. His irritation subsided as quickly as it had erupted as he studied the tormented features. In a much gentler voice, he asked, "How do you know this?"

With a distressed glance at his sister, Milo told the story of his carving, right up to the latest nightmare visitation.

The Shamans in the room had assumed positions of meditation as soon as Milo had begun. "They pass the words to those not yet arrived," a youthful voice next to Jon whispered. Startled, he turned to face the young girl seated next to him in full Chieftain raiment, hair braided in tight ropes down her back. A brief smile lit her sun-darkened face before she resumed an air of intense concentration.

Jon looked more closely around the room. Both Chieftains and Shamans varied widely in age: an elderly male Shaman accompanied the young girl beside her. Another middle-aged male Chieftain sat by an equally aged and male Shaman. Yet another team consisted of youthful male Chieftain and ancient female Shaman. Every combination was seated around the chamber. Jon thought sardonically of Alba's governing body—nearly all old and nearly all male. He promised himself that he would find out more about the nomad system. Shondral would be pleased.

Once Milo had finished and Jon had filled in his and Shondral's part, the Conclave looked expectantly at Halam. "I'm just a guide, no more. But I have been touched by the Shrine," he waited for them to complete their supplication, "and have been instructed to bring them there." He was now certain that Banifour and what the nomads called the Shrine were one and the same; the Shaman who had studied them at the door had confirmed this. Nomad legends describe it as a place of magic and holiness protected by the gods where the days are long and filled with sunshine and the nights are mild and filled with stars, where the trees bend their branches so that their fruit can be plucked with ease, and where clear spring water bubbles up from the ground. This would be heaven indeed compared to the parched and barren Plateau.

The nomads did not question the truth of Halam's words or the story of his three companions. They focused on the new knowledge they now had of their enemy and concentrated instead on the intricacies of planning war. The Shamans would do everything they could on the spirit level, and the warriors of the Plateau would fight any physical foe. They were a People of action.

Although Jon had decided on action himself not so very long ago, he did not like the sound of this at all. Helping Milo was one thing but to battle 'a black wave of hate' was too crazy even for him. He could handle himself in a dockside brawl, he knew how to filet a fish and so had a way with a knife, and he knew how to write a passable story. These were not much of an arsenal. Shondral squirmed out of his grasp; he had been crushing her hand and smiled a feeble apology. He would tell the Chieftains and Shamans gathered there exactly what he thought.

"This is crazy!" he spluttered.

Milo got to his feet in the silence that met Jon's outburst. The Conclave shifted its attention to him. "It is my duty to fix what I have done," he whispered into the hushed gathering. Without another word, he stepped through the drapes and was gone.

Halam pursed his lips and whistled a low note of admiration. "As much as I would like to argue against it, I know in my heart that he's right. All we can do is stand by him and offer what help we can." He rose and beckoned Jon and Shondral to do the same; they followed the sound of Milo's retreating footsteps.

Jon smouldered. "What can a band of backward nomads and four misled fools hope to accomplish with an enemy that can dematerialise and attack from the air?" he muttered. "The Shamans seem to have a similar talent but they use it for prayer not combat. How ready can they be? And how can anyone be ready to fight an army of beasts? What kind of beasts anyway? How many of them?" Halam hushed him and he walked in frustrated silence until they were seated around the central fire of their hut.

"There are events unfolding around us that no one fully understands, not even the perceptive Shamans," Halam began, "but I shall try to piece them together for you as best I can." He explained that the Guardians had attempted to erase all knowledge of Lifefire from Méadhon in an effort to abort the destruction they had foreseen. Only a handful of obscure myths and legends retained any reference at all to Lifefire; they thought to preserve Méadhon through ignorance. But Milo had somehow tapped into its power, lying there dormant, and unwittingly released its antithesis—a force that could result in the very destruction they sought to prevent.

Through Oriander, Halam had glimpsed Malissa's master plan even as the Shaman, Coccin, had done. She had armies of vile creatures that existed to do her will, she created poisons to force her victims into submission, and she sought to subjugate Milo as the sole perceived threat to her power. Malissa grew stronger every day.

But she had weaknesses: she did not have an infallible network of information. She did not know that Milo travelled to Banifour and for what purpose, and she could not see that he was accompanied and that he gathered allies.

Jon's ire fled with the smoke up the chimney. He would never be any use on this expedition if he questioned everything and believed nothing. He resolved to bury his doubts and to open his mind to Lifefire and to Guardians and to whatever Malissa was. A great weight lifted from his shoulders.

He looked up to see Shondral staring at him. For a fleeting instant, he felt that she knew of his internal battle and his change of heart. Then the feeling was gone. Strange.

"You carry the heaviest burden, Milo, but I dare not interfere. She would become suspicious and increase her efforts to make you one of hers." Halam put a sympathetic hand on Milo's arm. "It will not be for much longer."

Milo was relieved to understand at least something of what had happened two years ago. He was not out of his mind. He did not know how he could possibly defeat Malissa, he only knew that he would do anything to stop her. And, best of all, he was not alone anymore.

They decided on an early start in the morning notwithstanding the customary offer from the tribe to stay as long as they wished. They unrolled the bedding that had been placed in their hut and settled down for a much-needed rest.

"If Milo can use this power," Shondral

whispered into the darkness of the hut, "maybe I can too." The more she learned about Lifefire, the more she felt vaguely disjointed, as if a piece of her was missing.

"I agree, but I am an inadequate teacher; we must wait until Banifour." Halam sighed. *And pray we arrive soon.*

It was grey with dawn when Eich nosed past the door covering and bounded into the hut. Two oversized paws pinned Halam's shoulders to the ground while he greeted his master with exuberant, wet kisses. After a sniffing tour of the hut, he dashed out again. Jon's quick reflexes steadied the pot of porridge threatening to capsize in his wake.

"I'd say Eich's ready to go," Halam laughed and dusted himself off.

They folded the sleeping furs, ate a hasty breakfast, and crawled from the hut. Their horses and mule were tethered outside brushed, fed, and rested. As they packed their gear, a shy nomad girl brought an offering of food and, far more precious, woven blankets for their mounts. She showed them how to secure the ends so that the knot was flat and would not irritate the animals. The great warmth and endurance of the nomad horse blanket was well known to Halam and he was grateful to have them for the Mjorns. They strapped the gifts to the mule and led their mounts through the village.

At the edge of the village, Nepeta and Didyma stood before a gathering of their People. Chieftain and Shaman were robed in magnificent furs befitting a momentous occasion. Halam halted his party at a respectful distance.

The Shaman beckoned for Milo to approach. From an ornate box held open by a nervous acolyte, Didyma retrieved a glittering stone of crimson and gold. "It is called the *Flame of Life* and has been among our People for many generations," the Shaman explained as he threaded a leather thong through a small hole piercing it at one end. "It is our symbol of hope and victory." He placed it around Milo's neck and solemnly touched the boy's forehead with his own. "Invoke its name and we shall be at your side."

Nepeta presented them with spears of the finest precision and insisted that a tracker accompany them to the foothills. There were ways known only to the People that would save many hours' travel. A young man stepped forward and was introduced as Kilimandschari, named after a potent herb. He said they could call him Kili if they wished, then strode to where a young boy held the reins of a sturdy Plateau pony.

Nepeta spoke again. "Our Shamans will remain here to answer your call, and our warriors prepare for battle." He raised his voice so that the entire gathering could hear, "We will crush her beasts like grubs underfoot! We will destroy our enemy!" His People, fierce and unafraid, roared their battle cry.

The five led their horses through the pandemonium of shouted encouragement, racing children, and scampering dogs, and left the Rhudha Tribe behind.

***

In a few short hours, they began to understand the true harshness of the Dreven Plateau, and by the end of the second day, the memory of the colourful nomads had been consumed in the tedium of the plains. Only the occasional biala tree that jutted from the earth like bleached bone broke the monotony of the stunted grass. There was little else to alter the sensation that they moved through an endless tawny sea suspended beneath a never-ending arc of sky.

Jon's sea shanties that were comical at first had soured and his efforts at story telling languished.

From Jon's failed attempts, Halam decided that any further assay at good cheer would be resented and he concentrated instead on the mundane duties of keeping them moving and fed. Even Eich plodded along, his nose brushing the ground.

The single, saving grace of the Plateau was the glory of the starlit night. In the clear, still air, the firmament was alive with twinkling, silvery pinpricks of light. The dreariness of the day was forgotten in the engrossing diversion of tracing pictures in the stars and concocting lavish tales to go with them. Jon and Shondral competed to outdo each other, much to Milo and Halam's entertainment, until even they had run out of words and one by one, they nodded off to sleep.

The next day, Kili made one of his infrequent appearances. They had learned his routine quickly: he remained visible when the trail was faint but when it was clear, they saw no sign of him; at dusk, he brought roots and berries that he had foraged, declined to dine with them, and disappeared to stand watch. "We must ride long to reach the next water," he informed them. "At your pace," his upper lip

194

curled in just the slightest scorn, "three hours past sunset." At their unanimous groan, his dark brow furrowed. "You do not have to drink, but your animals must." He turned his pony and trotted away.

"I just wish he would have waited until later to tell us." Jon kicked at a clod of loose dirt sending a shower of dust in every direction. "It's one thing to have to ride half the night, but now I get to think about it all day."

Shondral stopped brushing her hair. "At least we'll have the stars to look at and, as far as I'm concerned, the longer we ride, the sooner we make it across the Plateau." Halam and Milo grunted agreement; the mind-numbing Plateau was getting to all of them.

The long day of riding continued into an equally long night. The blazing stars gave sufficient light to see the path without much trouble and they took turns in the lead position so the others could doze in their saddles.

The trilling of a night bird startled Halam; he had been nodding off. In the fog of his drowsy mind, an alarm sounded: they heard very little on the Plateau, much less a bird's call. Eich's yelp barely preceded the ominous shadows that rose up to surround them. The horses lunged, frantic to escape, but the shapeless hulks were impossible to hurdle. An acrid odour filled the air and with the first whiff, the animals ceased their struggles. The shadows grew taller, threatening to blot out the sky.

With his horse strangely placid, Halam noticed a curious surging motion. He dismounted and examined the ground. When he put his hand to it, he felt a warm, rubbery texture that faintly pulsated. He approached the nearest wall and pressed his hand to it—it was the same as the ground. He made a quick circuit of the perimeter; it encircled them completely.

"What is it?" Jon tried to steel his nerves for the answer.

Halam swallowed hard to clear the growing fear in his breast. "It's like nothing I've ever seen or heard of. Dismount everyone," Halam commanded, "and watch your footing."

They probed the thing that held them captive but could discover nothing of its nature or intentions. Halam kept Eich close by his side for he had succumbed to the fumes just as the horses and mule had.

Jon retrieved his spear and made a slight gash in the wall. The substance separated for a moment then closed tightly. He drew his knife and plunged it to the hilt slicing a large opening. As with the spear, it closed so completely that no trace was left.

Sucking sounds came from the direction of the sedated animals. Shocked out of its lethargy, the pack-mule unleashed a terrified scream as both of its forelegs sunk out of sight. It kept on screaming and screaming as its chest was swallowed and the silence rang in their ears when its head disappeared. In a few seconds, the entire animal had been absorbed.

They clung to each other, paralysed.

Shondral cried out—her foot was sinking into the ground. Halam and Jon gripped her leg and pulled. Milo added his strength and together they stopped the downward motion but could not free her. Abruptly, Shondral's sobbing subsided and her face grew still.

"This can't be happening," Milo screamed. "I will not let this happen!" He thrust his hands into the rubbery mass that held his sister and squeezed with all his might.

It hurled itself at them from every side. Jon was flung to his back and he watched, helpless, as the last sliver of the night sky was blotted out by the convulsions of the thing that had trapped them. A blinding flash seared his eyes and in the next instant, he dropped painfully to what felt like honest ground. He staggered to his feet and felt the hot breath of one of the horses near his cheek; he grabbed for the reins as much to support himself until his vision cleared as to keep the animal from bolting. He blinked the last smarting tears from his eyes and searched around him. The menace was gone.

His attention locked on Shondral. He scrambled to her side and a surge of relief flooded him as he saw her chest rise and fall. He cradled her head and tried not to look at her flayed foot.

Halam gently wrapped Shondral's injury and helped Jon lift her to Midnight's back, securing her with ropes and blankets. He then knelt over Milo who was the colour of ash and still as stone.

"We must get away from here," Jon urged.

Halam nodded, mounted his horse, and reached for Milo as Jon lifted him. He supported the boy before him with one strong arm around his chest.

With the other hand, Halam gathered his reins.

Leading Midnight and Lightning, Jon stumbled ahead and located the trail, eerily normal.

No more than an hour later, they found Kili's promised water in a shallow gully clearly marked by a nomad spear. Their horses had needed no marker, however, and had to be restrained in their eagerness to drink the shallow spring dry.

They lowered the still unconscious siblings to the ground and started a small fire. Halam carefully washed Shondral's wound in warm water laced with herbs. It was as if the outer eighth of an inch of her foot had disintegrated. She would likely not lose her foot but it would be very painful. He prepared a draught for her to drink as soon as she regained consciousness.

Milo had not stirred. Jon pushed back the strands of hair that stuck to his clammy forehead and made him as comfortable as he could. Milo's breathing was ragged and shallow, and a cold sweat beaded on his brow. He gave a violent spasm and was suddenly awake. Jon read the agony in his eyes and knew he had been in Malissa's grip. He drank in little sips from the cup Jon held and gradually his shaking stopped.

"How is she?" Milo rasped. His throat felt like sandpaper had been taken to it.

Halam gave the fire a last critical look and joined them. "She'll not be able to walk on that foot for awhile," he answered, "but it will heal."

Milo heaved a sigh of relief. "Then it was worth it."

"Oh, yes," Halam agreed. "And there's also the

198

small matter of having saved the rest of us too. We would not have made it out of there without you." He knew the boy should rest, but he must know. "What you did when you put your hands into that thing, did it feel the same as when you made Malissa?"

Milo chewed his lip. "It's hard for me to remember exactly; but I think it was pretty close. I just willed with all my might for the creature to go away." He lowered his eyes. "This last visit of hers..." Malissa had somehow sensed that he was vulnerable and pounced on him. She could have killed him had she known just how weak he was, but she had seemed distracted. "I think she knows about the Shamans."

Halam suppressed the sudden rush of anxiety. "They can take care of themselves," he reassured the boy. "Besides, it might take her mind off you for awhile."

Milo felt a surge of relief. He turned his head from Halam so the old guide could not see his face. How could he wish a problem of his own making onto anyone else? He was ashamed; he was the only one who should pay for his mistake, for his moment of blind rage. For the millionth time he felt the burning frustration of being unable to undo what he had done, to un-feel what he had felt. He had grown afraid to make even the simplest decisions. What if he made another mistake?

Halam placed a cool hand on his forehead. "You get some rest now."

Milo was more tired than he had ever felt in his life and succumbed to sleep, not caring if she waited for him.

The next morning, Shondral insisted they leave the area immediately. She glanced worriedly at Milo; he was pale and drawn. They could not risk another attack, and where was that nomad guide? He should have warned them of the danger. She said as much to her companions.

Halam's brow knit in worry. He had wondered the same thing, but he only shrugged and busied himself concocting something for Shondral's pain.

Her foot throbbed with every heartbeat, and she needed no encouragement to drink every drop of the greenish mass that Halam brought to her. By the time they had finished breaking camp, Jon and Halam lifted a giggling Shondral to her saddle. She ruffled their hair and teetered wildly until they secured her once again with blankets and ropes.

"Maybe we should all have a little taste of that," Jon suggested, eyeing the rest of the mash that Halam had made. "She's certainly in a good mood."

"Then we'd all sit down right here and have a gay old time." Halam grinned. "Tempting."

Shondral had just broken into a bawdy song that made Milo blush to his eyebrows and he tried to hush her. This, of course, made her sing even louder.

"One of us should ride beside her at all times," Halam said. "No telling what she might take a fancy to doing." Milo had begun to pay close attention to the lyrics and Halam suggested that Milo take the first shift. It might do the boy some good to keep his mind from his own worries for a time. Since the trail was clear, Jon and Halam both rode behind to keep an eye on them.

The foursome ascended a low rise in the undulating plain and Halam called a halt to take their bearings. In the dry air, the Mjorn foothills were clearly visible; they would reach them in two or three days. Halam looked back towards the spring and noticed something odd. After convincing Jon to stay with Shondral and Milo, Halam turned his horse back for a closer look. A sapling biala grew before his eyes, and in its delicate trunk the features of their nomad guide were unmistakably outlined. Halam knew with morbid certainty that if they returned to the site where the mule had been killed, they would find a similar sapling, but with the features of a mule on its surface.

It had been no animal that had assaulted them, but rather the killing throes of a desperate birth. Did the nomads know that they lived in huts made from the bodies of the dead? He was certain that their hut had had no likenesses on its frame and conjectured that the features must become subsumed as the biala grew to maturity. Halam shook his head—some questions were better left unasked. He would keep this information to himself; Ord knows his charges had gone through about as much as they could handle. But he would get word to the tribe of Kili's death, and how and where it had occurred.

They scheduled frequent stops because of Shondral's foot but nonetheless reached the foothills late the next day. There was more than one set of misty eyes at the sight of the first squat, scrubby bush they passed. It was green and it was beautiful.

They were tired but pushed on into the sparse vegetation. No one wanted to spend even one more night on the desolate Plateau.

"Why do the nomads stay there?" Jon wondered as he looked back across the wasteland. "It's so empty, so lifeless, so..."

"Not so," Halam interrupted. "We just do not understand its beauty. The nomads lead a very rich life; you saw their village."

It seemed a lifetime had passed since their meeting with the Conclave.

Chapter 10

Malissa spat on Jeorg one last time. How she loathed him. She ordered servants to bind the deep lacerations she had made with her fingernails. She wanted to torment him for a long time. And then perhaps she would manipulate him ever so slowly into something vile, something that crawled on its belly in the slime of her army's latrine. She would leave his mind intact so that he could feel every second of his torment and be unable to do anything about it. Yes, that is what she would do to him. She licked her lips in anticipation.

But first, she would review her army, her real army. She breathed the cloying swamp air deep into her lungs and summoned her commanders.

***

Weary but heartened, Aird scrawled a rough sketch of their clandestine operation onto a faded piece of parchment while Steven fetched the Uamhans and half a dozen of the most intact crew. They arrived bleary eyed, shoulders slumped—not at all the kind of people he needed them to be. There was no time to recover from the ordeal of the battle; every moment was critical. He knew that Jeorg suffered far worse for the damage they had done to Malissa's estate.

"Géodha," he entreated, "is there some marvel of yours that can keep us going for a few more hours?" Since their mind-to-mind encounter in Uamh, Aird felt an odd mixture of feelings for her. His anguish for his people's needless suffering was irrationally focused at Géodha and at the same time he desperately wanted to protect her from the grim reality she had been forced to face. She had worked for hours through what must have been a waking nightmare, and still she was here, ready to do more. In the harsh light of the Captain's quarters her pallor and drawn features were an eloquent statement to the strain they were all under. Yet her resolve was clear in the set of her mouth; she had more strength than Aird had imagined.

She looked at Maol who ran both hands over the top of his head before nodding. Maol knew that look well — easier to capitulate than face an hour of her relentless persuading.

"But you must promise to rest for at least two days afterwards!" Géodha tried to sound stern but knew it was an order even she would not follow should the circumstances demand it.

As she prepared the concoction, Aird described the rescue plan and what their roles would be. He watched their faces for the incredulity he expected to find. To his surprise, they accepted his scheme with only one or two modifications. Even Endel restricted his comments to fussing with his spectacles.

They swallowed Géodha's brew, gathered the necessary supplies, and left the ship in two pitifully small teams.

The six crewmen in the first team made short order of a gallon of rum, dousing each other with it. Suitably 'inebriated,' they zigzagged along the portside road where the taverns and brothels were thickest. On such a mild night, the doors were wide open and the outside tables were crammed with patrons, mostly sailors. Each of the *Pride's* crewmen selected a tavern and proceeded to loudly denounce the new tax the Council had recently passed. More tax on ships could only mean one thing: lower wages for them. It took no time at all to create a surly mass of bellowing men and screaming women, all in the mood for some action and they did not much care what form that action took. A mob soon choked the wide street and surged in a single, seething body towards the Council Chambers.

This was a much sought-after neighbourhood— the higher the status and wealth, the closer one lived to the Council Chambers. The residents prided themselves on their well-ordered manors that lined the boulevard. So the rabble that now disgraced the serenity along their front entrances was unacceptable. Their house servants and stable hands, gardeners and kitchen staff were given firm orders to discover the cause of this outrageous insult and to quell it immediately. Their shouts swelled the pandemonium up another notch.

The town's constables were too few and too slow and, frankly, incapable of handling such a large unruly crowd. The sea-folk usually stayed down by the docks and kept only each other awake with their rowdy behaviour and occasional outbursts of violence. This sort of uproar was unheard of in the genteel area surrounding the Chambers.

It was essential that the sailors from the *Pride* bring the horde to the front door of the Council Chambers. It did not matter that the Council never met at night, this crowd had a complaint and demanded to be heard.

One member of the team ran up the wide staircase to the double doors. With both fists, he pounded on them and shouted, "No tax! No tax! No tax!" in time to his thuds on the intricate woodwork. Before the second round was out of his mouth, the throng joined him in a deafening chant, stomping their feet and beating their hands on walls, stairs, pillars, and each other. They were having a marvellous time.

Inside the darkened building, a servant shuffled nervously in the doorway of the room that 'Malissa' had usurped as her headquarters.

"What?" she snarled. She disliked interruptions, exactly as much as she was supposed to.

"A mob, mistress. At the door."

The servant cowered to the floor but he was not fast enough to avoid an angry kick as his mistress stormed by. Her mannerisms duplicated the real Malissa with fine precision. Her role was to convince the town that Malissa herself was here; she must keep all attention focused on Alba and away from any rumours in the south. That was her sole purpose for existence; she had no will of her own. She thrust open the massive doors, scattering the sailors who stood on the other side, and surveyed the mayhem in the Square. A hideous snarl swelled from her throat and silence fell like a wet, stinking blanket over the crowd.

"No tax, you say." She advanced upon them, disdain in every step. "Well this is what I say, and you *will* do what I say." Her venomous glare swept over them. "There will be tax, as much tax as I command, and you will pay it. Then perhaps I will spare your miserable lives," she smiled with the same heinous effect as her master, "as long as it entertains me to do so."

She glared at the burly sailors who stood on the staircase and they fell to their knees. She strode forward and seized the beard of the one nearest and, with a sudden jerk, snapped his neck. Without a backward glance, she stalked back through the doorway in a swirl of black cloak.

The slain sailor remained in his supplicant's position, staring over his right shoulder. In dream-like slow motion, he toppled forward.

***

Much to Maol's distress, Teber had insisted on participating in the rescue attempt. After all, he had argued, how else could they swiftly find the Captain in that huge building and, he assured the elder Uamhan, Roinn's death had made him more wary than ever. No one remarked on the slight quaver in his voice or how his dark eyes blinked rapidly.

Aird, Riab, and Teber watched the disorderly crowd from the shadow made by the Council Chambers. The sailors had done a fine job; the noise would distract any guards and easily cover the sound of their entry. They pried open a basement window and crawled in, daggers drawn, and dropped into the empty storage room that Teber had scouted, the better to be inside when the exact location of the Captain was found. While Aird and Riab stood guard, Teber's spirit soared through floor after floor, twice, three times, seeking Jeorg Oprum. The Captain was not in the building.

The rescue team sat in the Captain's Quarters wondering what had gone wrong. The potion that Géodha had administered earlier kept them painfully aware of the disaster of their attempt—no Captain and another man dead.

Endel pounded his fist on the desk. "We must go over the chase between that farm of hers and Alba. We'll retrace every inch. There has got to be a clue somewhere." He stuffed his errant fist into a coat pocket. There had been quite enough violence for one day.

"I'm not sure what, but something was wrong at the Chambers. With Malissa, I mean." Teber's tremulous voice reflected the strain they all felt. Endel encouraged him to continue. "It's just that she was different somehow. Kind of... watery." His clear brow knit in futile concentration. "I don't know how else to explain it."

"We'll discuss her later," Aird snapped. "The Captain is still missing; that's what's important now." Aird had spoken more harshly than he had intended and turned away from the hurt in the boy's face.

Endel stepped into the breach. "Our men report that she's left the city again heading north. We must assume that she goes to Jeorg so when she gets to wherever she has him hidden, we'll find him. The men will leave trail markers for us. In fact, we should be readying ourselves to pursue."

"Perhaps the other far-seekers can also help," Teber offered. When no one reacted, he jumped to his feet. "Well, we can't just hide! She would find us! Maybe not today or tomorrow, but she would find us."

Riab put a comforting hand on his shoulder. "We all miss him, Teber. But we can't risk you and the others; you're too valuable. And she is very powerful."

The boy exploded from his grip. "It could take days, maybe weeks, to find her lair without us! What will the Captain be by then? She killed Roinn like that." He snapped his fingers. "Do you think she doesn't suspect that there are others like him? Do you think that she won't search until she finds us? She must see us for the threat that we are. Or, at least, that we could be." He rubbed a hand across his eyes. "If you let us help."

"Well said, young Teber." Aird's praise broke the tense silence. "We've got to use everything in our power because, as this brave lad has pointed out, she will search for the Uamhan far-seekers," he paused, a challenge in his eyes, "and it would be infinitely better if we found her first."

Diminished by two, the same team that had departed from Uamh a few short days ago left the port city of Alba to follow Malissa's route for themselves. They were determined to rescue Jeorg from her clutches.

The day was uncommonly beautiful but Géodha barely noticed. Between tending the wounded from the previous day's battle and preparing for today's journey, she did not have the time or the energy to spare so much as a glance at the immense sky over her head let alone admire its beauty or contemplate the metamorphosis it had made of her life. It was not until much later, when they were camped by the roadside on the way to Ked, that she began to recover some of her strength. And with her recovery came clarity of thought and she began to grasp how extensively Lifefire had been abused. "If she can take the creatures of Méadhon and transform them into fighting demons..." Géodha could not go on. She brought her knees up and hugged them tightly to her chest.

"She has unheard-of power and control indeed," Maol finished for her. "There must be some way we can bring her out into the open, make her more vulnerable."

"I'd surely love to get my hands on her." Aird snapped the thick branch he had been using to prod the fire.

"Truly." Maol sympathised with him; he had immediately recognised the close bond between the Captain and the First Mate. "But I think that sheer physical force will not be enough. You saw her creatures, you heard what she did to that sailor." He shuddered.

"I know you're right, Maol," Aird looked at the Uamhan through the firelight, "but I just don't know any other way to stop her."

Maol did not reply for many minutes, eyes closed, deep in thought. "Lifefire has many, many uses," he began in a low voice so the others had to lean forward to hear him, "and though I admit I have never seen it used for evil before, and it goes against all that I believe, I also must admit that it can be done." He manoeuvred himself into a more comfortable position. Géodha wondered what he was getting at and she concentrated on every word, for on the rare occasions that Maol was serious, he seldom hypothesised nonsense.

"Those Uamhans who study such things have surmised that there is a finite amount of Lifefire on any given world and *that* amount is equal to the sum total of all things on that world—living and non-living. Everything has its share. Now let us suppose that Lifefire is twisted radically from its original purpose. For example, a grain of sand is no longer a grain of sand but rather an insect, what do you suppose happens?" He looked at his puzzled listeners, wondering if he should tell them what he suspected. Yes, they must know. Only by putting their minds together would they be able to stop it.

"I think that it can unbalance other Lifefire it comes into contact with. The men wounded in battle yesterday had a peculiar, vacant stare about them. At first, I attributed it to trauma and shock. But, today, when I checked in on the most serious cases...," he looked aside, hesitating to continue.

"What? What has happened to them?" An edge of panic crept into Aird's voice.

Still looking into the darkness outside the small circle of firelight, Maol whispered, "They had lost the spark of soul or intelligence or whatever it is that makes us human. It was as if an animal's eyes looked back at me."

Géodha's sharp intake of breath told Maol that she, too, had seen it. "We must warn them," she cried, "the ones we left behind to care for them. They could be in danger!"

Endel looked at the small group around him; they could spare no one to send on such a mission

211

and their horses were exhausted. He shook his head as if to wake himself from a bad dream.

"Can you do nothing for them?" Aird's bellow of fury resounded in the still night air. "With all the magic powers you have? Are you going to let them become *hers?*" He stormed from the campsite.

"We are just not strong enough to undo her manipulations." Riab put a comforting arm around Géodha's shaking shoulders.

Aird had gone beyond the reach of the fire's light. He seethed with anger and sought the night to still his raging heart. He must remain level-headed, it was his strongest ally. He could return to the ship and warn them, but if even the Uamhans could not save them, what could he possibly do? To suppress the anguish he felt for his men, he concentrated on the safety of this rescue party. He could hardly believe that they were the only ones left capable of enduring the rigours of the road. Endel could look after himself but he was not familiar with the land and its dangers. The Uamhans were far worse: Maol was stalwart but the journey had barely begun; and Géodha, Teber, and Riab were fit but inexperienced.

His clenched his jaw, grinding his teeth together. Alone or with a brother, Aird would track her wagon until it was found. There would be no question of resting, he could do that later. He chafed at the delay of having to stop for even the few hours they needed to regain some strength. He chafed at the need for wagons to carry supplies. The only thing that stopped him from heading out on his own right now was the combined healing powers of Endel and the Uamhans; he had a sick feeling that those powers would be badly needed.

Aird returned to camp and was relieved to find Endel and the Uamhans stretched out in their sleeping sacks. He could not have tolerated their sympathy; he would have said or done something stupid. He checked the fire and appointed himself to stand watch.

It began to rain shortly before dawn. The clues that had guided them disappeared in a sea of mud. In dismal spirits, Aird volunteered to question some of the local farmers and, as he predicted, they had not noticed a wagon travelling at high speed. In fact, they had seen no wagons at all, nor had they seen the *Pride's* men who had been tracking Malissa.

As Aird trudged through the sodden fields back to the others, a rider materialised through the downpour heading in the direction of the camp. Even with his speed and proximity, the horseman would reach it before him. He pushed his legs to the limit and skidded into the copse of woods that concealed their party just as the intruder dismounted. At Aird's battle cry, the stranger pirouetted to face him, eyes wide. It was Steven, the *Pride's* cabin boy. Aird aborted his leaping kick, somersaulted to one side, and narrowly missed the jagged edge of a boulder.

The Uamhans stared, mouths open. "I'm glad you're on our side," Maol managed to say.

Aird made no excuses for his actions; he would protect them and would use all his training and instincts to keep them safe.

Steven had recovered from his alarm but his expression forewarned them—he did not have glad

213

tidings.

"They burned her, sir, they torched the ship." He addressed Aird but could not look at him. "It was the middle of the night. They took oil and dumped it everywhere and set it on fire. Then they walked overboard into the sea as calmly as you like.

"It was the ones wounded in the fight that done it, sir, and there weren't enough others on board to stop them. By the time the alarm reached the few of us on shore, we could do no more than keep her from sinking."

Aird's face was grey; his head slumped to his chest. He shrugged Géodha's hand off his arm and wandered away from the camp. At Endel's headshake, she did not follow him.

"Come, Steven." Endel needed to do something to keep from visualising what he had just heard. "Let's get you dry and put something warm in your belly. The rest of you might as well start breaking camp." There was nothing anyone could do about this latest blow. They must push it from their minds and continue their search; it was the only hope.

Aird returned by the time they had finished. Géodha flinched at the hardness in his eyes, the tense muscles in his jaw, and the thin line that was his mouth.

"The farmers saw nothing," he belatedly reported. "We have little choice: we must send Teber aloft."

Earlier that morning while Aird questioned the farmers, Maol had contacted Féadan in Uamh. Communicating using the far-seekers was rather tiring for those so used; they had to return to their

214

bodies to 'mouth-speak' the questions and answers. But it worked and Maol deemed it necessary. After the first long trip to Uamh to let them know what was needed, Teber carried Maol's words a little better than half the distance to the Mjorn Mountains where he met one of the junior far-seekers. They then exchanged Maol and Féadan's words and returned to their respective bodies to deliver the messages. Féadan agreed, after Maol shocked him with the consequences, to let the five junior far-seekers participate in the search for Jeorg Oprum. At the first hint of Malissa, Féadan insisted, they were to pull out; they were not to go anywhere near her. Maol knew what Féadan's acquiescence had cost him; Teber was Féadan's son.

Maol conveyed to the rest of the group what he and Féadan had discussed. "We will just have to trust that they can sense Jeorg before Malissa senses them," he concluded.

Aird absorbed this in silence, studying the tree to his left. "Good." With his face turned to the side, the knotted muscles in his neck were clearly visible. "Can they offer any other assistance?"

Maol shook his head. "But he has his research team working day and night on the negative Lifefire phenomenon. They may come up with something useful." When Aird's brow furrowed in scepticism, he added, "After all, they did find a cure for the Captain."

The briefest glimpse of a smile touched Aird's face before granite resolve slammed back into place. He told them of a plan he had worked out during the night: they would travel directly to Ked.

An old friend of the Captain's lived nearby who, Aird was certain, would allow his home to be used as a base. The greater distance from Alba and Malissa's estate might offer some protection for Teber as he led the other far-seekers on the search, that is, of course, if she wasn't near Ked herself. One thing was certain: far-seeking would be more effective than trudging through farmers' fields. They agreed to this without discussion and turned to finish loading the wagons.

Aird bid Steven farewell with orders to set up a relay of riders from Alba to Ked. He would need to know immediately if Malissa returned to the port.

Teber, his eyes downcast as Aird and the others spoke, felt tendrils of fear grip his mind. Why had he been so careless? He could have convinced them that he must have Roinn with him in order to fly, that he simply could not do it with the other, more inexperienced far-seekers, that his ability was inadequate, that—and he admitted the real reason to himself—he was terrified.

Chapter 11

Spirits were high the following day despite the loss of their mule with the supplies it had carried. Fortunately, Halam had decided to try the nomad blankets before the attack and so their horses would have this small comfort in the mountains. They had made excellent time, they had the provisions their horses carried, fresh water trickled in numerous streamlets fed by the mountains, and Milo had slept peacefully three nights in succession. It was with much lighter hearts that they tackled the rolling foothills.

Ord shone on them all day. It was more like a pleasant picnic excursion rather than a journey to some mystical place seeking Guardians thousands of years old. Halam led them slantwise across the hills, ever north and west, toward the highest peaks in the Mjorn Mountains that brooded in lavender twilight.

Eich patrolled ahead and to either side of the group. He did this in almost perfect silence, padding with delicate precision over fallen twigs and dried leaves, and when they reached the Greengard forest, the needles that covered the ground in a dense mat muted his passage completely.

They camped that night near a rambunctious brook strewn with boulders that the feisty mountain runoff was determined to batter down to size. Over the last few days, they had settled into a comfortable routine: Milo and Jon fetched water and searched the nearby bushes for firewood, Shondral prepared the vegetables and roots for supper, and Halam, with Eich by his side, tended the horses.

The huge dog dropped to a crouch in mid-stride, a warning rumble in his chest. Halam's head snapped up even as he drew the wicked-looking dagger from the sheath strapped to his calf. He searched the brush where Eich glared but detected nothing in the gloom. With every ounce of concentration, Halam sought the familiar sounds of his three charges. Shondral was at the stream and he could hear Jon's footfall approaching from behind. Where was Milo? He softly whistled the danger signal.

Jon was at his side in seconds and Shondral shuffled into view in the next moment. Eich sniffed the air, moving his great head slowly from side to side.

"Shondral, with me; Jon, with Eich." As he breathed his command, Halam drew a circle in the air with his hands. The two teams moved apart, daggers drawn and fangs bared.

Droplets of sweat trickled down Jon's back. He breathed silently through his mouth, one hand clutching the thick fur at Eich's neck. Every few paces, he stopped to listen, but it seemed that even the ravenous mosquitoes were stilled.

Shondral crept behind Halam, gripping his belt for support with one hand and clutching her cooking knife in the other. The tension choked her, but she was strangely elated—she sensed none of the vileness of the beast that had pursued them to Camelia.

Halam dropped to one knee and pointed to a

bundle of wood. There was no sign of a struggle; Milo may have left it to be gathered on his return to camp. *Return to* camp! He signalled to Jon and they emerged into the camp's clearing as one.

Eich growled menacingly then grew still at Halam's hand signal and did not attack the peculiar figures surrounding Milo. Though bound at wrist and ankle and gagged, he seemed otherwise unharmed. He was frightened, certainly, but appeared to have his wits about him.

Milo's captors were no bigger than children six or seven years old, with arms that hung to their knees. One of them struck a spark to the kindling Milo had been assembling and its features leapt into eerie definition. It was impossible to tell its exact colour, which seemed to blend with the greens and browns and blacks of the forest. Tufts of mottled fur covered its legs and feet, and poked through the collar and sleeves of a short leather tunic. Only its face from brow to chin was bare. Two cat's eyes with vertical pupils reflected the oranges and reds from the firelight. The fleshy snout that separated them tapered into human-like nostrils quivering in tandem with the pursed mouth immediately below. It had styled the somewhat longer fur on its head into thick spikes protruding every which way. In the flickering light, no ears were visible.

Hanging from a thong around its neck was a tube about seven inches long: a blowpipe to propel the ugly darts that protruded from a pouch at its waist. A quick glance at the other creatures gathered around their campsite showed similar weapons around each neck.

"What are they?" Jon whispered.

Instantly, deadly blowpipes were pointed at Milo. They had very good hearing, wherever their ears were.

Halam carefully lowered his knife to the ground, never taking his eyes off the central figure; Jon and Shondral followed his lead. Unarmed, they waited.

The leader twittered and snuffled, perfectly emulating a thrush, a merlin, a yampré, a kestrel, a cat, and a hawk in quick succession. Three of his cohorts soundlessly scaled nearby trees and four others vanished in the direction of the horses. The remaining two positioned themselves on either side of Milo, nostrils flaring.

Gazing at each of them with unnerving feline eyes, the leader spoke. "Ourrrr Forrresssstt," he circled a long arm about his head. The sound was high and warbling; it grated on the edge of tight nerves. "Whhhyyy?"

Halam extended his hands, palms up, in what he hoped they would interpret as a sign of peace. "We mean no harm," he said slowly. "We travel to the Mountains."

"Whhhyyy?"

"We seek the Shrine." Halam decided that the truth could do no harm. He also had a very bad feeling about lying to these creatures.

The leader twittered and snarled at a furious pace and the two guards jumped to act on his commands. In a few heartbeats Shondral, Jon, and Halam were gagged and had their wrists bound, and Milo was dragged to his feet. Two of the half-feline half-man individuals hoisted Shondral onto one of the horses; they were not unaware of her injured foot.

Single file, the four companions were led into the Greengard. They marched through the night without respite. The path was riddled with roots and moss-covered rocks, and they had to work their way around fallen trees. Fatigue and thirst eroded their strength as surely as the winter snows had deteriorated the forest trail.

Milo squeezed his eyes shut to clear the gummy haze that blurred his vision, and lost his balance on a slippery stone. With his hands bound, he could not break the fall and landed painfully on his side. Jon hastened to kneel beside him even though he could offer little assistance. In an instant, three of their captors dropped from the trees above their heads, hauled them to their feet, and shoved them back in line; these were dangerous creatures.

The third time Milo fell, the leader let them sit on the ground and paced impatiently while they rested. Their gags were removed and they were at last given a little water.

"Little is known of the Barbardensi," Halam breathed, his lips barely moving. "They were thought to have been totally annihilated during the Great Cataclysm. They worship the things of nature, particularly the trees, and are said to be highly superstitious. But that was long ago."

"Sssilence." With a lightning blow, a guard sent Halam sprawling in the dirt. Only Halam was re-gagged.

Barbardensi, Jon repeated to himself. *People of*

the barbar.

In the first blush of dawn, they heard the sound of rushing water: the River Quiem. They scaled a low hill and, without the tons of earth to muffle it, the roar was deafening. This was not just the sound of the river, but of the great Royo Falls itself. Clouds of cold mist billowed high above the cataract and chilled them with its icy touch. They rounded a bend in the path and in the distance glimpsed the serene ribbon of water that would soon plummet into the abyss. At the next turn, the chasm yawned before them and the pounding water obliterated all coherent thought.

The lead guard advanced to within a few feet of the brink and peered at the deluge. Its drenched fur clung to its body and the coifed points were plastered to its head. It turned abruptly to the right and walked directly into the water.

Jon refused to believe that they were to be sacrificed to some barbarian water deity; water had always been his ally and he clung to the conviction that it would not abandon him now.

Shondral shut her eyes, gripped the pommel of her saddle with vice-like intensity, and prayed she would not succumb to an attack of vertigo. She would focus on how tired and dirty she was, on how much she wished they had never left the sweet comfort of the School, and even on the pain in her foot—on anything but the sickening drop into the river far below.

The horses' eyes were bound and they were led through a dense curtain of spray. Beyond it, a crude passageway had been carved by the unremitting pounding of the water. Death was inches to their left and the constant spray made the footing treacherous. The four companions could not offer each other even the smallest comfort. They were islands, alone in the grip of a shared nightmare.

Thoroughly soaked and cold to the bone, they emerged on the other side and descended once again into the arms of the Greengard. Whatever their fate, at least the Falls were not to have them.

It took all of Halam's will simply to stay on his feet; the forced march had long ago numbed them. He had scarcely noticed the latest peril though the cold and wet sent uncontrollable shivers through his entire body. He must persevere. He must go on.

Mid-morning, their captors increased the pace and forced them into a staggering shuffle. First one foot, then the other foot, then the first one again. Jon vaguely remembered being this miserable not so long ago. The memory crystallised and cleared his mind like a soft cloth wiping mist from a window. He could see Shondral's slumped shoulders beyond the furry points of the guard that separated them. Her hair hung in damp clumps, snarled and muddied. His heart tightened in anguish; anger flashed hotly through him. It brought him fully alert for the first time in hours and Jon studied their surroundings. If they were to escape these creatures, he had better know something of the lay of the land. They skirted a corrugated wall that rose vertically into dense forest. He squinted at the greenery, puzzled by how it could grow sideways out of sheer rock. They passed beyond the wall and he realised his mistake. It was a barbar tree—a colossal barbar tree.

His stunned mind registered odd fluctuations in the air above his head. He blinked rapidly to make sure his eyes did not deceive him, for descending all around them on inch-thick vines were hundreds of 'short-points,' as he had nicknamed the Barbardensi sometime during the endless march.

They were blindfolded for the second time on their journey and though they saw nothing, they sensed a great number of the creatures all around them. Some snatched at their garments and were gruffly slapped away by the guards. In the next moment, they were brought to a halt. Harnesses were secured around their waists and under their legs to form a rough sling. In the midst of shrill orders, much snarling, and general cacophony they were hauled off their feet and straight up for several minutes.

One by one, they reached a platform and were released from their harnesses. When all four had arrived, they were led a short distance into an enclosure—at least it felt less open than it had a moment before. Inside, one of the guards untied Jon and gestured for him to release the others. It turned on its heel to stand watch outside the leafy slats that served as the door to their prison. One guard was more than enough to restrain them, dizzily high as they were in a barbar that shaded a jumble of craggy boulders far below. Unfettered, they sprawled there, aware only that they no longer had to move.

Shondral opened one eyelid, gasped, and scuttled on hands and knees to the centre of their cell, drew her knees tightly against her chest, and

224

buried her face in her arms. Milo crawled over to comfort his sister and noticed a bucket in the corner behind her. After cursory inspection, he drank a ladle of the sweet water and carried it over to Jon.

Jon hunched over Halam's prone figure. Halam had not been able to speak since the Barbardensi had re-gagged him, but even in the depths of his own misery, Jon had noticed how the forced march had taken its toll on Halam.

"How is he?" Milo asked.

Jon shook his head. "Not good." Halam's forehead was hot and dry, and his breathing shallow.

For reasons known only to them, their captors had left Halam's assortment of small pouches on his person and Jon carefully detached them from his belt. He fervently hoped he would know the contents of some of them. Milo removed his cloak and arranged it flat on the floor; it would not do to drop anything through the cracks. They carefully emptied the pouches onto the least dirty parts of the material.

Jon thought he recognised a seed Halam had used to soothe Milo after one of his nightmare episodes. It might help Shondral. "Is this what he gave you the other night?" he asked. Milo shook his head; he had been too exhausted to think of anything but what Malissa had inflicted on him.

After one look at Shondral's huddled form, Jon decided to take the chance. He gently pried up her chin to show her what he had but she would not open her eyes. "It's alright, Shonny, this will help." He carefully brought the medicine to her lips and

225

she managed to swallow it with the help of a little water. Shuddering, she pressed her pale face back into her knees.

"We have to break Halam's fever," Milo warned. He had seen this kind before; it could be deadly.

Somehow, through the phobia that paralysed her, Shondral perceived that they could use her help. She took a shallow breath. "Does he have a leaf that's oily to the touch and smells like mint?" She kept her eyes shut and did not move.

Jon and Milo brought their noses into action and found one that matched the description. "Now what?" Jon asked.

"Crumble a piece about the size of your fingernail in a little water and make him swallow it," Shondral answered. "Watch his throat. Make sure it moves."

Together, Jon and Milo managed to administer the herb. Halam's breathing grew easier.

"Keep him warm and raise his head a little."

They covered him with Jon's cloak and stacked the emptied pouches beneath his head.

The relaxant had dulled the worst of Shondral's fear and she inched her way over to examine their work. She silently thanked her mother for the patient instruction on herbs and natural healing. "Good. Now dip those in the bucket," she pointed to a mass of black, ropy roots. They absorbed the water and expanded into tuberous shapes not unlike sea worms. Jon wrinkled his nose at the revolting-looking stuff and waited for her next instructions.

"We eat them." Her white teeth flashed in the dirt on her face. In no time, disgust firmly set aside, they devoured the repulsive but energising meal.

"Now it's my turn." The bandages on her foot were long overdue to be changed; the cloth was damp and dirty. She buried her apprehension.

Jon positioned himself so that she could not immediately see her foot and held her hands while Milo carefully unwound the dressing. Her brother was quiet. Jon waited for confirmation of the grisly truth. He feared that the worst had happened—it was infected and she would lose her foot. He held her tightly.

"Tell me," Shondral's tone, though soft, demanded an answer.

Milo raised her foot so she could see the healthy, pink skin where they had expected corruption.

Shondral squirmed in Jon's embrace. "For heaven's sake, Jon, let me see." She stared. "I don't understand. I couldn't feel anything, but I thought it was shock."

She locked eyes with Milo but he was as puzzled as she was; it had not been his intervention. He had not used his power—or whatever it was—to heal her.

Jon swallowed. "It seems that unusual," he hesitated, "abilities run in your family."

A commotion sounded from without and their door banged open. Three more guards had appeared and made it obvious that the captives were to follow. Shondral kept her eyes on them as she placed water near Halam's sleeping form; they did not interfere and left Halam to rest.

The taller humans had to crouch to get through the opening and, beyond their cell's platform, was a swaying catwalk no more than twenty inches wide. Jon gingerly stepped onto the rickety structure. He spared an instant to look up and glimpsed a whole network of walkways linking the branches of the barbar. Young Barbardensi dashed along them and shrieked in glee as they leapt from one to another.

"Keep your eyes straight ahead." Jon hoped he sounded more confident than he felt. "Just pretend this is the boardwalk along the harbour." His feeble attempt at a helpful suggestion grated on even his own nerves. He had thought he was so clever with a ready turn of phrase, perfect for any moment. But this kind of moment went way beyond any kind of moment he could have envisioned.

Shondral moved like one possessed. The sedative was wearing off and she had to rely more and more on her own strength of will. The ground far below sang to her, beckoning her to come join it. She kept her eyes fixed on the head of the guard in front of her, studying it with such ferocious intensity that all else became fuzzy and indistinct. She knew every strand, every point, every subtlety of the furry thatch. Shaky and pale, she entered a large, solid chamber and immediately felt better.

It exuded a warm peaceful feeling, like curling up in a favourite chair. Afternoon sunlight danced through the verdant foliage that curved above the open chamber. A solid wood floor wove around the massive trunks that supported it, and rugs fashioned of many-coloured fronds were strewn about.

As they neared the far end of the room, a low table came into view and around it were seated three Barbardensi, the first old ones they had seen. Their fur had lost its lustre and was tipped with silver. Tiny rivulets creased the ruddy brown faces, and the cat eyes had a milky cast to them.

The guards dropped to their knees and their arms formed a "Y" above their heads. In a moment, they were dismissed and the prisoners bade to sit.

Long after the last footfall had faded, the three elders continued to study them. There was no discernible reaction, but that was not so much because there was none, but rather because the humans had no idea how to recognise a Barbardensi reaction when they saw one. By unspoken agreement, they relied instead on their experience with the nomad Conclave and remained passive under the scrutiny.

"We wish to know how Méadhon fares," wheezed the central elder, breaking the lengthy silence, "and why you travel through our Forest."

Jon drew breath to speak but was cut off before he could utter the first syllable.

"This one speaks," it pointed to Shondral. "The sounds are more... pleasing to us."

Shondral was grateful for her training at the School—the School, it seemed to belong to another lifetime. Having no idea where to begin, she delivered a concise narrative of events since the Great Cataclysm, touching only on major events. She told them of the co-operative farmers' groups, of Ked and Mriss, and how bridges spanned the

River Quiem. She told them of the hamlets and of the tribal nomads and of the fen villages. And, lastly, she told them of Alba and the wonders of the newly discovered lands whose ships harboured there. She glanced at her companions, and then continued on to answer the second part of the question.

The three Barbardensi sat motionless throughout Shondral's monologue and for some time after she had finished. Then, as one, they nodded. "Your words both please and puzzle us. On the one hand," whereon the central elder held out a delicate paw, "you tell how prosperous and grand is the land, then on the other, you tell how danger threatens us all. How can both be true?"

Shondral ransacked her mind for an analogy that would not only clarify the dichotomy but also inspire them to offer assistance. Any and all allies were welcome. She stared at the floor and let her eyes wander around the room. She had an idea.

"When blight strikes a grove of barbar..." She stopped as they hissed in dismay and surged to their feet.

"Whhyyyy do you say thisss? Have you sssseen thisss?" the elder on the right demanded. The one on the left stormed towards her, fur bristling.

Shondral bit her lip; she had thought only to use an analogy they might understand. "There is no blight," she hurried on. "It is just a story to help explain in a way you might understand."

Their ire cooled as suddenly as it had heated and they returned quietly to their seats. "A story," the leader repeated. "Continue."

She could not change her strategy now. Resolved to do everything she could to convince the Barbardensi and to quite likely save their lives at the same time, she went on. "It does not infect all the trees at once. It begins with one, spreads to a second, then to a third, and soon the entire stand is diseased." Their eyes grew wide and their nostrils flared. "But until the blight touches a tree, it remains healthy. It is therefore possible to stop the destruction of a grove by severing the blight in its beginnings. So, although the grove is prosperous and grand, it is possible that the danger of blight could threaten its very existence." The elders were clearly upset. She feared she had struck too harshly at the heart of the Barbardensi.

"Telll usss." In its disquiet, the central elder had lost the refinement in its speech. "Could the evilll dessstrooy the Forresstt?"

Shondral felt a stab of doubt, but she must see this through. She glanced at the anxious expressions on Jon and Milo. "Yes," she answered firmly.

A renewed flurry of commotion ensued. Their powerful arms gesticulated wildly and delivered hammer blows to the tabletop. This was definitely a reaction. There was no sign of feebleness or age as the debate among the elders reached painful decibel levels. The argument reached an ear-splitting crescendo then it was over. The reverberations echoed in the hall and inside the heads of the three companions.

Young Barbardensi appeared with heaping trays of food and drink and the elders ate with the same gusto as they had argued. Their plight momentarily set aside, Jon, Shondral, and Milo sampled the strange food set before them. At the end of the meal, servants brought bowls of steaming water to cleanse hands, and retreated with the remnants of the meal.

The central elder addressed them. "We have served the Forest from before the Holocaust. Her roots reach far into the earth and hold it securely even when the world crumbles. We offer ourselves in whatever way She requires. She is our Home, our Food, and our Protector. Whatever threatens the Forest is our enemy." It clapped its paws. "We will now meditate on whether to favour you or return you to the earth."

They were stunned into silence by that final comment and, before they could ask for clarification, were escorted from the hall to different and larger quarters nearer the hall. In a curtained alcove at the back of the room, Halam rested on a mound of leaves and his herbs had been placed within reach on the floor beside him. He was weak but his colour was much better. He smiled at them and held up a hand. "Refresh yourselves first. I can wait a few more minutes to hear what has been happening."

Bowls of water and their own spare clothing had been placed near the door. They quickly washed and changed so that they might have a few precious moments together without gags or guards. Jon quickly summarised their encounter with the elders, growing more agitated with the telling. "Return us to the earth?" he hissed. "We have to get out of here!"

"You have kept us alive, Shondral, and for that we are in your debt," Halam patted her knee, ignoring Jon's demand. "We know so little of the Barbardensi. We must be very..."

A snuffle from the doorway ended whatever else Halam wanted to say. He gave them a beseeching look which he hoped with all his heart conveyed to them to remain silent. They just did not know enough.

With Jon and Milo supporting Halam, they were ushered into a hall no longer cloaked in solemn majesty but arrayed for a dazzling festival. The domed foliage was woven with intricate patterns of light that sparkled and danced like an aurora on a clear winter night. Hundreds of Barbardensi cavorted, skirting barbar limbs here, embracing others there, springing to circle the ones overhead and landing exactly in step, exactly in time, to the orchestration of bird calls and animal sounds that somehow coalesced into a song of the forest.

Their escort politely urged them along the periphery of the room. The song dimmed into the background as they neared the table of the three elders. They, like their fellow Barbardensi, were dressed for the occasion. Flowing robes, iridescent in the glow of a thousand lanterns, had replaced their short leather tunics. Silvery droplets were sprinkled on head, hands, and feet so that from top to bottom, the Barbardensi shimmered and blazed, no longer the muddy little 'short-points' but rather the resplendent caretakers of the mighty barbar.

The four companions were seated

conspicuously apart from each other with younger Barbardensi separating them. Food and drink were brought and consumed with the same enthusiasm as a short while ago. When they were sated, the elder who had spoken that afternoon rose to his feet.

"The Forest is content." It had not raised its voice and had spoken in common Méadhonian. Nevertheless, the gathered throngs raised their voices as one in a trill of jubilation and continued their song and dance with renewed exuberance.

"I am called Ocimum, and these are Agastache and Saponeria, or as near as our names can be spoken in your tongue." It bowed in turn to its fellow elders. "We speak for all Barbardensi. The young among us," it gestured to the other Barbardensi who sat with them, "study your speech and we wished them to be present to learn what they may."

He—Jon decided arbitrarily that it was a 'he' for there appeared to be no way to distinguish between male and female, if there were even two sexes at all—arranged his robes more comfortably. All eyes at the table were on him, never once straying to the feverish activity twenty paces beyond.

"The Forest is first child. Her roots are the centre where all roots meet. This is the binding force, this is the gift, and this is the love of the Forest. Without Her embrace, the World would be as particles of dust in the wind, lifeless."

The Hearth was suddenly dim and silent. The Barbardensi knelt, arms raised, facing some part of the barbar.

"The Barbar is first child of the Forest and we are the Children of the Barbar." Ocimum chanted the story of his birth, the first of the Barbardensi...

***

Ocimum had awakened. The supple bark of his sapling womb protected and nourished him. He revelled in crushing delicacies from subterranean rock and in drinking the pure water of underground rivers. For an ageless time, the communion of the Forest seeped into his thoughts.

When the Mother saw fit, he was shown the glorious purpose of their union: the Tree would feed and cleanse the World and he would care for the Tree. Together, they would sustain the World. Soon, there were hundreds of Barbardensi; they appeared wherever a Barbar Tree graced the World. But the men of Méadhon, too, grew numerous, and they destroyed the Trees and slaughtered the Barbardensi. After sewing many of their own people into the soil, the few remaining Barbardensi joined together to protect the more remote stands of Barbar, away from the ones who would harm their Trees.

The men of Mriss were the most despised. A great hissing erupted in the Hearth. The Barbardensi had worked many seasons to enhance the Barbar so that its bark became like rock and they had rejoiced for many seasons. But the enemy learned new ways to slay the Tree. They solemnly vowed to return to the earth any man of Mriss found near the Forest.

Since that dark time of slaughter, the elders had decreed that all trespassers be brought before them. Some had not survived the march and were sewn deep within the timberland. Others had not smelled right and had to be sewn immediately. Curiously, they withered the sod that was placed on top of their resting-places.

***

Halam sat bolt upright. "Where? When?" he burst out.

The filmy cat eyes moved to his face, blinked once, twice. Ocimum had never been interrupted before. No Barbardensi interrupted a telling, for they were a long-lived race and had time enough to say everything. A young student chirped a few notes. Halam would never know how close he had come to experiencing, personally and immediately, what being returned to the earth was like.

Ocimum pursed his lipless mouth into a tight ball, his nostrils dilated. "Yesss. I forget you have pitiful short lives, gone faster than morning dew. Another will speak with you of this. Go now."

Their escort returned them to their quarters. They could hear the festivities blossoming once again in the hall. Jon shook his head. "Don't they ever stop?" he wondered aloud. The others had already settled on their leaves, oblivious of the clamour in their exhaustion. He followed suit.

Milo had been awake for two days and Malissa lay in wait. He tensed in dread anticipation of what her twisted mind had in store for him. But it was different this time; she did not gloat or make demands, she simply asked him questions. She asked about his friends and his family, about what he liked to do and about his favourite places, and about his concerns and problems. She seemed genuinely interested in everything he had ever thought or done.

The interrogation was pleasant and without coercion and, with seeming innocence, arrived at the incident when he had animated the wooden doll. Milo was weary by the forced march and lack of sleep and had been lulled into complacency by the long conversation, and he also felt a certain affinity for her need to find out about herself. He recounted the entire story. What harm could it possibly do? She asked a few more questions about inconsequential events then bid him goodnight.

That evening, Milo told them of Malissa's inexplicable behaviour. They unanimously suspected an ulterior and diabolical motive. It was too unlike anything she had ever done before. Powerless to offer Milo more than encouragement to be careful and to not trust anything she said, they turned to their present situation.

"We need to find out everything about the people who didn't 'smell right' and then leave as quickly as we can," Jon proposed. "I, for one, cannot bring myself to trust these short-points."

Milo snorted at the nickname and nodded in agreement. "They're so different from us; you can't tell what they're thinking. For that matter, you can't tell anything with those cat faces."

"We do know some things, though," Shondral said. "Like their devotion to the forest and their ability to communicate with it. They can be dangerous, I agree, but maybe they can protect us while we travel through the woods." She shivered at the unbidden memory of the demon's face inches

237

from hers, reaching to strangle her, its foul breath overwhelming her senses.

"What you all say is true," Halam concurred. "And there are three other factors to consider. One: the witch is up to something new with Milo; two, she's had ample time to dispatch more trackers." He paused to let them absorb this. "And, three, our journey will become more hazardous as we approach the Mountains. We need all the help we can get, however strange."

Jon and Milo glanced at each other. "Well, when you put it that way..." Jon said for both.

At that moment, a Barbardensi appeared at the door. It could have been one who had sat with them at the feast or one they had never seen before. Aside from the elders with their greying fur and myriad wrinkles, the only other distinctions among Barbardensi were slight variations in height and tunics. The four outsiders certainly had no way of knowing who stood before them.

"I am called Tanacet," he said, "and I will tell you of the wrong-smelling ones." He clapped his paws for food and drink, and after they had eaten, began his tale.

"We travel swift and far when the Forest calls." They nodded in wry agreement. "Six darknesses past, we found intruders hacking branches from trees." He shuddered and drank from his cup. "We put them back in the earth to rest until their madness leaves them." He looked at each of them. "What questions do you have?"

"Where did you find the intruders?" Halam asked.

Through a discussion of plant species, bird migration, and the direction of the sun, they were able to pinpoint the attack north-east of Ked in the heavily treed area that separated the farmers' fields in the lowlands from the domain of the Dreven Plateau. It was considered a dark and dangerous place and seldom traversed.

Tanacet trilled in what sounded like glee. "We make the Forest wear a bad disguise."

When they were children, Shondral and Milo had been entertained and frightened by legends of ghosts that lurked in the wild Greengard thickets. The tales said that the unfortunate mortals discovered there after dark were never heard from again except as mournful wails begging for release. The stories were more than enough to deter the hill-folk; they knew of no one who had ventured into that particular stretch of forest.

"How many were there? What were they like?" Milo asked.

"Five. All different. One very tall and could run very fast. One with arms as strong as Barbardensi." He seemed to find this mystifying. "One small and round that we find in the tall one's pouch. One like a snake on the ground." He waved a paw at Shondral. "And one like you."

Shondral gripped Jon's arm. "What do you mean like me?" She had turned very pale.

Tanacet turned to her. "Like you. Same fur, same face, same bigness."

Halam paced in the small area, his hands clasped behind his back. "Malissa is far more dangerous than we had imagined." He turned to

239

Tanacet. "Can you tell the difference between Shondral and the creature?"

"Oh, yes." He snuffled in her direction. "Smell different."

"Have you found other intruders like those ones?"

"No."

Halam confirmed that there were no more questions from his companions, and asked his last one. "Do you know if your people will help us in our quest?"

"The Three decide."

"Thank you, Tanacet."

When the Barbardensi had left, they brooded in silence, piecing this information together with what they already knew or speculated.

"Right. Let's review the situation again." Jon waited for their attention. "Malissa's trackers are close behind us, she can emulate our likenesses, and she is trying a whole new tactic to get control over Milo. On the positive side, the nomads gather to assist us and the Barbardensi may ensure that we make it to the tree line of the Mjorns. Then we're on our own until Banifour. Does that about sum it up? Have I missed anything?" he paused. "And do we have any other choice but to go on regardless?"

Shondral sat on the floor hugging her knees. She was used to Jon's propensity to clarify the facts and get started, and he was usually right. But something bothered her. "Halam, why can't the Guardians just reach out and destroy Malissa? They have such incredible power; they must be able to do something."

240

He sensed her mounting apprehension and knew his answer would not satisfy her. He sat beside her and put an arm around her shoulders. "Shondral, if they end our struggle for us, we would forever lose control of our lives on Méadhon. I don't pretend to understand how or why; I can only repeat what they told me. They are bound by their own laws, and cannot interfere. They are here only to monitor and can intervene only when total destruction is imminent. And even then, only as much as they have already."

She looked through him. "I hope it is enough."

A meal was sent to them with instructions that the elders would grant another audience when a decision had been made. They were confined to their quarters and took advantage of the time to catch up on much needed rest.

By the third day, they were jittery and ready to go. And by the morning of the fourth day, they had pieced together an escape plan. Shondral participated in the scheming even though she knew she could never go through with it—it meant climbing down hundreds of feet of vine.

Before they could execute any breakout plan, they were summoned to appear before the elders. There was no indication of what their fate might be, and it seemed to their untrained eyes that the three had not moved since they had last seen them.

"You will save the Forest and the Forest will keep you safe. The People will protect you and help any who defile the Forest to cleanse themselves." They rose to their full height of four feet and raised their voices in a soul-wrenching incantation, modulating the sound to harmonise with the earth and the air and the sky and the sun. They became one with creation, and the four understood, for a brief instant, the joy of the Barbardensi.

Chapter 12

By nightfall, the small caravan from Alba reached the outskirts of Ked on the shores of the River Quiem. Tradesmen, craftsmen, and artisans gathered at this vibrant northern outpost to sell their services and ply their wares. The town was also a natural focus for the local farmers and many of the Kedish had dwellings both in the town and on their outlying parcels of land. During the winter months, the town was convenient for schooling the children, not to mention the pleasure of company at local taverns during the long nights.

Even though the town was not as crowded at this time of the year, and a couple of wagons would not be an unfamiliar sight, they kept to quiet side streets and were inspected only by a lazy cat stretched out on a frayed porch swing. Aird had visited Ked a number of times en route to his home on the Plateau and he knew two or three very fine inns. But it would be better if no one knew of their presence, for what they did not know, they could not inadvertently mention where Malissa's spies might overhear. Besides, their destination was not much further.

They turned north-west and followed the gentle banks of the river. All signs of civilisation gradually dwindled and the road deteriorated to parallel ruts in the dirt.

"This must be it." Aird pointed to a dense screen of foliage.

For all her keen observational abilities, Géodha could not discern any sign of a path or opening. "It certainly hasn't been used much." Even though the intensity of the nomad sometimes made her nervous, she was nevertheless impressed by his skills. "However did you spot it? I can barely see my hand in front of my face even with my Uamhan abilities." Her left hand glowed slightly from the light of her luminous eyes.

Aird shrugged. "I'll see if he's home," he said over his shoulder, and disappeared into the brush.

"He's lived in the wilds most of his life," Endel offered, "and reading the land is second nature to him. I think that's why the sea fascinates him so much; it's a whole new challenge."

Aird returned shortly and guided the two wagons through; his stony face revealed nothing. Though she had known him just a few days, Géodha missed his dancing eyes when he laughed and worried about the depths of his anger. Sometimes a man did not think clearly when revenge filled his mind.

She faltered. Was not her mind clouded too? The outside world was so *big,* and it was a continual discomfort to have the heavens directly overhead with no protective mountain in between. She and Maol had discussed it, but his excitement overwhelmed any disquiet he might feel and he was convinced that she would soon overcome the nagging remnants of her phobia. Riab feverishly studied everything in sight, and for Teber, this was a grand adventure. At least it had been until the battle. *Enough brooding,* she scolded herself. They had a mission to complete first. Only then would she grieve for Roinn and contemplate the mind-boggling repercussions of the freedom to come and go from Uamh.

The undergrowth they struggled through opened onto a clearing dominated by a pond directly ahead of them. They gave it a wide berth; the lily-dotted pool was spongy along its perimeter, a perfect trap for wagon wheels. The moon chose that moment to peek out from behind a cloud and they could make out a rambling structure with a sizeable garden tucked close to one side and a large barn on the other. The original house was obvious by its styling, apparent even in the faint light. Several additions stretched out behind it like mismatched afterthoughts. The soft glow of candlelight warmed the largest of the windows.

A slight creak from the front porch brought all eyes to bear on what had first appeared to be part of the house, so closely did the old man blend in with the aged timbers. The creak was repeated as he shifted in his rocking chair studying his callers. Wisps of smoke curled from the pipe in his gnarled fist and he motioned with it for them to approach.

Aird went to their host and sat on a low bench near his feet. The others clambered down from the wagons and remained standing, uncertain what to do next.

"Captain Gaski," Aird said, "I would like to present Géodha, Maol, Riab, and Teber. They are from a most unusual village called Uamh, but I will let them tell their story. And Endel Laurs. Jeorg may have spoken of the *Pride's* Doctor." He turned to the grizzled seaman, sat a little straighten "And this, my friends, is Captain Arthon Gaski who sailed that worthy vessel, *Stormbender*, for sixty-three years. Jeorg learned everything he knows from this man."

A tiny woman bustled through the door at that moment bearing a tray heaped with mugs and a frosted pitcher. Riab rushed to her aid.

"Arthon Gaski, where are your manners? Why haven't you brought out chairs from the front room to make our guests more comfortable?" She looked imploringly at them. "You really must forgive him." She rounded on Arthon again. "He never remembers that not everyone is as comfortable as he is." She turned to her guests. "Now. Who are these lovely people?"

Aird stood to repeat his introductions, and with a courteous bow introduced them to Arthon's wife, Elli.

Riab and Aird followed her into the house and soon everyone was seated on the veranda in deep-cushioned chairs with a cool cup of fruit juice. Elli lit a few lemony-scented candles before perching on a stool beside her husband.

Arthon squinted at Aird and in a surprisingly strong voice said how glad he was to see him and meet his friends, but would he please explain their reason for seeking out an old, retired sea Captain. His sharp eye had not missed the tension in the First Mate's face nor the strain in his voice when he spoke Jeorg's name.

"And," he added, "how is Jeorg anyway? I haven't seen him in, oh, a good eight years. Young devil he was, too. Did I tell you about the time, when he was just startin' out as my cabin boy, when he..." He shot an irritated look at his wife. "Now why are you poking at me like that? It's been a while since I've had a fresh audience," he finished somewhat petulantly.

"Well by the look on Aird's face," she retorted, "and if you'd pay more attention to others than to yourself, you'd've seen that it's about Jeorg they've come." She softened her reprimand with a worried smile and a pat on his arm. "Now listen for a change."

Géodha hid a smile behind her hand and, out of the corner of her eye, she glimpsed Teber stifling a chuckle.

Among Aird, Endel, and Géodha, the story unfolded. "And so we respectfully request the honour of your hospitality for a few days and would welcome any suggestions you might have," Aird finished, and hoped their hosts could absorb this fantastic tale.

Elli and Arthon looked at each other and communicated their thoughts as only two people married for sixty years can do. Arthon nodded and turned his attention back to his guests. "We welcome you to the Gaski homestead for as long as you wish and I, for one, will not sit idly by while young Jeorg is in trouble." He pounded the arm of his chair for effect and sent a dozing tabby scurrying from his lap.

"That's settled then." Elli took over. "First, let's get the horses settled and show you your rooms. Then you'll have a good, hot meal before you start all your planning and scheming." She wagged a finger at them. This time, they all smiled.

Arthon pushed himself to his feet. "Just take what you need from the wagons and I'll see to the horses. No arguments," he said firmly. Elli stood on tiptoe to kiss his cheek and he gave her waist a quick squeeze. His pipe gripped firmly between his teeth, he strolled to the first wagon and introduced himself to the placid mare who waited patiently for attention.

They gathered their things and followed Elli into the house. She kept up a running monologue as she opened windows to air out stuffy, unused rooms. She told a story about how Arthon would come home from a voyage and, before he left, she would be pregnant again. He'd done that fifteen times. And every five years or so, they'd had to build another room onto the house, swearing that this would be the last one.

When she was certain her guests had everything they needed, Elli bustled up the erratic hallway. "When you're ready, join Arthon in the front room," she called back as she turned a corner and disappeared from sight.

"Now there's a ball of energy," Riab voiced their unanimous opinion. "I wonder what she really thinks of our strange tale?"

Aird snorted. "Oh, I'm sure we'll find out." He turned to his pack. "Let's get settled then."

Dinner was a lively affair. Elli was in complete charge and, soon, sated and more cheerful than they had been for days, they relaxed in the front room with a glass of Arthon's home-made plum brandy, the perfect finish to Elli's delectable cooking. She had not allowed any talk of business at her table.

Bad for digestion, she'd said.

And so it was with a lighter heart that Aird broached the subject again. "Arthon, I could think of no better place to come, and I truly hope this will not mean hardship for you and Elli."

"Of course not, of course not," Arthon insisted. "You did the right thing, coming here."

Elli sat in an overstuffed rocking chair, idly caressing Seadog, their marmalade cat. "Near as I can tell, that woman, what was her name? Oh yes, Malissa, could be anywhere by now. I don't see as you have any choice but to send young Teber here and his friends out flying." Her eyes lit up, "That must be incredible!" She hastily returned to the topic and added, "Strictly looking for Jeorg, mind you."

Arthon nodded in agreement. "You reading my mind again, woman?" He smiled at her. "That's where we start," he paused, fingertips touching under his chin, "but what do we do when we find him?"

"If we had a far-seeker regularly check Alba," Riab said, "we would know if she returned to the Council Chambers." He sat on the edge of his chair. "She would surely want to check on her captive now and again. She could lead us right to him!"

"I'm afraid that Féadan, that's our Researcher in Uamh," Maol added for the benefit of the Gaski's, "would not permit any such surveillance. You know what she did to poor Roinn." He shook his head sadly. "We must concentrate that effort on Jeorg alone."

Frustrated, Riab stood and paced behind the

chesterfield.

"Well, then," Arthon got back to business, "I suggest the far-seekers start beyond the circumference of her farm and search for Jeorg in ever-widening circles. You'll have to figure the height and width of your fly-overs." He shrugged. "Without additional clues, I don't see any other way."

"We don't have to hold back the far-seekers while we figure out what to do when we find him," Aird broke in. "Can you start tonight?"

"Certainly. I should have thought of it myself," Teber replied, and proceeded to make himself more comfortable for the journey away from his body.

Riab hunched beside him and put a hand on Teber's shoulder. "If you sense a sign, any sign at all, of danger..." He shook him gently; everyone in the room nodded in time with his admonition.

Teber laughed. "You can be very sure of that!" He rested his head on the cushion Elli had provided and was soon far away from the warmth—and worry, he added—of the Gaski's front room.

An acute sense of direction that was one of the properties of far-seeking sped him unerringly towards the Mjorn Cliffs south-west of Ked. As planned with Féadan the previous day, one of the junior far-seekers was aloft cavorting above the waves near the cave entrance. He happily recognised the pulsating golden glow of Embar, the only girl among the far-seekers. He gently touched her luminous glow with his own so as not to startle her.

"Teber! Welcome back!"

He tried very hard to conceal how glad he was to see her and to be home. He had not realised how much he missed his friends.

"Hi, Embar. Please gather the others. We go to search for Captain Oprum. And," he added hastily, *"tell my father that we won't go anywhere near Malissa."*

While he waited, he relished the complete freedom of going anywhere, of seeing everything, of soaring over the wonders of the world. A sudden stab of sorrow pierced his joy. Roinn would never be with him again. And Malissa lurked out there somewhere, waiting like a spider in her web. She had no right to terrorise everyone! They would just have to stop her.

He penetrated the tons of rock to his home, suddenly needing to see the familiar fields and buildings. For the first time, he felt a little suffocated by the mountain on every side. Disconcerted, he raced back outside to the rendezvous point.

The arrival of the others dispelled such alarming thoughts. They were anxious to be on their way, but Teber felt obliged to add his own warnings to the ones his father had doubtless just given them.

"I know Féadan has already warned you." They groaned their confirmation of Teber's comment. *"Just remember that we stay together no matter what. Understand, Garl?"* Garlasco was the newest far-seeker and was still stretching his 'wings.'

Teber was glad, and not for the first time, that the far-seekers could see each other. In this state of

251

mind-away-from-body, they looked like softly glowing miniature clouds complete with distinctive colourings. Garlasco was a deep blue, Achisu was reddish, Filyos and Bayan were lighter and darker shades of green, and Embar was golden. His own colour was white with streaks of orange.

Although Féadan had explained it often enough, Teber still had difficulty thinking of himself as connected in any way to his body. Sure, what he experienced flying had to be processed by his brain, but it was just that it did not *feel* like it.

Regardless of what he thought or did not think, it was time to go if they were to complete any search patterns before they needed to return. That was another thing his father was working on: how to spend longer periods of time aloft. It seemed that a soaring spirit faded in proportion to the time spent away from its earth-bound body. He would have to watch their colours carefully.

With the Sea of Orchès guiding them on the right, they touched each other in a "V" formation. Together, they flew at speeds none could hope to match alone and their senses were heightened to perceive the most minute details around them. They studied the busy animal life below in its frenzy of hunting or being hunted, resting or nursing. They passed cottages on the seashore: one with a young couple making love (did Embar turn a deeper gold?), another with a farmhand sorrowing over the loss of his prize bull, and a third with a family sitting down to a late supper. If they concentrated, they could pick up the conversation and aromas wafting up through the night air. But their purpose was not to eavesdrop on the details of domestic life; they sought the anger or frustration or despair or, worse, the pain of a captive man.

They reached the northern arm of Alba's protected harbour and Teber directed them inland on the first sweep that would bypass the town and take them beyond Malissa's estate. He remembered the farm all too well and with an effort, dampened his feelings so the far-seekers touching him would not share his grief.

Teber estimated that they could finish four sweeps before they tired. That should bring them near Mriss—not a bad night's work. But at the end of the third run, Embar's cloud had faded and grown dim. Teber ordered a speedy return to Uamh and encouraged the others to use their strength to buoy her the remaining distance. Féadan would be furious with him for taxing her! He had forgotten that it was Embar who had been on watch so, of course, she would already have been a little tired when they started.

He arranged to meet them again in ten hours and left for Ked. He sunk back into his body, muttering that they had not found the Captain. Riab lifted him from the couch and carried him to the quiet bedroom at the end of the corridor.

***

They watched, fascinated, as Teber's body relaxed and sunk a little further into the cushions.

Elli in particular was keenly interested in the research and experimental studies of such a marvellous ability. Riab was hard pressed to answer her probing questions.

Arthon chuckled. "You were afraid to sail, and now you want to fly!" He shook his head. "I swear, woman, I'll never know all there is to know about you."

"A good thing, too," Elli retorted. "Better to keep you guessing." She winked broadly at Riab. "You were saying?"

"Oh, yes." He swallowed his grin and continued his explanation. "Féadan's goal was to discover a safer, faster way to contact the outside world than by the ill-fated boating expeditions." Maol and Géodha murmured confirmation. "He hypothesised that since we seemed to fly in our dreams, perhaps we could fly at will, with purpose and control. He had everyone on the research team hooked up with wires and smelly paste night after night." He wrinkled his nose at the memory.

"After months of study, Féadan discovered the exact part of the brain that controls dream-flight and manipulated it using Lifefire techniques. The result lies on the couch before you: controlled flight complete with acute sensation." He shone with pride.

Elli sat lost in thought for a few moments. "Has he tried the manipulation on older people?" she asked.

"The theory so far has been that young people adapt more easily to the radical change, the total severance, of mind and body," Riab answered. "To be honest with you, Féadan has not tried it on anyone past adolescence."

Aird, too, was awed by the possibilities of soaring over the waves. And he knew how fascinated Jeorg was with Géodha's outrageous idea of crossing the ocean of space. But Jeorg would not be going anywhere until they found him and dealt with Malissa.

"My friends," Aird said, "shall we put our formidable resources together to plan Jeorg's rescue?"

Elli lowered her eyes, embarrassed at having taken time to indulge her own fantasies.

"Don't fret Elli," Aird waved her concern away. "We can't do much until Teber finds him."

"If Jeorg had been in the Council Chambers," Riab stomped his boot on the hardwood floor, "your plan would have worked. I say we try the same scheme when we find him." He folded his arms on his chest and waited for discussion.

Arthon took a deep breath. "It was very dangerous, what you tried, and it was lucky that a mob developed and drew her out. Chances are you won't be able to count on that again. And until we know the exact location, we won't be able to devise a credible distraction. Fire comes to mind, but that's too hard to control. We could end up burning down more than we bargained for. A stampede of some sort would be effective, but we'd have a hard time ourselves." He spoke to himself, his listeners forgotten. "Pirates!" He jumped up. "That's it!" He sat down again, rubbing his hands together in anticipation.

"Pirates!" Elli sniffed. "Crazy old man."

No one came up with anything better, so they spent the rest of the evening listening to Captain Gaski recount tales of pirate attacks he had personally witnessed.

"You're making this up," Elli accused him.

"They might give us ideas," he said, unperturbed.

They established a system of watches so that when Teber returned, someone would be there to either guide him to bed or to alert the others if he had any news. When first one then another of her guests stifled yawns, Elli ushered them off to bed taking the first watch.

Frustrated, but certain that he was doing all he could, Aird managed an uneasy sleep, his first since Jeorg had been captured.

Chapter 13

Shondral breathed a heartfelt sigh of relief as her feet touched solid ground. But she also felt a curious sense of loss, a far cry from her abject terror when she had first arrived. From their quarters high in the barbar, which they had come to learn was the largest in the grove, she had observed the Barbardensi going about their tasks. Every morning, the young ones collected dew from the broad leaves, always leaving some behind for the tree. Other Barbardensi could spend the entire day examining a branch, or smelling and tasting the earth at the base of a trunk. The trees must eventually grow old and die and she wondered what the Barbardensi did in such a catastrophic event. She wondered if, someday, she would get the chance to find out.

A furious babble of snorts and shrieks jerked her back to the business of the moment. She spotted Eich in the middle of a melee as he wove his way around the guards that scrambled after him. He turned his head, great tongue lolling out, as he bounded over the top rail of the crude stall in which they had kept him penned. In his wake sprawled a jumble of dusty, infuriated Barbardensi. Nothing and no one would keep Eich from greeting his human.

Their horses grazed at the back of the same enclosure and appeared well tended. Jon and Shondral fetched them while Milo checked their belongings and Eich slobbered over Halam. In short order, the horses were saddled, packs were secured, and the four companions were ready to take their leave.

Barbardensi were everywhere, curious to see whom the Three had chosen to protect. Tanacet detached himself from the crowd along with several others; they would accompany the humans to the fringe of the Forest. He handed them lengths of material and gestured for them to blindfold themselves explaining that all routes to the Barbardensi's forest home must remain protected from the outside world regardless of their exalted status. No Barbardensi could remember when humans were treated with such deference.

Long after the sounds of the small tree folk had dwindled, Tanacet permitted them to unbind their eyes and pointed the way towards the Mjorns. Before Halam could ask how he and his friends planned to protect them, Tanacet had vanished into the foliage overhead. Shrugging, Halam signalled for them to continue.

The temperature dropped as the day progressed, and they changed into warmer clothing. By late afternoon, their breath fogged in great clouds and the forest had substantially thinned. Reluctant to leave this scant shelter behind, they made camp earlier than usual, claiming the need to ease back into the saddle. Halam snorted at Jon's slow, careful dismount.

They found plenty of dead wood to coax into a fire. The hot coals would last well into the night. By the time they had taken care of the animals, eaten, and gathered yet more firewood, they were content to call it a day and snuggled into their sleeping blankets.

Milo was surprised when, once again, Malissa contented herself with gentle conversation. He was more than happy to oblige her if it kept the terrible agony away. The ride had tired him and soon he was drowsily chatting about his sister and her friend, Jon, and their stories of Alba and the School. Milo secretly envied the close bond between them and yearned for the day when he could permit himself to love again.

"And where are they now?" Malissa wondered.

"Who? Jon and Shondral?" Smiling, he answered, "Why I expect they're right where they dropped, on the other side of the fire pit."

Her savage wrath forced the air from his lungs and pressed him to the ground.

"They should be dead!" she spat. Her rage engulfed him, consumed him. She unleashed her seething impatience at having coddled him for the past few nights and threw an uncontrolled storm of agonising torture at Milo. Everything she had ever done to him before was doubled, tripled. Searing fire stabbed his chest. The intensity of the pain wrenched him from Malissa's grip and into the far worse pain of what he had done.

He drew in ragged gasps of the crisp night air. "She knows you're here," he whispered through clenched teeth. "I am so stupid."

Eich had prodded Halam awake at the first sounds from Milo. The old guide was beside him, peering into his face. "Be still, boy," Halam commanded as he probed for damage. "You fended her off far longer than any of us could have. Now don't move," he repeated more gently, "while I wrap these ribs of yours." He blamed himself for not keeping a sharper eye on Milo; he had dismissed the possibility that she could physically harm him. In the uncomfortable light of retrospect, he had known that her power must be growing more formidable and it made perfect sense that she would use it for this. He would not underestimate her again.

"Get some water boiling, Shondral, and fetch the green pouch from my saddle bag; it's the smallest one. And, Jon, come help support him." He could at least ease the boy's breathing and help him get some rest.

Milo gripped his arm. "I'll be all right." He shuddered; fine beads of perspiration slipped down his temples.

Shondral handed Halam the pouch, her face a mask of worry. He inserted two fingers into the opening and retrieved several odd-looking twigs that he dropped into her open palm. "Put it in the water and stir until it turns a muddy brown. Won't take long." Shondral poured the steaming contents into a mug and gave it, handle first, to Halam. He examined the contents and raised Milo's head a little. "Drink. It'll help you rest."

Halam encouraged him until the last drop was gone and as his eyes fluttered closed, signalled Eich to lie alongside Milo. Eich sniffed Milo's sleeping form, padded around in his customary three circles, and settled in on the colder side away from the fire.

"He should sleep through the night, but I'm afraid we will have to take our rest in shifts," Halam said. "His system has had quite a shock and we need to keep him warm. We need to keep the fire blazing. I'll take first watch." He raised his hand as Jon and Shondral sputtered in protest. His stern look sent them back to their blankets but it was a long time before either of them slept.

Morning was a perceptible greying of sky. Clouds hung low in the sky, burdened with moisture. Jon groaned. Snow. They would have to find or build a shelter; Milo was in no shape to be jostled about on a horse. He stood to stretch stiff muscles in the way Jikal had shown him. When he felt limber enough to move quietly, he left the others sleeping and meandered through the trees, idly gathering wood, and thought of home. He could just imagine the juicy rumours about their disappearance. Jon chuckled to himself. Actually, he didn't think it would create too much of a scandal; it was common knowledge that he and Shondral were very close. And his father and uncle liked her.

Jon remembered the last time that the four of them had had supper together. Uncle Kory, with a look a malicious glee in his eyes, told Shondral about the time that Jon and his friends tried to trick one of the old fishermen into thinking that his catch had spoiled. It was easy enough to do: you just had to put a few really rotten fish on top of the good ones and anyone would think that the whole haul was bad. The idea was that old Herm would then throw his perfectly good fish into the midden. Jon and his co-conspirators would wander by, extract the fish, and sell them for whatever they could get. Easy. But Herm had seen all the tricks there were to

261

see and had engineered quite a few of them himself when he was a lad. So when Jon and his friends dug their hands into the waste pile, faces flushed with the success, their howls of surprise and pain were heard the entire length of the fish market. Old Herm had replaced his catch with a particular nasty type of stinging jellyfish. The red welts on the hands and the forearms of the culprits identified them to all. Jon's father had made him work a full week with Herm—a thoroughly unpleasant task for, although Herm lived and worked on the water, he seldom bothered to use any of it on himself or his clothes.

Jon smiled; he was quite glad that his uncle did not know about some of his other escapades. Or maybe he did. His uncle was uncanny and had made Jon squirm on more than one occasion with pointed comments. It was exactly his uncle's ability to observe things like the colour of the mud on Jon's boots (that put him in the wrong place at the wrong time) that had taught Jon the importance of the little details. As he grew older, this became a critical skill on the road to becoming an Historian. He considered himself very lucky to have had an uncle like Kory who was willing to share so much of his knowledge with a young, pest of a boy. It made up, Jon told himself, for the huge amount of time that his father spent out on the water.

Halam was rousing himself as Jon returned with an armload of wood. "I'm afraid our young friend," he pointed to Milo's sleeping form, "will not feel very well today." He vigorously rubbed his face in a futile attempt to conceal his distress. "We'll find a more sheltered site and settle in for a

262

day or two." Jon nodded his agreement and turned to add fuel to the still-warm coals of the night's fire.

Shondral opened her eyes, met Jon's, and smiled 'good morning' to him. She struggled out of her blankets and, after neatly folding them, crept to Milo's side. Aware of her gaze on him, Milo opened his eyes a crack. For a moment he was in Morbella; Shondral always woke him for breakfast. The ache in his chest and the worse ache of how he had revealed them to Malissa destroyed the pleasant illusion. He turned his head away from her. "I'm sorry," he muttered. Shondral tried to console him but it was Halam's broth that gave him peace from his misery.

Once Halam had scouted a suitable location for their camp, he and Jon gathered fallen boughs and constructed a crude shelter that would keep out the worst of the wind. Shondral remained with Milo to keep an eye on him and to pack loose items for the short move to their new camp. Just as she was finishing, Halam and Jon appeared, carrying two sturdy poles. They secured several blankets between the wooden supports and carefully lifted Milo, who was still asleep from Halam's potion, onto the makeshift stretcher.

Milo woke shortly after they had arrived pleading that he would burst if he could not make use of the facilities. Laughing, Jon and Halam helped him to his feet. His face turned grey. "Once I'm up," he gasped, "it's not so bad." He made a valiant attempt to walk by himself, then gladly accepted Jon's supporting arm. As soon as they were out of sight of the camp, Jon left him his privacy. "I'll be right here, if you need me." Jon tried to sound serious but he knew his grin gave him away. He sauntered about a nearby clearing, admiring the fresh growth of spring. A shadow crossed his path and he looked up expecting to see storm clouds scudding beneath the overcast sky.

Instead of a moisture-laden cloud, hideous black birds wheeled above him, their naked heads swaying back and forth. Jon watched in morbid fascination and felt a pang of sympathy for whatever it was they were hunting. Suddenly, one of the birds folded its wings and arrowed towards the earth, the others swiftly joining the attack. They shot over his position and headed unerringly towards Milo. "No!" The denial hissed between his lips. Yelling at the top of his lungs, Jon grabbed a branch at his feet and raced to Milo's defence.

Milo glanced up at Jon's shout and stared, transfixed, at the sinister birds plunging towards him. The air seemed to darken around him and filled with a foul, rancid odour. They toyed with him, buffeting him with powerful beats of their oily wings. He struck back with his fists, but they effortlessly darted out of reach. Their stench made his head reel and the pain in his ribs blinded him. The largest of them turned its blood-red eyes on Milo and screeched, outstretched talons dripping with venom.

Jon stormed into the foray, oblivious of the Barbardensi materialising from the brush. He thrashed at the flapping wings and one of the birds squawked in surprise. It separated from the whirling mass and dove at him. Jon brandished his makeshift weapon like a sword and slashed at its head and shoulder as it flew past. It jolted in mid-air and continued on its trajectory to collide into the trunk of a tree. Jon wasted no time pondering his stroke of luck and ferociously resumed his assault.

The birds began dropping to the earth with a sickening, moist prattle in their throats. Jon halted, bewildered. A Barbardensi flitted past him and dispatched one with a dart from his blowpipe, but not before it had gripped Milo's shoulder with its talons, piercing through cloak and tunic to the flesh beneath.

Milo felt a lance of pain constricting his lungs. In the instant that the poison reached his heart, a great calm descended on Milo. In idle curiosity, he watched Jon perform a slow-motion dance of destruction among the black birds. He saw a dart glide through the air and nestle itself into the breast of one of the birds. Stunned, the bird's wings remained outstretched and it glided in a graceful descent to disappear in the tall grass. Eich drifted into his line of sight with Halam and Shondral. His sister's hair floated behind her—it was the most beautiful thing he had ever seen. She would miss him and for a moment he felt sadness. *Jon will take care of her.* That thought brought him to the happy contemplation of love and how he really did have it in his life. It had not forsaken him—he had forsaken it. Now he knew better; now he could rest.

Halam and Shondral burst upon the scene directly behind Eich.

"Do nottt touch birdsss!!!" Tanacet shrieked. Halam hastily restrained Eich.

Using wooden hooks and nets made from vines, the Barbardensi gathered the dead birds and dragged the carcasses into the forest.

Shondral ran to Milo as he crumpled to the ground, eyes staring. She supported his head, careful not to jar his broken ribs. "I'm here, Milo." She brushed his hair back from his forehead, a gesture she knew he hated, but she could never help herself.

Halam knelt on the other side of Milo and felt for a pulse, for the warmth of breath from his slack mouth, for any sign of life. With a trembling hand, he gently closed Milo's eyes. Shondral looked up at him, unbelieving. "Don't say it," she whispered, "just don't."

Halam lowered his head and closed his eyes. "I'm so sorry."

Jon dropped to the ground beside Shondral and wrapped her in his arms. Shondral took a shuddering breath and released it in a low sob. Jon rocked her back and forth; they remained that way for a long time.

As darkness approached, Halam murmured that they should think about burying Milo. Shondral nodded. They used a blanket for a shroud and reverently placed Milo's body in the shallow grave that Jon and Halam had scraped in the hard ground. Shondral lowered the blanket to see Milo's face one last time and kissed his brow. In the fading light something sparkled on his breast; the *Flame of Life* blazed as it reflected the last rays of the sun. Shondral gently removed the nomad talisman and placed the leather thong over her head.

Halam busied himself stirring the embers of their fire back into a hot blaze and prepared a broth to warm numbed hands. In her grief, Shondral did not notice that he added a smidgen of white powder to her cup. She drank it automatically and as her eyes began to close, Halam and Jon guided her to her sleeping sack. Eich curled up beside her, comforting her in his own way.

"What do we do now?" Jon asked in a hoarse whisper. His sorrow, frustration, and anger were compressed into a painful knot in his chest. His dearest friend in the world was scarred for life, and he knew that were it not for the Barbardensi, they would all have suffered Milo's fate. For the first time, he did not smile as he thought of the diminutive short-points.

"How can we hope to stop Malissa without Milo?" Jon snapped a twig he had been worrying. "He was the key."

Halam stirred the fire with a branch before adding it to be consumed. "We must continue." His features tightened in resolve. "Shondral must take Milo's place."

Jon sat for a moment looking at his hands in his lap. When his eyes met Halam's, Halam knew he had some persuading to do.

"Remember when you first came to see me?" Halam asked. "It was then that I felt the power in Shondral. And in you too," he added, "though not as strong."

Jon stared at him in disbelief, but did not interrupt.

"How else can you explain her foot? She must

267

have healed herself. She may be even more powerful than Milo; the Guardians will know. We have to go on." He put a hand on Jon's arm. "Who else would believe what we have seen? Who else would do something before it's too late? Before Malissa becomes too strong for anyone to stop?"

"And before she murders someone else," Jon growled. His eyes flashed with vengeance, but to place Shondral in danger went against every fibre in his body. Couldn't he do it? Maybe he had enough of this 'power' Halam talked about.

"On one condition," Jon insisted. "We wait until we get there and know for certain that there's no other choice before we mention anything to Shondral." He had no trouble making this condition since he had decided that *he* would take Milo's place.

Having come to an acceptable agreement, they ate a little, and Halam rolled into his sleeping sack. Jon would take first watch; they would not be caught unaware again.

Shondral woke before dawn, disoriented and hungry. Her chest ached and she wondered if Milo's chest felt this bad. Milo! How could he be dead? Painful barbs dug deep into her heart. She threw off her blankets and stumbled to the low mound that marked where her brother lay. Eich padded silently in her wake and stood by her, supporting her with his broad back, as the flood of sorrow coursed down her cheeks.

At last, the well of tears exhausted, she saw what she must do. She dried her face on her sleeve. She would take Milo's place; she would fix his carving. Wasn't she his sister? Couldn't she always do anything he could do? If Jon and Halam chose to turn back, she would sneak away at the first opportunity. They would only argue and she was in no mood. She returned to camp, and kept her plan to herself.

Halam looked up and brought her a bowl of stew. She hesitated. "You didn't by any chance add a little something extra did you?" Although she was grateful for the night's oblivion, she needed her wits about her now.

"So. You saw through my ploy," Halam said, unrepentant. "I assure you that this is strictly for nourishment." He offered her the bowl again.

She accepted it this time and no one spoke until stew, bread, and cheese were consumed. Jon watched her over the top of his mug; she was pale and remote, and had a firmness about her mouth that told him more clearly than any words she could have said that she had made up her mind about something. She had a plan and it didn't take much thought to figure out what she was up to. He would stay close by her side.

"So. What have you two decided?" She tried to sound as neutral as possible. "Do we continue?" Halam's relief was so obvious that Shondral smiled a little. She looked at Jon and cursed the way he could so easily see through her. He knew that she was determined to continue regardless of what he and Halam had decided. She bit her bottom lip to hide her consternation and nodded. She had work to do on her subterfuge skills. "Right. Let's go then."

Cold drizzle, which did little to raise their

spirits, congealed into snow at the edge of the tree line. As they left the forest, Jon turned in his saddle to salute the invisible Barbardensi.

They trudged into a land that grew more barren over each rise. Halam pointed out the peaks they would travel between and, in a not-too-distant valley, he assured them that they would find the place called Banifour. His mood was somewhat lighter with their destination imminent. But even as they gazed at their goal, the light snowfall grew heavier and obscured it from sight. The storm intensified and they tied their mounts together for safety. Visibility deteriorated until all they could see was a blinding white sheet and the howling wind ripped their voices away.

Jon pulled his hood further over his face; he couldn't see anything anyway. He wondered in a brief moment of panic if his horse was still tied to Shondral's or if he wandered alone to be swallowed whole in the icy jaws of some bottomless crevasse. His numb fingers checked and re-checked the taut line. Jon fervently hoped that Halam was as good a guide as he claimed to be because they would not make it through the night without shelter. He looked up from a close study of his tribulations and into a dirty brown shadow that surrounded him in the next instant. He howled defiance and flourished the sturdy stick he had brought with him from the forest, the one he had used to attack those ugly black birds. Whatever this new threat was, he would not go down without a fight!

Shondral's muffled laughter penetrated his battle-fevered mind in mid-flail. He freed one hand from its mitten to rake the snow and ice from his eyes. The weary faces of Halam and Shondral smiled up at him. He surveyed his surroundings, and to his acute embarrassment, saw the cave that Halam had led them to.

"Come, Jon, get off that poor mare and calm 'er down." Halam offered a steadying arm.

"I thought... I thought..." he stammered, then broke into a grin, cracking the rest of the ice off his face.

He blessed Halam's foresight in hauling dry wood with them, though it had meant an hour of foraging before they had set out that morning. Milo's horse was able to carry the extra load. Soon, firelight flickered off the damp rock walls and a soup of savoury herbs and dried vegetables simmered in the coals.

"How far back do the caves go?" Jon asked. His curiosity was one of the first things to thaw.

"I've not been through the whole maze by any stretch of the imagination," Halam replied. "Some say they twist and turn for miles." He lowered his voice conspiratorially. "Some even say they go as far as the Sea."

Warmed by the nourishing meal, the hiss and snap of the small blaze lulled them to sleep, one day closer to Banifour.

In the depths of the night, Shondral woke. A dull glow was all that remained of their fire and she could see nothing beyond the shadowy shapes of Jon and Halam. There it was again! A scrape, from the back of the cave. The nature of the cavern made it impossible for her to judge the exact place it came from or how far away it was. Her breath came in short, harsh gasps and her heart pounded so hard that it obliterated any other sounds. With considerable effort, she slowed her breathing and unclenched her hands. She spied Jon's 'sword-stick' near the fire and slowly reached for it. It would give her some protection and she could use it to prod the others awake without letting whatever was in the cave with them know about it. She squinted across the dying fire and stifled a yelp. Halam's eyes glinted back at her. He shook his head from side to side; she lowered the wood to the ground. The horses, tethered near the cave entrance, snuffled and pawed at the thin layer of snow that had drifted into their shelter.

The scrape sounded again—much closer this time. Halam leapt to his feet, his bloodcurdling howls echoing through the chamber.

Jon sat bolt upright, his sleeping blankets puddling in his lap.

Halam stomped his feet and brought his hands together in resounding claps, and his bellowing increased in volume. Shondral pressed her hands to her ears and through squinting eyes saw Jon do the same.

Halam stopped, panting for breath, and continued to survey the darkness long after the reverberations of his rampage had died away. At last he turned and dropped onto his dishevelled sleeping blankets. Eich sat next to him and put a protective paw on his thigh. "An Ice Bear," he explained, his voice raw.

Jon rekindled the fire.

"Yes, keep it blazing. It's one of the few things they don't like. Not that it could hurt them, with hides like the granite walls of this cave. It's the colours that bother them." He grinned at them ferociously. "They also don't like loud noises much."

"But what are they? Where do they come from? What do they look like?" Jon blurted.

Halam rubbed his hands before the fire. "The first one I ever saw," he smiled, "was high in the Sgeir Range." Shondral's indrawn breath brought another, gentler smile to his lips. "Oh, yes, I've been there too. I explored a great many places when I was a young man."

Jon was spellbound. He loved tales of places he had never been and of things he had never seen; it made his blood sing. It was his great hope to witness it all with his own eyes someday; he would become the famous Travelling Historian who brought tales of faraway lands to the people. Not that such a position existed. Yet.

"There he stood, all twelve feet of him, glistening like a diamond filled with the purest cream. Picture a bear," Halam told them, "only much larger. Now add scales the size of your hand and an eight-foot tail that tapers to a series of barbs. Now I didn't actually see him do it, but it is said that with that tail, he can dislodge chunks of rock from the mountainside. He then pulverises it with his paws to find the crystals he feeds on." He picked up a clump of dirt and made a fist, spraying fine particles of dirt into the air. "His hind legs were about as thick as this," he made a circle of his arms,

273

"and help power that incredible tail of his. But his face," his eyes focused on some distant place, "his face was incredible—like a child's, curious and innocent. It was mostly flat except for a large protruding jaw, but in that expanse of smooth surface were eyes like milky-blue clouds." As one, they peered into the cavern, desperate for a glimpse.

"I moved closer," Halam continued. "That's when he dropped to all fours and flashed three-inch teeth at me—nothing childlike at all about them. Needless to say, I moved back in a hurry. He let me stay a little longer but was obviously agitated and began to pace back and forth. It was only then that I saw the three smaller Ice Bears behind him, more delicately featured and probably females. Still facing him, I slowly retraced my steps out of the gully where I had found them." Halam heaved a tremendous sigh.

"It should be dawn soon. Eich and I will stand watch." He quelled their protests and when all was quiet again, his thoughts returned to that different place and time.

The weather was more co-operative the following day and the horses were anxious to depart, unsettled by the lingering scent of the Ice Bear. They were careful to leave the cave as they had found it and strode out into the frosty air.

The Mjorn Mountains, garbed in a flowing cloak of snow, soared into the brilliant blue sky, painful to look at. The morning light conjured a glittering spectacle from the pristine whiteness and their breath formed tiny crystal clouds. Pillows of drifted snow crested like waves on a sea drained of colour. Their route would be more circuitous in order to bypass the largest of them. It would be a beautiful yet strenuous day.

They made passably good time and stopped for lunch in a hollow swept bare by the wind. Halam hurried them on, anxious to reach the copse of trees that was visible at the far end of the valley. It would protect them from the worst of the weather and provide firewood to replenish their dwindling supply.

By late afternoon, they had reached it. Shondral and Jon removed the saddles and packs from the horses and brushed them down. The horses ignored their ministrations, however, intent as they were on the tufts of grass that poked through the light covering of snow. Halam was busy assembling rocks to contain their fire and, without turning from his task, sent them to fetch wood while he prepared dinner. They returned quickly with the first bundles, anxious for something hot in their stomachs. Seven trips later, Halam declared that there was enough to last through the night and they sank onto the deep pile of boughs he had gathered for their beds. They passed an uneventful, though very cold, night.

The next two days were copies of the first except for Halam's spirits, which rose higher and higher. He could feel it, he said, and pushed them harder. But it was the keen noses of the horses that found it first, mid-morning on their fourth day in the Mountains. Like young colts, they pranced through the grey mist that shrouded Banifour from all but those who were welcome there.

Jon was instantly reminded of Halam's back

yard. This was the template. The animals demanded grazing time and their riders were more than happy to acquiesce while they relaxed in the warm sun unfettered by cloaks and boots. Jon looked into Shondral's eyes as they bit into the succulent fruit he had plucked from a low-hanging branch. Impulsively, he kissed her and they bubbled with laughter when their lips stuck together, glued by the syrupy juice. The sound of splashing water drew their attention away from each other and to Eich and Halam frolicking in the lake. They needed no further encouragement.

Sated and refreshed, they were reluctant to leave the corner of paradise they had found, but their ominous mission soon over-shadowed even this momentary respite. They saddled the horses and rode to find the Guardians.

Halam led them north-west through giant spruce and pine trees laced with delicate vines. Flowering shrubs adorned both sides of the path. Brilliant yellow birds the size of Shondral's little finger chirped happily and dove in and out of the blossoms sampling the sweet nectar.

They came upon a sprightly brook and, although it was shallow and not very broad, it was spanned by a sturdy bridge. Halam whooped with glee and encouraged his stallion into a trot. Jon and Shondral, lulled by the beauty and peace around them, kept their pace slow, unwilling to shatter the fragile magic of the moment. The trail widened enough to ride alongside each other, and so it was that hand-in-hand they emerged from the forest to stare at the Great Hall.

Halam waved to them from an airy gazebo but they did not notice. Their attention was riveted on the glorious edifice in front of them. Spires tipped in gold formed a staircase of shimmering peaks that soared gracefully to the lofty pinnacle. Panes of jewelled crystal covered the entire facade in an intricate web-work that astounded and delighted the eye. Pillars of blue-white marble flanked an arched entranceway at least forty feet high. The portal was slightly ajar and it seemed that the burnished copper was etched with diamond and emerald.

"Welcome to Banifour."

Jon bit his cheek, and gingerly ran his tongue along his wounded flesh.

"So sorry. Didn't mean to startle you."

"I'll be fine, thank you." He blinked and focused on the short, portly man beside him.

"Please join us for a cool drink while we get to know each other. Your horses can wander where they like." They dismounted and took the packs and saddles off the horses, leaving them to graze.

"My name is Oriander," he announced as they arrived at the gazebo where the others waited. "I'm sure Halam has mentioned me." He smiled a toothy yellow grin and introduced his fellow Guardians, Ushival, Risto, and Aoineadh. When everyone was seated, his expression grew serious and he took Shondral's hand in his. "We share your sorrow."

Shondral swallowed hard. A single tear rolled down her cheek and blazed for an instant as a perfect miniature of the Great Hall was reflected in it.

"We do not have to explain the evil to you,

though you have seen but a small sample. And she will not stop," he emphasised every word with a light blow to his thigh, "until Méadhon is completely and utterly destroyed!"

Jon studied the Guardians. There was concern in each face, but no fear. He supposed that they could return to wherever they had come from if things got out of hand, if Malissa won. "Pardon me if I'm out of line," he interrupted, "but with such power," he waved his arm to encompass the valley, "would it not be a simple matter for you to destroy her? Why bother taking a chance with us?"

The Guardians were silent, eyes out of focus. "Very well," Oriander muttered under his breath. "It seems I have been nominated spokesman." He looked at Jon and Shondral. "Although, as you have guessed, we could overcome Malissa, it would be just as terrible a blow to Méadhon as what she herself has planned.

"A world that supports life, any life, is the most valuable thing in the universe. And Méadhon supports a spectacular variety—a rare find. However, it was learned long ago, long before Méadhon existed, that for another race to interfere is to destroy, just as Malissa wishes to destroy. It would take a little longer perhaps but the result would be the same." He stood with his hands folded across his belly and paced in a way they would come to learn was his habit whenever he lectured.

"You see, the Lifefire of each planet is intertwined with it, is one with it. It is part of each individual blade of grass, each flower, each rock, each animal. Each of you. It binds Méadhon with a unique energy that, if manipulated in the least way by someone not of Méadhon, would cause a chain reaction that would take a great many years to recover from, if ever. You see, it has the unusual property of reversing itself, of annihilating itself, rather than allowing an outsider to tamper with it. Banifour was brought here at incredible expense so that we would not be tempted to touch Méadhon's Lifefire. Not that we ever would," he hastened to add.

"Although Guardians are assigned to monitor and intervene only when total obliteration is imminent, we *can* teach you to tap Méadhon's power for yourselves, to control it, to wield it," he put a hand on Jon and Shondral's shoulders, "to eliminate Malissa."

"Why us?" Jon persisted. Oriander's answer may have satisfied his intellect but his emotions were by no means persuaded. "Why not some great hero or a holy man or, better yet, some lunatic? I just don't understand why it has to be us." He grumbled an apology and strode from the patio. Confronting Malissa was no longer some distant, remote quest contrived from dubious clues. And she could kill! He needed time to digest the awful truth.

Shondral's arm slipped around his waist and, when they were out of sight, he turned to hold her. "I'm afraid for you," he whispered into her hair. "I couldn't bear it if you were hurt."

"We have to try, Jon. Don't you see?" She gripped his arms and forced him to look at her. "It has to be us because of what we already know about this power and because we have some small affinity for it. How long would it take to find someone else? We're here, now. If she is not stopped, nothing else will ever matter." Her eyes filled with tears. "And we have to do it for Milo."

They held each other for a long time before rejoining the others.

Oriander waited for them to return and did not comment on their lengthy absence. He guided them through the Great Hall and let them pause to admire the tapestries. They entered a corridor at the far end of the Hall and followed Oriander through one of the numerous nondescript doors along either wall. Halam's stories had somewhat prepared them and they accepted the alien vista with only a modicum of stupefaction. A lavender sky dotted with a dozen silver moons served as the canopy for a landscape that swayed with delicate feather trees of soft pinks and startling crimsons. The collage faded into the horizon like ripples on a fiery sea.

Laughter and music drifted from the other side of a small knoll. To retain some small sense of the ordinary, Jon tried, unsuccessfully, to find the musicians who performed such exotic harmonies. They topped a low rise and, in the shallow valley beyond, Halam, Ushival, Risto, and Aoineadh lounged on a quilt vast enough for three times their number. At the centre, crystal bowls overflowed with fruit and tiny, delicate cakes. Ushival graciously gestured for them to make themselves comfortable and offered tall glasses of a beverage that refreshed like a cool spring night. Eich rolled on his back a short distance away, his coat glossy in the silver light, and his tongue lolling out of the side of his mouth. Shondral laughed gaily at some comment of Ushival's, easing Jon's heart.

Soon, a full stomach, the excitement of the day, and the weariness of the long road culminated in a huge yawn. His eyelids began to droop and he stretched out on the enormous blanket. It moulded itself to his contours and he gave in to sleep.

***

Oriander was a patient teacher, going over the simple steps until Jon and Shondral silently screamed with frustration. There was some trick, or some twist, or some sleight of mind that they simply could not master. They persevered as long as they could each day until even the wonders of Banifour could not relieve their sense of defeat.

"How did Milo do it?" Shondral demanded after one such exasperating day. She looked at Oriander. "Well, how did he do it?"

Oriander closed his eyes briefly at her impatience; he must treat her with care and compassion—he needed her and he had never needed anyone. "Milo," he said the name gently, "was a special boy. He had the same innate ability to use Lifefire as all Méadhonians but he also had a desire, albeit a negative desire, to change something so badly that without knowing what he did, he forced opened the dormant channel between himself and the world around him. I surmise that because he was an artist, he was more sensitive than most and perhaps that was a deciding factor. It must have been very painful for him." Shondral nodded, Milo had said something about hot pins in his head. "For poor Milo," he patted Shondral's hand, "using

281

Lifefire was a harsh, unpleasant experience."

Saddened by the knowledge of this additional torment that Milo had suffered, Jon and Shondral returned to their endless practice exercises.

The longed-for breakthrough came at the end of the fifth day. Shondral yelped with glee. She had transformed a piece of dried fruit into a huge red apple. "If only we could have done this on the trail!" She bit into the succulent fruit. Oriander laughed and hugged her, effusive with praise. Shondral picked up another piece and repeated the feat more easily. She did it a third time, even faster. In short order, all of Shondral's practice fruit had been transformed.

Jon grunted something indecipherable, intent on his own piece of dried fruit. He strained, sweat prickling his scalp, but when he opened his eyes, the same wrinkled slice of peach stared back at him.

Shondral jumped to her feet, flushed and excited. It took a few seconds to absorb the despair on Jon's face. She sobered. "You'll get it, Jon." She smoothed back his dishevelled hair and retied it for him.

Oriander came up behind him. "You try too hard, Jon. Let it happen. But enough for today." He clapped him on the shoulder. "Time to celebrate!"

For the next two days, Oriander drilled them. But Jon could not overcome his block although he could sense it and knew its shape. He tried to go through it, or over it, or around it until he thought his brain would explode. "A strong desire and maybe artistic abilities," Jon fumed. "That combination must have happened hundreds, no, thousands, of times." He glared at Oriander. Shondral knew what troubled Jon—he desperately wanted to spare her the battle with Malissa; he wanted to go in her place. She had no choice but to let him work it out on his own.

Oriander looked away, his eyes glittering with anger. *Would this boy not just shut up and concentrate?* Of course, others had discovered Lifefire before Milo's blunder. The huge difference was that Oriander had been instrumental in making those other 'discoveries' happen. He smiled to himself; the last time had yielded results nothing short of spectacular—the Great Cataclysm he believed it was called. He must admit that things had gotten a little out of hand and the Keepers had questioned him deeply. But he had covered his tracks well and they could not trace the experiment back to him. He had been even more cautious this time. Oriander would place additional blocks on Jon's conduit to the enormous forces of Lifefire. He did not need a nosy busybody asking questions. He composed his face and turned to the black-haired youth. "You are right, Jon," Oriander agreed. "The combination of emotion and art has doubtless occurred before. Milo must also have had some deep insight into the working of the world; he must have been quite intelligent." *Let the young upstart chew on that for a while.*

At the end of the eighth day, Jon conceded defeat and left Shondral with Oriander. She, at least, had uncovered her vast potential. She could transform anything into what she wished it to be, and move it with ease from one place to another.

283

His consolation was that he would be at her side to protect her while she focused on manipulating Lifefire.

Halam found him later that night at the lake where they had first revelled in Banifour. They sat motionless for a time, comfortable with each other from their long days on the road. "You'll be leaving soon." Halam was a disembodied voice beside him.

Eich leaned against his leg and Jon absently scratched his soft ears.

"Shondral is strong, very strong," Halam continued, "and, with you beside her, guarding her, you'll make it."

The bile rose in Jon's throat. "I should be the one confronting Malissa." He surged to his feet and angrily hurled rocks into the water. He spun to face Halam's shadowy outline, and just as quickly as his anger had flared it dissipated. His shoulders slumped. "What if something goes wrong? What if she isn't strong enough? What if we can't protect her?"

Halam did his best to reassure Jon, but he had other disturbing news that must be told. "I'm afraid I won't be going with you." Jon was too stunned to say anything. "Oriander and the other Guardians are convinced that it would be a mistake, and perhaps even endanger the mission. They won't say exactly why or how, just that my presence would be an unnecessary risk."

Jon burst out laughing. "A risk," he managed between chortles. "You'd be a risk." He knew he verged on hysteria and bent down to splash some water on his face. "Sorry, Halam. It's just so absurd to think that one person, bringing our vast entourage to three," he flung his arms out to encompass an imaginary army, "could change the odds."

He kicked at the turf. "These Guardians seem to have trouble explaining a lot of things. And why is it that Oriander is the only one that actively helps us? What's wrong with the other three? Don't they have the same interests at stake? I don't know what to think of their so-called benevolence sometimes. Maybe there's something in it for them." He dared Halam to deny his accusations.

It was not the first time Halam had to deal with Jon's sceptical nature. He patiently outlined the dilemma and brought it to its inevitable conclusion. "Just the two of you would make a better team. And," he paused to emphasise his next words, "would have a better chance of success."

Jon was by no means content as they stretched out on the fragrant grass to spend the night under the stars.

Jon and Eich explored the perimeter of Banifour the next day. He needed to clear his head and to focus on what was important. If he could not take Milo's place, he could certainly be there for Shondral and do whatever was necessary to protect her. He ate the fruit that grew within easy reach, and refreshed himself in a crystalline waterfall when the sweat trickled down his back. Eich joined him in a swim and sent drenching sprays of water his way with powerful slaps of his front paws. Jon retaliated with a miniature tidal wave of his own. They battled each other until Jon, laughing and exhausted, crawled into the welcome shade of overhanging trees. Eich shook rainbowed arcs of water from his fur and basked spread-eagled in the sun. Pleasantly tired, they returned to the Great Hall for the evening meal.

Shondral entered the cosy dining room in deep discussion with Oriander. The others arrived and, without ceremony, they ate from the steaming platters before them. Jon noticed that Shondral barely touched her food, her attention in some faraway place that he would never experience. The bitterness surged again and he thrust it back into its dark corner—it was a waste of time and energy and he renewed his resolve to concentrate on what he *could* do.

Shondral's gaze passed through him at first, and then slowly focused. A wan smile touched her face; she looked tired and confused.

"What is it?" he asked in a low voice, reluctant to attract attention.

She shrugged her shoulders. "There's just so much." She stared at her plate. "Oriander says we should leave tomorrow."

Jon stared at her. "But you've barely had time to get over..." He stumbled to a halt, cursing himself.

She reached for his hand under the table. "I'm doing it *for* Milo." Her weary expression transformed into one of fierce resolution. He caressed her hand hoping that he somehow conveyed his total support.

Oriander called them together shortly after lunch the next day. Shondral appeared in a gown that matched the sky-blue of her eyes. Her hair

286

shone like fire and was bound with a circlet of silver around her brow. Jon was speechless, and a little cowed by the aura of power that surrounded her.

She gestured regally. "Your dagger, sir." Jon mutely drew his dagger and handed it to her. She concentrated briefly and a sword, scabbard, and belt flashed into existence. She handed it to her astonished friend. He studied the exquisite workmanship and automatically tested the edge on the blade. She touched his travel-worn clothes and, before he had the time to take another breath, he stood in soft leather boots, trousers, silk shirt, and a rich fur travel cloak that hung from his shoulders. Jon strapped on the sword and vaguely noticed how the silver sparkled against the midnight black of his fine garments. She smiled brightly at him and she was Shondral again, totally familiar but forever changed. He tried to concentrate on what Oriander was saying.

"...the best we can and we dare not delay any longer. Please be careful and return to us safely." He embraced them.

Halam came forward. "Just believe in yourselves." He hid the moisture in his eyes by hugging them quickly and walking back to Eich's side. He stiffened. "He wants to go with you." Halam's face was white but his eyes were fierce with pride. Oriander nodded and Eich trotted over to Jon's side.

"We'll bring him back to you." Jon was not at all sure they could keep that promise but he was elated to have Eich with them. The big dog often sensed danger before they did and, more importantly, Eich would protect Shondral with his life.

The three travellers stood close together in the circle formed by the outstretched arms of the Guardians. There was a brief sensation of vertigo, and Jon, Shondral, and Eich stood ankle deep in the muck of the Raylorn Fen.

Chapter 14

The next two days were the longest in Aird's life. Although the Gaskis kept them busy doing chores around the farm, the waiting was worse than sitting out a storm on the Plateau. At least there, you knew the storm would end.

The far-seekers had completed their third attempt at finding Jeorg and had reached Ked itself. They reported heavy traffic for this season, which Arthon attributed to the unusually dry spring weather, but no sign of the Captain. The next foray would take them outside civilised areas, which would make it easier for them to spot pockets of activity. Unfortunately, it might also make it easier for them to be spotted.

With the assistance of the youthful far-seekers, Féadan was kept informed of any plans that the team at the Gaski's formulated. Meanwhile, he and his research team attempted to duplicate Malissa's feats. They were reluctant to pervert the natural course of Lifefire and, not surprisingly, had made little progress. When Jeorg was found, they had to hope that their existing strengths would be up to the task of freeing him from Malissa regardless of how she had chosen to subjugate him.

Aird sighed and applied himself to the task of drawing up contingency plans. If they found Jeorg in the Mountains, they would need climbing equipment and warm clothes in addition to the standard requirements of horses and food. If they found him on the Plateau—and Aird hoped with all his heart that Jeorg was there—he would call upon his brothers to give them the assistance they needed. If he was east of the Kobaska Hills, he did not know what they would need and knew of no one who had ever been to that remote land. If Jeorg was south, they would need a craft capable of navigating the River Quiem, by far the fastest way to reach the southern lands; in fact, Arthon had left early that morning to see if anything was available. Aird rubbed his eyes, not sure how much longer he could compile lists of items they may or may not need.

He had never been good at waiting, and he chafed to do something, anything, that would bring him closer to Jeorg. He had had to stop himself at least a dozen times from simply saddling a horse and galloping away. But in which direction? He clenched his jaw and forced his mind away from the torment that he imagined Jeorg must be suffering. He was driving himself into a useless frenzy. There was nothing he could do and he knew it. Teber rested now and could not fly again until later that night. With a second sigh, Aird stretched muscles unused to sitting so long, strode to the door, and continued walking at a brisk pace towards the low hills bordering the Gaski's homestead. He broke into a ground-eating lope as the ground started to rise; perhaps if he wore himself out it would ease some of his frustration.

Géodha watched him leave from the kitchen window where she was helping Elli to prepare dinner.

"He'll be fine once he's doing something again." Elli had come up behind her and put a sympathetic hand on her shoulder. "It's the waiting.

It gets to us all."

Burying their anxiety, the two women attacked the bread dough on the floured board.

Later that night, a yawning Teber joined them in the front room. He was tired but his determination easily overcame the fatigue. This was the first time he had been put in charge and he needed to succeed at finding Jeorg Oprum and at keeping the other far-seekers safe. If he was successful, his father might finally let him try some of the things that he knew he could do—some of the things that he and Roinn had talked about. So far, Féadan had kept the far-seekers on a tightly controlled program. Sometimes it felt more like a leash.

Elli bustled off to fetch the stew and bread she had warming for him in the kitchen. They discussed Aird's contingency plans and Arthon's queries regarding a boat while the boy ate his fill. Maol glanced sidelong at Teber and was concerned at his waxy pallor and sunken cheeks. After tonight, Maol decided, the young far-seekers must rest for at least two days. He did not look forward to what Aird would say.

"How far do you think you'll get tonight?" Riab asked.

Teber pushed his empty bowl aside and moved to the excellent map Aird and Arthon had drawn. "We should complete two sweeps tonight. From here," he pointed north-west of Ked to the Royo Falls, "to here," his finger formed an arc to the fork in the road that led to the Kobaska Hills, "and down to here," he completed a curve that would take them beyond the Lakes of the Claw in the Raylorn Fen, far to the south-east of Alba.

"You've covered more ground than we could have done in months," Aird congratulated him. Teber flushed with pleasure. "After tonight, though, you must rest." His words were gentle but his voice was steel. Maol smiled to himself; the lanky nomad was not, after all, insensible to everything but rescuing his Captain.

Teber stretched out on the pallet Elli had prepared for him. He knew that later, someone would carry him to his bed. But for now, it allowed his watchers to remain together. He smiled at them before closing his eyes to commence the breathing and relaxation exercises necessary to divorce mind from body. With a snap that was audible to his ears alone, Teber hovered above his body for a moment before he soared through the Gaski's roof to the starry glory of the summer night.

He met the others at the agreed upon place, just above the cave entrance. Féadan would not let them travel towards Teber.

"He treats us like first-time flyers, and we've been nearly everywhere! And I, for one," Garlasco blasted dangerously close to the others, *"am not the least bit tired!"* He executed an intricate series of rolls and twists to demonstrate just how not tired he was.

If Teber made Garl stay behind tonight it would unduly strain the others. He would have to watch him even closer; Garl was getting a little too cocky and might do something stupid. Teber gritted his ethereal teeth and signalled the "V" formation to start the night's search.

In the flight over the dense Greengard south of the Mjorns, they detected nothing but the wild animals of the forest and Teber was glad to reach the spectacular Royo Falls. Over four hundred feet high, the tower of water cascaded in a deafening roar to smash on the boulders far below, smoothed into bizarre shapes from decades of the merciless pounding. Angelic arms of spray reached out to them, sparkling and dancing to an ancient music. They played for a time, weaving in and out of the powerful downpour, their shrieks of delight audible only to each other. Energised, they continued their journey to the fork and on to the Eastern Arm of the River Quiem in high spirits.

Like a silver knife, the River separated the deep forests in the north from the dank swampland in the south. They huddled closer together, revolted by the sightless, loathsome creatures that dwelt in the mire below. Teber projected reassurance to his team; the winds of the Sea would soon cleanse this filth from their senses.

The first of the Lakes of the Claw came into view with its own set of horrors. A water snake out of all proportion to its cousins in the north slithered beneath the foul surface where it preyed on slugs that fed in turn on maggots oozing through the remains of a decomposing carcass. Embar sobbed and curled in upon herself, dampening her senses. Teber adjusted his flight path so that he was beneath her, supporting her.

As one, Filyos and Achisu exclaimed and pointed to a greenish glow speckled with pinpricks of ochre light, eerily out of place. The group circled high above and sent the tiniest fibril of awareness towards the weird phenomenon.

They came to within a breath of the trap.

A deadly web hovered over the swamp as far as their senses could extend. In the fleeting brush with it, they comprehended full well its purpose: to suck their mind-out-of-body essence into itself. Garlasco's agility whipped their trajectory back on itself but not before Teber resolved the points of light, which he at first thought was a vast swarm of fireflies, into campfires—hundreds of them, with thousands of creatures crawling around in the fetid smoke. Malissa's creatures.

They jarred Embar back into full awareness and raced with all their strength in a direct line to the Mjorns, disregarding the interdict to fly near Alba. Teber chanced a glimpse at the port and nearly jolted the others into an uncontrolled spin. For the second time that night, Garl's quickness saved them but Teber spared no energy to thank him. His mind was numbed by what he had sensed: a second lethal web surrounded the entire town.

At the Mountains, Teber left his charges with an improvised schedule for the next contact and arrowed to Ked.

His body was still in the front room where his companions continued their discussions. Glancing in his direction, Elli let out a small shriek at his open eyes. Questions filled the room as they scrambled towards him. Arthon's authoritative voice penetrated the commotion, and ordered them to at least give the boy time to re-orient himself.

Silent and fidgeting, they waited while Teber composed himself and sipped the Maol's hastily prepared restorative brew.

Teber recounted what they had seen and, although they had not penetrated either web, he felt certain that Captain Oprum was in the vast army camp in the Land of the Claw. After all, they had not found him when they searched the Council Chambers in Alba.

Aird had him tell the story over again and, this time, asked questions about every detail. Arthon listened, his fingers steepled under his chin, but did not interrupt. The nomad sat unmoving for several moments when Teber had finished. Nodding, he rose abruptly.

"I think you're right, Teber, and the fastest way to travel to that Ord-forsaken land is on the river." He turned to face Arthon. "Is that barge available?" Arthon nodded. "Good. So unless there is a very good reason to delay," he caught their gazes one at a time, "we leave tonight."

The Gaski homestead burst into a flurry of activity.

Maol regarded their dilapidated conveyance. "Are you certain this is waterproof?"

"Oh, yes. Old Bart uses it all the time to transport his grain to the market in Mriss." Arthon slapped the helm, which promptly emitted an impressive groan. "See, finely tuned!" He chuckled at his own joke until tears streaked his weather-beaten cheeks. Maol's expression remained grim. "She'll do fine." Arthon reassured him, still smiling. "Just looks bad."

They loaded supplies and boarded. Arthon and Aird comfortably slipped into Captain and First Mate roles, and before dawn, had manoeuvred the bulky craft into the middle of the broad river.

Elli and Teber waved until a bend in the river hid the barge from sight. Teber had no choice but to stay and rest, and she would have slowed them down, but it was very, very hard to see Arthon off on another voyage. "The old fool," she muttered through trembling lips.

Their retreating footfalls sounded hollow and forlorn on the wooden dock.

The Northern Bridge loomed over them. For the first time, Arthon was grateful for the slovenly watchman and they slipped beneath its expanse unnoticed. His passengers would remain hidden throughout the journey; it would not do for the town to gossip about a barge on its way south with nothing for cargo but a group of strangers, and there were fishermen scattered the entire length of the river from Ked to Mriss who would like nothing better than to have a bit of unusual news to share. It would be dinner time when they reached Lake Thungal and, with Arthon's reputation demanding respect, they hoped to glide around the town and on to the far side of the Lake without having to fabricate a story about what he was doing with Bart's boat—though Arthon claimed he had several ready, just in case.

Endel and the Uamhans made themselves as comfortable as possible in the dark, dank shed that crouched on the deck near the stern of the barge. Its purpose was to protect the more fragile goods during transport. Endel snorted; he supposed that they qualified as 'fragile goods.' They chose to ignore the skittering noises coming from the inky corners, and spent the interminable day resting or going over their plans yet again.

It was late afternoon when they heard Arthon exchange pleasantries with the watchman guarding the bridge near Mriss. After a brief pause, they were waved through. Aird and Arthon guided the barge around the perimeter of the town and sailed to the lake's south shore on the last breath of the evening breeze. Dusk had fallen when Aird's sharp eyes found the mouth of the inlet that would allow them to push even further south. Because of low rainfall that spring, the tributary soon became unnavigable and they were forced to pole the craft into a shallow cove at less than half the distance they had hoped to travel on the waterway. Aird dropped anchor.

Endel, Riab, Géodha, and Maol crawled out of their concealment, stretched cramped muscles, and breathed the fresher though somewhat cloying air of the Raylorn Fen. They shared a cold meal and Aird suggested they get as much rest as possible. He would take the first watch. The night seemed to last forever while the bullfrogs delivered their throaty symphony.

At daybreak, they concealed the barge with fish nets laced with fronds and tree bows scavenged from the shore. It would not hide the boat should someone chance into the inlet but it would pass unnoticed from a distance.

Preparations were complete and it was time to go. Aird, Riab, and Endel huddled a short distance

297

from the others.

"Well, what are you three waiting for," Géodha asked, impatient to be on the way, "a personal invitation from Malissa?"

Endel looked up but did not react to her question. He cleared his throat and straightened his shoulders. "Where we go today is unknown. We may encounter only swarms of insects and quagmire up to our chests, or we may face creatures that we have to fight or run from. It would seem to make sense, and we can vote on this," he hastened to add, "that only the fittest of us should undertake this last part of the journey." He lowered his eyes; he could not look at Maol and Arthon. "Besides," he continued, "a couple of people should stay and make sure that the barge is here when we return. We could rescue Jeorg, but without transportation, we could still fail." He removed his spectacles and polished them rather more vigorously than necessary.

Arthon's complexion had reddened during Endel's little speech and he took a deep breath to berate all youngsters who failed to realise the advantages of long experience, who would make stupid mistakes without his guidance, who had no way of knowing what skills would be needed, and who had no right to deny him an adventure just because his legs were not as strong as they used to be. Maol put a restraining hand on his shoulder. Arthon whirled to vent his ire at this convenient target.

"He's right. You know he's right," the elder Uamhan calibrated his voice to penetrate Arthon's anger. "We'll only slow them down and a smaller force might have a better chance of success. Besides, chewing mosquitoes is not my idea of an adventure."

Arthon visibly deflated. He kicked aside some of the leafy camouflage and disappeared into the barge's shed.

"Don't worry about him," Maol consoled Endel, "he'll be fine once he's had a chance to cool off and think it over. Now go, before my own good sense fails me."

Endel, Aird, Riab, and Géodha set off at a brisk pace into the still darkened woods. Aird estimated they would reach the perimeter of Malissa's camp by sundown.

The character of the land began to change within the first hour. The trees, at first tall and lush, seemed to recoil upon themselves and shrivel into stunted and convoluted travesties. The forest floor became damp and spongy; the sodden earth was defiled by a sickly green slime that smothered it like a noxious blanket and concealed the depth of the stagnant muck. They were forced into a convoluted route in search of more solid ground.

Aird prodded the mire with a stout walking stick and guided them from one relatively dry spot to another. Progress was tedious and slow, made even more unbearable by the teeming insects. Unfortunately, that prediction had been realised with a vengeance. In the sweltering heat, they were forced to don travel cloaks with the hoods pulled low over their faces and secured at the throat. Their precautions did little more than give the swarms a mediocre challenge. They struggled on in dismal silence.

Aird's hoarse cry pierced through the incessant buzz; he pointed to an outcrop of rock visible through loops of mossy vines. He increased the pace and jabbed his stick in the slimy water, spewing heavy veils of sludge in every direction. In moments, they struggled atop the first firm land to be found in hours and collapsed for a sorely needed respite.

Riab was the first to stir and rummaged through their provisions for water. Aird reached to grab the flask from his hand as the Uamhan drank deeply.

"Go easy. It has to last."

Riab glared at him, still forcing the tepid liquid to his lips. Ever so slowly, he relented. "It's this place," Riab muttered. "It makes a man crazy." He handed the flask to Aird and moved to the edge of the rock. He sat on a stony outcrop and closed his eyes to blot out the dismal landscape.

Soft pressure on Aird's arm brought him out of his own dark thoughts. "You must remember that he is only just out of the mountain. This is all so new to us," Géodha shuddered, "and some of it is…" she gestured to their surroundings. Aird covered her delicate hand with his and noticed how a few days of sunshine had polished her beautiful skin to a golden glow. Their eyes met for a moment and Aird felt a fleeting warmth course through him that had nothing to do with Géodha's Uamhan powers but everything to do with his growing attraction.

Endel had watched the altercation with Riab from his self-appointed lookout spot and sympathised with the Uamhan; this was another not-so-pleasant example of life on the surface. He opened the bag of medicinal supplies and prepared a small dose of cumbas leaf for each of them. It would ease the sting and itch of their bites.

An odd gurgling sound interrupted Riab's self-pity. He morosely studied the direction from which the next revulsion in this land of revulsions would come. The sound repeated, much closer this time. Alarmed, he stood to vacate his lonely outpost just as a fissure opened at his feet. A pallid tendril shot toward his booted ankle. At the same time, a second filament wrapped itself around his arm. Transfixed with horror, he watched helplessly as he was drawn into the gaping maw of the rock.

The scrape of boot on stone caused Aird to glance at his recalcitrant friend. In one swift motion, he leapt to his feet, dagger drawn, and raced to Riab's side. Endel was there an instant later.

Aird slashed at the strand around Riab's ankle and winced when his thrust met its unyielding surface. Jarred out of his deadly quiescence, Riab drew his own knife and stabbed at the tendril around his wrist. His hand had turned white and he could no longer feel his fingers. Inch by relentless inch, he was being pulled toward the widening crevice that now pulsated with bubbling juices.

"Hold still!" Géodha's shouted command surprised the three men into stillness. She carried a vial of liquid that emitted curls of acrid smoke when she removed the stopper. Recognising what she held, Riab dropped to one knee and brought the tendrils side by side. She carefully poured the contents across them in a straight line, shaking ever so slightly. Minuscule gashes appeared on the surface revealing dun-coloured tissues beneath. Into these gashes, Géodha sprinkled the rest of the toxic solution. The ground beneath them convulsed and, one after the other, the tendrils released their grip on Riab and slithered out of sight.

Endel and Géodha helped Riab to his feet; Aird grabbed their packs, two in each hand. Heedless of what lay beneath their feet, they leaped off the rock and ran for the nearest clump of vegetation. Daring a quick glance over his shoulder, Aird urged them to greater speed. He never told them of the grey mountain that loomed and swayed, deep rents writhing with dozens of serpentine limbs.

Their frantic escape drove them deeper into the Fen. Roughly at its centre, five ragged strips had been gouged out of the land: the Lakes of the Claw. There were many tales about how the Lakes had been formed, and none of them were pleasant. It was into the very palm of the Claw that they must penetrate.

Aird was confident they would succeed; to think otherwise would be more dangerous than the encroaching darkness. He had found loyal allies in the Uamhans whose skills and knowledge had saved Jeorg once before and he fully expected them to be able to do it again. He knew he was being unreasonable but he couldn't help himself; he needed to believe it. Endel, of course, would go to any length to see his friend and Captain alive and safe. Aird fervently hoped the price would not be too high.

The Fen drew dusk greedily to its breast. They had covered perhaps three-quarters of the distance Aird had hoped they would, but it was better that they rest before embarking on the last leg of their perilous mission. He led the small group towards a stand of sickly, deformed shrubs; perhaps a campfire could be concocted.

Try as they might, no spark would ignite the pile of brambles Géodha and Endel had collected, along with a patchwork of scratches that quickly inflamed. Disgusted with this latest insult from the swamp, they agreed to a double watch and huddled close together, not for warmth but for the simple contact of a fellow human being.

Aird and Géodha had the first watch and aside from the ever-present insects, one or two mysterious slithers, and an ominous rumbling far to the south, the quagmire surrounding them was still. They did not speak, but frequently sought each other's eyes.

When it was time to change the watch, Riab and Endel woke immediately at Géodha's touch. Riab probed his right hand and foot and though they looked normal, sensation had not yet returned. Apparently the rock creature preferred its victims helpless and inert.

In the hour before dawn, Riab's sharp ears detected the rustle of brush to the west of their camp. Something large approached. Endel's stiff back told him that he'd heard it too. They woke the others. With precise hand signals, Aird directed them deeper into the scant shrubbery in order to put as much distance and foliage as possible between them and whatever lurked in the obscurity of the bog. In total silence, they waited.

"...of course I'm sure they're here! I saw them didn't I?" Shondral was tired and her patience was wearing thin. "Hello?" she said a little louder. "We're friends." Her contralto voice was as distinct as a church bell amid the guttural chorus of the swamp. She wiped sweaty palms on the infinitely more practical breeches and tunic that had once been her blue gown. This was no place for finery.

"They need some proof," Jon whispered in her ear. He made certain that Eich stayed by his side.

Shondral smiled. "I wear the *Flame of Life,* a gift from the shaman Didyma of the Rhudha tribe." Jon gave her a little hug.

The abrupt snap of twigs introduced a tall man's silhouette against the spectral flush of dawn. "I am called Aird of the Isastis Tribe. You are welcome to share our camp." He knew with all his heart and soul that someone who had knowledge of the talisman was a trusted friend, but someone who actually wore it had been given a rare honour.

Jon and Shondral followed Aird to the camp and sat on a bit of dry ground while the others joined them. She noticed the teepee of brambles and branches and self-consciously touched a dirty index finger to it. It smouldered, resisting her at first, then gave in to the inevitable flame that would consume it. With a power of its own, the small fire drew the six together, etching their features in its dull orange glow.

Eich pushed his way between his two friends and dropped to his belly in a huff. Jon laughed, a sound very much out of place in the Fen, and ran his hand over the big dog's head.

Shondral studied their new companions as they, in turn, were studied. The tall one that had greeted them, Aird, must be the leader of the expedition. His dark, brooding eyes were deeply set in a rugged face—a face the colour of the tawny earth of the Dreven Plateau. The woman next to him, as pale as he was dark, was delicately featured, apparent even in the uncertain firelight. A very young man sat next to them, with hair that was likely golden in the sunshine. He had a kind face that events of the world had only recently touched. And, closing the circle, sat an unremarkable man of middle age who futilely rubbed at his spectacles with a grimy handkerchief. He looked strong and capable.

Shondral and Jon knew that this group of people was purposely camped on the fringe of Malissa's territory. Earlier, Shondral had sent forth her mind and encountered Malissa's web. She tested its strength and was satisfied that she could breach it undetected. She had returned to her body via a more northerly route and it was then that she had sensed the four humans in the midst of the interminable marsh. She had delicately touched their minds and discovered, to her delight, that they shared a common enemy. Incredibly, she and Jon had found allies.

They exchanged sketchy descriptions of their adventures thus far, each in awe of the other. The Uamhans were ecstatic to find that Lifefire was indeed known by others, and were even more enthused to learn about the Guardians and Banifour; Shondral and Jon marvelled that a civilisation such as the Uamhans described could possibly exist, let alone thrive. Aird and Endel then told of Jeorg's poisoning, healing, and subsequent abduction.

Aird was heartened by the shamans' participation and asked Shondral if he might see the fabled *Flame of Life*. She drew it from beneath her tunic where it reflected the firelight in a thousand shards of gold and ruby light. Aird covered the precious jewel with his hand.

"We do not want to reveal our position by such beauty." He stared at his own hand as if he could see through it to the wonder beneath. Shondral replaced it within the folds of her clothing.

Endel cleared his throat. "Would you consider a joint effort?"

Practical as ever, Aird thought. Of course! The girl would be able to pinpoint Jeorg's location and Jon could help with their 'diversion.' They spent the rest of the morning discussing their covert operation.

Jon pondered the total insanity of what they were about to do: six ordinary people (well, mostly ordinary) and one ordinary dog (well, mostly ordinary) staging an assault on a powerful and hideous force—a force that could crush them like bugs underfoot. But somewhere on this journey he had discovered that there was nothing on Méadhon that could stop him from trying. Amazed at himself, he realised that he would even die if it meant that the world would be safe again. That Shondral would be safe again, and that no one else would suffer as Milo had suffered.

For the second time, Endel had to ask a

member of their party to stay behind. Riab fretted but he knew better than any of them that his hand and foot were unreliable and might fail him at an inopportune moment. Before the others set out, they gathered wood and left him rope from which he could make some type of conveyance for Jeorg, in case it was needed. If no one rejoined him by the following dawn, he was to make all haste to the barge and to Mriss, and somehow convince the town-folk of the great danger that gathered its forces on their doorstep.

After a lunch marvellously enhanced by Shondral, they left the camp and Riab, and arrived at the periphery of Malissa's web without mishap. There, they rested as best they could until nightfall.

The campfires Teber had seen were lit one by one until the firmament smouldered blood red stained with wisps of sooty smoke. Tortuous shapes loomed thirty feet tall in the chimerical hell-vision before them. Bulky masses were being turned on spits by brutes they vaguely resembled; crude weapons lay in bundles, the ragged blades scarlet as if already dipped in the gore of men; hundreds of creatures plodded here and there, performing obscure tasks.

Shondral prepared to project her spirit over the encampment; she could provide valuable details for their foray. She took several slow breaths, closed her eyes, and was gone. It seemed that far-seeking was not solely a Uamhan discovery; Féadan would be eager to learn of this.

Jon supported Shondral's inert body. For the thousandth time, he wished for the key to Lifefire and found some small consolation in that even these Uamhans could not accompany her.

He would have had additional consolation if he knew that, at that moment, Shondral wished she had never heard of Lifefire. Her spirit quailed at being alone, a single bright mote in an endless sea of darkness. The size of the camp staggered her. She thought of Milo and resolutely endured, instinct guiding her to the centre of the vast encampment.

A structure jutted out of a low hill. It was a square box of a building with no adornment or window to mar its smooth sides. A single chimney escaped from the flat roof. Shondral gathered an additional smidgen of Lifefire to conceal herself in the way that Oriander had taught her. She gave herself no time to think about how afraid she was or how foolish she was, and dove into Malissa's stronghold.

The opulence conflicted so dramatically with the squalor outside that Shondral was unable to discern specifics for the instant it took to adjust to the mellow candlelight. Rich tapestries covered the walls and muffled the sounds of the mustering army; a curtain sectioned off sleeping quarters complete with a canopied bed; the work area boasted a solid barbar table carved over its entire surface and sentried on each side by a divan wide enough for three. A sideboard overflowed with liquors and delicacies from exotic ports.

And there, in a corner away from the light, was Malissa. She sat in a chair that sprouted wings on either side like some carnivorous bird ready to enfold its prey. She was younger than Shondral had expected. Her white face was relaxed and composed, almost pretty. Not the face of a cold-blooded murderer.

Shondral dared to approach the still figure. Malissa's eyes were closed, her breathing deep and regular. Though Shondral had seen only Oriander in this state, she recognised it immediately. *That's what I must look like right now.* Shondral contemplated the irony that both she and her nemesis soared above the earth, Malissa likely searching for her, and here she was, 'standing' before the empty husk of Malissa's body.

A spasm of racking coughs, faint but nearby, snapped her attention from the morbid fantasy of studying Malissa's face. She wheeled about seeking the source of such misery.

In a dirt hole beneath Malissa's feet crouched an emaciated, pitiful human being. Shondral involuntarily dampened her sense of smell; he must have been living in his own excrement and vomit for days. He moaned, and curled himself into a tighter foetal position, hoarding the meagre warmth of his body. Shondral yearned to comfort him, to release him, to take him far away. She did the only thing she could do, and returned as fast as possible to the others.

Shondral could not meet Aird's or Endel's eyes. "We need to rescue Captain Oprum as soon as possible. He's... not doing well." Their anguish stood out vividly in the ruddy glow from the campfires a hundred yards away. Her heart went out to them; she knew what it felt like when someone you loved suffered. Action, she knew, was the best remedy. Shondral smoothed a patch of dirt with her hand and using a sturdy twig drew a crude map of the encampment. They plotted the safest path to the building, though 'safe' was laughable.

That task done, Endel encouraged them to rest; they would rescue Jeorg while his captors slept all around him.

Shondral fretted over the necessary delay because *now* would be a good time to go in, while Malissa's mind projected. But she knew Endel was right; they would have to reach the building first. It was her own battle she over which she fretted. She, and she alone, would face Malissa. It gnawed at her confidence, leaving her weak and afraid. A warm arm went around her and she rested her head on Jon's shoulder.

Snores and grunts polluted the air. The army was as foul in sleep as it was awake. Aird convinced Jon that he would serve Shondral best if he were part of the 'pirate' diversion. Jon prayed they would not have to resort to it, for the unspoken truth was that it would be suicide—a last resort to reach and destroy Malissa. To occupy his mind, he learned the various escape routes should things go awry. He learned these things but he knew he would ignore them if Shondral needed him.

Their faces and hands blackened with mud, and their strength and purpose fortified with everything Géodha could give them, they entered one by one through the opening Shondral created in the invisible barrier. The dark forms on the dark ground made a difficult, but not impossible, maze for them to navigate. Malissa had set no guards. Who could pass her intricate web-work? And if the impossible occurred and they did, what harm could they possibly do besides provide a little sport for her army?

Géodha blessed her foresight in bringing olfactory suppressants; she could practically see the stench. She wondered how Eich was coping with his more powerful canine sense of smell. Distracted, she stepped on an out-flung hand. Endel and Aird were at her side, ready to silence the brute, but her light weight had been barely noticed and the sleeper was content to gather his arm beneath him. They stared at each other and continued, more vigilant than ever.

It took two precious hours to wind their way to the only prominent rise. Shondral repeated her earlier visit and was immensely relieved to report that Malissa was still aloft. Aird and Shondral approached the unprotected door while Géodha, Endel, and Jon, with Eich at his side, crawled beneath the scrubby brush at the base of the low hill.

The door opened easily under Aird's gentle shove and he and Shondral stepped into the building. The candles arrayed around the room guttered in melted wax, furtively illuminating Malissa's face. It took all of Aird's self-control not to skewer her where she sat, smugly lording it over his friend, but he had promised to leave her untouched. The Guardians were convinced that she must live to reverse the damage she had done; otherwise, it might not be possible. Shondral stood to one side, her eyes never leaving Malissa's face, because if her spirit should return in the next few minutes...

Aird raised the thick carpet where Shondral indicated. A trap door was outlined in the floorboards. He reached for the latch and, bunching his muscles, pulled hard. It opened quite easily and his momentum came close to throwing him off balance. He steadied himself and waved away Shondral's concerned look.

A dead, rotting smell assaulted their nostrils; Shondral was hard pressed to keep from gagging. Aird plunged the candle she handed him down the narrow shaft. A wooden ladder descended to a platform and to a second trapdoor. Beneath it Aird knew he would find Jeorg Oprum.

Aird climbed down and lifted the door. A figure whimpered in the dark. Aird reached for the filthy arms that Jeorg had immediately wrapped around his head when the door opened. With hoarse cries and feeble attempts to kick his assailant, Jeorg was lifted up through the floor into the candlelight. Shondral gasped once, retrieved a soft-looking throw from one of the divans, and covered his tortured body. Glaring pure venom at Malissa, Aird lifted a now motionless Jeorg over his shoulder and disappeared into the night.

Fighting against every instinct to flee, Shondral remained behind. She clung to the hope that Malissa would be momentarily disoriented as she re-entered her body and would be tired from a night's searching. Shondral shoved one of the divans over to face Malissa and sat, waiting.

Chapter 15

The 'pirates,' too, waited in growing anxiety.

Maybe Aird and Shondral had been caught and could not signal? Maybe they were unconscious? Maybe they were already dead? Jon shook his head. Questions like this would make him do something rash.

After only a few minutes that were somehow stretched to feel like an eternity, Aird's tall form, distorted by what had to be Jeorg's body draped over his right shoulder, appeared in the doorway. Shondral would be next, Jon thought, but the doorway remained empty. He squirmed from his hiding place, and rushed forward to grab Aird's arm. "What about Shondral?" he whispered urgently.

The seaman stopped to stare at him. "She's the only one who can deal with that witch. You know that." Aird shrugged to position Jeorg more comfortably and continued on towards the others.

Without another thought, Jon turned and hastened to the building, Eich at his heels. He would stay with Shondral, and was inordinately grateful that Eich would also be with them.

Géodha heard the soft tread of Jon's boots heading away from them and knew the futility of trying to change his mind. She spared a quick glance over her shoulder just as he and Eich slipped inside Malissa's stronghold and closed the door. Her stomach clenched at the desperate hope embodied in those two young people. Sighing, she turned away to face the challenge of retracing their steps to the opening in the web.

Riab had explained that Malissa's army was fabricated from the familiar animals of Méadhon. Aird tried to keep this firmly in mind as he crept through the encampment but he would be haunted by what had been done to these poor creatures. He thanked the gods that Arthon and Maol had remained behind, safe from this physical and emotional ordeal. In the same breath he cursed himself for allowing the Uamhans and Endel to convince him that only Shondral could overcome Malissa, even though she did have the *Flame of Life*. Aird's thoughts were a swirling mass of the difficulties that lay ahead but his heart was light; Jeorg's welcome weight on his shoulder somehow made any obstacle surmountable.

In the darkness beyond the web, Endel called a brief halt. Aird gently lowered Jeorg to the ground and the doctor managed to force a little water into his mouth. Jeorg had been silent during the tense retreat through the camp but now fought Endel's ministrations with all his pitiful strength. It seemed he preferred to die of thirst rather than suffer what he thought in his fevered mind were more of Malissa's machinations.

They quickly rejoined Riab and secured Jeorg to the crude stretcher that the Uamhan had constructed from sleeping blankets and sturdy branches. The three men shared the task of carrying the still form of Jeorg Oprum while Géodha's keen night vision kept them from sinking more than ankle deep in the muck. At daybreak, the feeble sun helped her to keep them pointed northward toward their hidden barge. Except for short breaks to change stretcher-bearers and to drink and eat a little, there was no question of stopping.

Throughout the long march, Riab glanced over his shoulder so frequently that his neck muscles complained. Every rustle, every breath of air, every dull slap of mire was the rush of attack. It sapped his strength. It was so impossible! They had simply strolled in and taken the Captain! He stopped in his tracks as an ugly scenario leapt, fully formed, into his mind. If Shondral were defeated, their success would be empty; that hoard could overrun anything in its path no matter what they did or where they hid. This vision of death and devastation obliterated the tiny bud of hope that Jeorg's rescue had caused to germinate in Riab's heart. His legs began to move again of their own accord and he limped blindly to what was likely meaningless freedom.

Late that afternoon the bog solidified and, tired to the point of stumbling along, they attempted to increase their shuffling pace. The barge couldn't be much further.

Arthon shouted from a treetop and scrambled down with the agility of a man thirty years his junior. He rushed to assist them with their burden and asked a long stream of questions not bothering to wait for the answers.

The barge no longer seemed like the decrepit transport they had journeyed south in, but rather a haven of pure luxury. Aird insisted they pull out into Lake Thungal immediately. A wide band of water separating them from the shore gave him a badly needed, if illusory, sense of security.

Maol and Endel heated water and bathed Jeorg as best they could. They dressed his wounds and forced a little warm soup laced with painkillers and sedatives down his throat. He slept easier but it would be many weeks before Jeorg Oprum returned to his former physical vitality; it was uncertain how long it would take for his mind to heal.

The despondency that shrouded Riab was apparent to them all. Maol rubbed his hand over his bald head, momentarily regretting that he no longer had a thick mane of hair to run his fingers through—it had been far more satisfying. He took Riab outside on the deck and quietly spoke to him, the soothing murmur of his voice gradually smoothing the lines of tension from Riab's face. The old healer then gave all the rescuers a little something from his bag of medicines. Rest was what they needed, and the tiny white pill would help them have a dreamless sleep.

As soon as it was light, they began their journey up the River Quiem. Claiming to be sufficiently rested, Aird assisted Arthon with the duties at helm and sail. Their exhausted passengers slept through the day and into much of the next night under Maol's watchful eye. It took three days of tacking against the current to reach Ked.

Elli laughed through her tears and Teber jumped up and down and ran among the small entourage like a puppy.

Jeorg had been awake for the final day of the voyage but would not believe that he was no longer in Malissa's clutches. He raved that she could look like anyone or be anything, and sullenly refused to speak to them. The Gaski's gave him their bedroom. It had a wonderful view of the garden and the fields, and you could see the stars on a clear night. "Good for a man's soul," Elli maintained.

***

Shondral remained motionless when Jon and Eich let themselves in; she dared not let her vigilance lapse for even a second, though a flood of relief washed over her.

Jon stared. It was his first look at the woman who had murdered Milo, poisoned Jeorg Oprum, manipulated uncountable humans into her puppets, twisted Méadhon's wildlife into monsters, and threatened to destroy the entire world. Incongruously, she looked harmless. He surveyed the rest of the room before joining Shondral on the divan that she had positioned facing Malissa.

Eich padded over to Malissa and sniffed her hand that dangled over the edge the chair's armrest. Satisfied, he jammed himself on Shondral's other side and proceeded to clean swamp mud from his front paws.

Shondral desperately reviewed all that Oriander had taught her. Her strength, he said, was rooted in her devotion to the land and to all the living things that dwelled upon it. Why could she feel none of that devotion now, when she needed it most? Instead, her mind was filled with fears—fear of not knowing what to do or when to do it, fear of not trying hard enough, fear of not being good enough, fear of failing all those who counted on her, fear of letting Milo's death remain unavenged. The elusive diamond within her, that bright spark of *something* that she had first glimpsed while on the plateau, dimmed until all that remained was a faint wisp of its memory.

Eich growled deep in his throat, and leapt from the divan to stand in front of Jon and Shondral.

A cruel smile twitched on Malissa's lips. Her mouth opened wide and from it disgorged the terrible sound of her laughter.

"This is rich," she gasped. "I search under every filthy rock on this mud hole of a world and here you are." She erupted into another paroxysm of demonic glee.

Eich's fur stood rigid along his spine, his massive shoulder muscles quivered. Jon reached down to put a hand on the dog's back; he suspected that physical force would be useless.

Malissa glanced at the trapdoor near her feet. "I see that you have taken my toy from me. Now, was that nice? But no matter; he was hardly entertaining anymore. Oh, I almost forgot," she smiled, "too bad about Milo." At the look of shock and outrage on their faces her smile widened. "Well," she paused, "enough chit chat."

Malissa locked eyes with Shondral.

Shondral's spirit was wrenched from her body and hurled far above the Fen. Dazed, she groped for her bearings.

A dark cloud veined with silver buffeted her from below. She strained to control her erratic flight and was struck again. The faint ghost of familiar laughter surrounded her, swallowed her. In blind panic, Shondral shot away from her tormentor, not caring where she went.

The Raylorn Fen flashed beneath her. In another instant, the broad expanse of the Sea of Orches glittered in the moonlight. She pushed herself harder. At last, far out over the water, Shondral stopped and warily extended her senses, seeking Malissa's evil taint. She reached above and below, all around. Nothing. Shondral had escaped for the moment.

She descended closer to the Sea, comforted by its familiarity. How could she defeat a force this powerful? Why hadn't Oriander prepared her for something like this? She did not know how to fight such a thing; nothing in her life had ever taught her to be ruthless and calculating, to be vengeful and hurtful. And yet somehow she must find the strength within herself to do this thing. With a calmness that would later astonish her, she straightened her 'shoulders' and felt a flood of confidence rush through her. She would do whatever it took because she must.

The stars guided Shondral to the coastline and, soon, the sparkle of the Sea gave way to the flat black of the land. Pinpoints of light caught her attention—stars reflected in the nearest Lake of the Claw. She altered her course slightly. As she neared, the shape of the lake looked somehow odd to her senses: it was not quite as long and slender as she remembered and the stars reflected in it were not quite right.

Then Malissa was upon her, surrounding her, smothering her.

Shondral struck with all her power, grimly resolved to break Malissa's hold, and angry with herself for falling into the trap.

Nothing happened.

She focused her power and, needle-like, jabbed it into the wall of her prison.

Nothing.

She changed the focus. She struck again and again.

The darkness intensified and became more stifling. Dismayed, Shondral realised that it was using her own power against her.

***

Jon stared from one woman to the other. Both were oblivious to the world around them. Shondral had stiffened when Malissa's eyes met hers, and then she had slumped into the cushions of the divan. She was pale, but her breathing was regular.

Malissa had not changed position at all, even when she had filled the room with her hideous laughter. He could kill her right now, while she was separated from her body. Her spirit would find no home. Or would it? Would she simply take over one of the beasts outside? And what if he harmed Shondral by attacking Malissa? He did not understand enough about how this worked and, besides, the Uamhans and Aird had said that it was Shondral's battle. Shondral's battle? He quashed the intense burn of frustration that welled up in him. However much that he wished it otherwise, he could not do this thing for her. He cradled Shondral in his arms, and rested his cheek on her hair. *I give you all my strength.* He remained that way for a long time.

***

Shondral screamed, without a mouth to form it

or lungs to breathe it. She could sense nothing in the void: no light, no air, no life. Time had no meaning when there was no way to gauge its passing. How would she know when it was time to return to her body for rejuvenation? She would know, she realised. It would be when she was too weak to hold herself together and could only watch as her form dissipated into tiny motes of fading light. In the end, she would not even have that comfort. She shrank in upon herself and clutched the solitary spark that was her essence.

Despair as black as the abyss choked Shondral. This was the end. She had failed everyone. She had failed herself. Lost in a morass of self-pity, knowing she was going to die, she bid a melancholy farewell to the things in life that mattered most to her. How she had loved the hills around Morbella—when spring covered the meadows with brilliant flowers, when summer's lazy days were cooled by a sweet-scented breeze, when fall blazed with vibrant colour, and when winter sparkled in white majesty. She would never see those hills again. She remembered the joy of a Dryx birthing and the lucious pleasure of fresh Dryx cream. She remembered the happiness in her home. She remembered Milo; he had died trying to do what she was not strong enough to finish. She remembered Jon and felt his love flowing through her. She could hear how he said her name with such tenderness.

The void seemed more grey than black, or was it just an hallucination as she weakened? Probably, but she didn't care. She continued to relive the special moments from her life. She remembered the first time she had seen Jon. He was sitting alone in a corner of the Library, his hair had escaped its thong and framed his face with smoky wisps. His intensity drew her like a moth to a flame.

Her prison became more opaque.

Something was working! Her thoughts were weakening Malissa's grip. Before she lost the moment, Shondral returned to that time and place in the Library.

Jon must have felt her staring and looked up to meet her eyes with his direct, penetrating gaze. Her heart did a queer flip and she flashed him a wide smile before she could stop herself. His eyebrows rose, a look of confused astonishment on his face, then he smiled back at her. It was better than the best sunrise.

Abruptly, Shondral was free from Malissa's grasp. She glowed with renewed energy and power and shot after the dusky blotch that fled before her.

Malissa and Shondral reached their bodies in the same instant, but Shondral was ready this time. She took Malissa's hands in her own and for the briefest moment marvelled at their delicacy.

"Flame of Life!" Shondral's fierce cry shattered the air.

***

Jon doubled over with wracking pain. His head threatened to split into tiny pieces and his eyes refused to open. Nausea churned in his belly. He was sprawled face down in a field, this much he could tell. He forced his eyelids apart and, as his vision cleared, discerned Malissa's limp body a few feet away, Shondral supporting her. He struggled to his hands and knees, breathing deeply to keep his stomach under control.

Shondral cradled Malissa's head in her lap. Eich, unperturbed by events, sniffed the prone woman's cheek and raised his great head to Shondral. He seemed to nod once and sat on his haunches to observe.

Jon rubbed his eyes with the heels of his hands and blinked furiously. He stared at Shondral, unable to turn away. She began to glow, lit from within. Brighter and brighter, unbearably bright.

Shondral placed her hands on Malissa's head. "I give you what Milo did not," she said, in a voice that came from everywhere and from nowhere. "You are whole." The woman beneath her hands took on a radiance of her own. The tableau held for a moment, then Shondral's hands moved to stroke Malissa's hair.

Jon's senses were beginning to function although the inside of his head felt like pins and needles were dancing about. From Shondral's description, he thought he might be in the small clearing where Milo had patiently and lovingly carved his gift, never knowing that he had awakened his talent for wielding Lifefire, never knowing that he would unleash, embodied in Malissa, a Lifefire twisted with betrayal, revenge, and hate. With a clarity he would later understand was Lifefire at work, Jon knew that Shondral had summoned all the love and trust, compassion and generosity that she felt for everything in the world around her, and had fused it to the woman before her.

Milo's gift was at last in balance, its burden lifted.

Malissa's eyelids fluttered open as though from a long sleep. She sat up holding Shondral's hand and smiled shyly at Jon; her eyes matched the soft green grass. She looked small and afraid. "Where is this place?" she whispered.

Shondral put a comforting arm around her shoulders. "This is where you were born."

The strange woman looked around the clearing in amazement and rose gracefully to her feet to examine her surroundings more closely. It was a warm summer morning filled with the sweet song of birds, the buzz of insects, and the whisper of tall grasses in the gentle breeze. Eich padded alongside her, manoeuvring his scruffy head under her hand. She laughed delightedly and rubbed his ears. "I'm glad. I like it. I like it very much."

She turned a puzzled face to Jon and Shondral. "There is so much I seem to have forgotten." Her hand flew to her mouth. "I don't even know my own name!"

Shondral was overwhelmed. This innocent woman had moments ago engulfed her in black terror. "Mila," Shondral murmured, inspired, "your name is Mila."

She thought about it then nodded her head. "Yes, that sounds right. Mila." With her hand on Eich's back, Mila wandered to the edge of the meadow to exclaim over a profusion of daisies.

Shondral remained where she was, kneeling in the grass. Only moments ago, the deepest despair had been replaced by the soaring joy of Lifefire

324

coursing through her. As she slowly regained her equilibrium, the fact that she was close to her home crept into her thoughts and with it came the anguish that she must now tell her parents of Milo's death.

With Jon's help, they decided upon a simplified version of the last few weeks, leaving out much of what had actually happened. Her parents would have enough to cope with. Jon agreed to take care of Mila and to come to the house later that evening. Shondral hoped that it would give her parents enough time to absorb her story; there would never be enough time for them to absorb their son's death.

When Jon and Mila arrived at the door that night, the Laracyls invited them into their home with their usual, if somewhat subdued, grace. They thanked Jon for his help when the birds had attacked Milo. And wasn't it nice to meet another of Shondral's friends, and with such a nice name.

***

Oriander and his fellow Guardians sat in a circle, eyes closed. They had been like this for nearly two days. Halam knew that they 'watched' the struggle in the Raylorn Fen, and that they observed Shondral in particular. The waiting was worse than anything that could have happened—well almost anything.

As one, the Guardians smiled. Halam straightened from the slouch into which he had sunk, hoping there was news. The Guardians opened their eyes and looked very satisfied. Halam could contain himself no longer. "Well? What happened? Are they all right? Is Malissa dead?"

Oriander looked at him. "Calm yourself,

325

Halam. All is well. The girl performed beyond our expectations." Oriander did not elaborate. "You will receive your instructions and then you will be returned to your home." He sniffed. "And you will take those smelly animals with you."

In what seemed like the next moment, Halam stood on shaky legs in his dooryard with Midnight, Lighting, his own Mabel, and Milo's horse, who had never been given a name. He decided he would take the extra horses to the Laracyls. Shondral, at least, would return there and he would find out more than the Guardians were willing to share with him.

***

Eich had been restless all morning, pacing back and forth in front of Shondral's house. Mila fretted over his behaviour and tried to distract him by throwing sticks, one of his favourite games, but to no avail. In the middle of one of his circuits, Eich stiffened. His ears shot up and his nose quivered. In the next instant he bounded out of the yard and pelted down the road. Mila shouted for Jon and Shondral and they sprinted after him. They dashed around the corner of the lane and skidded to a stop.

Eich had pinned Halam to the ground and was busily slobbering heartfelt kisses all over his face. Halam thumped the big dog's sides and after several joyous moments, gently pushed Eich off him and over onto his back to administer a vigorous belly rub. It was then that Halam noticed his audience: Jon and Shondral with huge smiles on their faces, and a third person with a look of bemusement on her face.

Halam pushed himself to his feet and was accosted a second time, by a fierce hug from Shondral, though she avoided coming into contact with his drool-smeared face. Jon pounded him on the back and shook his hand. *If all his welcomes in Morbella were like this*, Halam thought, a wide grin threatening to split his face and his eyes a touch watery, *why he just might make the trip more often.*

Eich nudged the back of Halam's leg and padded over to Mila who was now smiling at the obvious joy of this reunion. "Halam, meet Mila," Jon introduced. "We've already told her all about you."

Halam walked over to her and was struck by the childlike innocence in her eyes. "A pleasure to meet you, Mila," he said, "and it seems that my great brute of a dog here is also a friend of yours."

Eich had insinuated his head under Mila's hand. "Oh, yes. He's wonderful!" Mila bent to hug Eich's furry neck.

"We should be getting back," Shondral interjected from where she was renewing her acquaintance with Midnight. "My parents will be wondering where we raced off to."

Jon insisted that he and Halam stable the horses and under that chivalrous guise took the opportunity to recount to Halam the abridged story of Milo's death that Shondral's parents had been told. He then filled Halam in on events since their dramatic departure from Banifour. And who Mila used to be.

Halam nodded, not surprised at all. "It is as the Guardians said. I'm only glad it's over and that no one else was hurt." The two men held each other's gaze for a moment, a look of mutual satisfaction of a job well done in their eyes. They finished tending the horses and strolled to the house.

Not without a little dismay, Shondral's parents shook hands with the 'crazy man.' Halam could be very charming when he chose to be and he entertained them all with amusing anecdotes throughout dinner and into the evening. For the first time since Shondral had delivered her devastating news a few days ago, her mother laughed.

On the morning Halam prepared to return to his home, it was with many promises to visit the Laracyls whenever he was in town and to write to Jon and Shondral.

Two weeks after Malissa's rebirth, Jon, Shondral, and Mila saddled the horses and left for Alba by way of Ked. Jon and Shondral knew that that was where Jeorg Oprum had been taken and, from what little they had learned, they hoped that the Gaski's would welcome an innocent young woman into their lives. A long shot, but they could come up with no better plan.

***

Jeorg rested comfortably in the bright, airy room. He could feel his strength returning to him day by day. He exercised faithfully. He drank the concoctions that Maol and Endel insisted were good for him. He did everything they asked. It seemed only fair that they could do the one thing that *he* asked. All he wanted was an answer. He remembered nothing of his last days with Malissa and the days before that were a bewildering haze of pain. He, more than anyone else, deserved to know

Malissa's fate.

That morning, his impatience got the better of him and, wobbling slightly, he stood beside the bed. He was still amazed at how thin he was, but three weeks of Elli Gaski's cooking was filling him out again. He could hear the low murmur of voices in the next room; he knew that Aird and Endel and the four Uamhans remained as guests of the Gaskis. Steeling his resolve, Captain Jeorg Oprum shuffled to the door that opened onto the front room.

Arthon immediately came to his friend's aid and helped him into a comfortable armchair. "We wouldn't want you to be breaking a leg, now would we? You never listened when you were this tall," he put a flat hand next to Jeorg's elbow, "and you still don't listen!"

"You're a fine one to talk, Arthon Gaski!" Elli spread a quilt over Jeorg's legs. "Don't you pay him no mind, young Jeorg, he just doesn't like someone else getting all the attention." She tucked the blanket under his feet and tweaked one of his toes.

Laughing at the familiar antics of his dear friends, Jeorg looked up and choked on his own breath. Two strangers faced him from across the room.

Aird rose to his feet. "These, Captain, are the two people that Méadhon owes its very existence to," he bowed deeply to them. "Meet Shondral Laracyl and Jon Montrai."

The girl's eyes flashed wide while the boy's dark complexion grew darker. They reached for each other's hands.

"You're embarrassing them," Elli tisked.

"But it's true," insisted Aird.

"We h-had a lot of help," Shondral stammered, "and couldn't have done anything without Halam, or the Guardians, or the Barbardensi, or the Shamans!"

"Wait a minute, wait a minute," Jeorg sputtered. "Can you indulge a poor, sick man and tell him what this is all about? Who is Halam? Guardians of what? And Barbarbar... whatever that is." He lowered his voice. "But most importantly, is Malissa dead?"

Jon cautiously raised his voice. "In a manner of speaking, yes. Sort of."

Jeorg threw his hands in the air and resigned himself to cryptic answers and more tall tales.

The story gradually unfolded. Elli served them bread and fruit, and Arthon kept the wine flowing. Jeorg asked a question now and then, and was beside himself with curiosity about Banifour. He shared the Uamhans' desire to seek out the Guardians and to study with them. Shondral did her best to discourage this and, in the end, convinced them of the Guardians' pledge of non-participation. She knew in her heart that they would never even be able to find Banifour; it revealed itself only when the Guardians wished it.

Shondral would teach them everything she had learned there, though, and she and Géodha excitedly discussed plans for introducing Lifefire to the people. Perhaps a school.

At a polite cough from Jeorg, Shondral continued her story, her eyes bright and her colour high. "But it was the power of the Shamans that gave me the chance to complete Malissa, to give her what she needed." Aird sat straighter. "They knew her essence had to be brought into balance, and that it had to be done in the exact place where it had been first created. I didn't know the true purpose of the talisman," she drew out the *Flame of Life* for them to see, "until that very moment when I cried out its name. The Shamans' power instantly filled me with the knowledge of what I must do and carried us to the hillside outside Morbella where Milo..." Her voice caught, and Elli was at her side in an instant. After a sip of wine, Shondral went on. "Where Milo's gift went so terribly wrong. I finished what he had begun." She untied the nomad talisman from around her neck and wrapped it in a square of silk. "The Shamans asked me to bring it to you, Aird, so that you can return it to them on your next journey home." She reverently handed it to the awed nomad.

***

While Jeorg had been recuperating, Aird and Géodha had travelled to Alba. Shops were closed and shutters fastened. The harbour was still except for the swoop and cry of the gulls. The conversation in the few inns that were opened was filled with rumours of pestilence and war.

Aird and Géodha thought it wise to remain silent and unobtrusive until they could locate the members of the Council Triad. It took two days to gather the Triad together and a further two days to convince them that the danger was past, that Malissa was defeated. But it was Géodha's cure for Malissa's poison that finally turned their fear into

331

hope. Nedral, the eldest Triad member, sobbed openly.

Although slow to believe the truth, once they did, the Triad wasted no time in setting the wheels in motion to restore their community to its former vigour. They declared a public holiday and opened the coffers of Malissa's house to pay for it. It was then that the young girl who had been altered to become Malissa's duplicate was discovered. She huddled in a corner of the basement, trembling and shaking, not knowing where she was. One of the town clerks fainted dead away as he recognised his own daughter, missing these past two months.

The townspeople were eventually coaxed out of their homes, but it would be many days before the easy bustle returned.

Aird secured craftsmen to refurbish the scorched *Pride* and the Triad insisted on overseeing the project. They pleaded with Aird to bring those responsible for Malissa's demise to Alba for commendations and rewards. The town needed a celebration, and the townsfolk needed to see their heroes.

As Aird and Géodha relaxed in an outdoor tavern the night before returning to Ked—Géodha insisted on sitting under the stars—a traveller told them a strange tale of animals and birds emerging from the Fen in great droves. Without her control, Malissa's 'soldiers' had reverted to their true forms and were returning home. And to the great joy of many families, some of the children who had gone missing were found wandering in the fields beyond Malissa's encampment. They were one and all emaciated and ragged, and had no memory of what had happened to them. Teams of searchers had been immediately assembled to look for others.

***

"You're certain that, Mila is it?, is perfectly harmless?" Jeorg was decidedly upset that Malissa's body still roamed the earth.

They had unanimously agreed to tell Jeorg nothing of Mila's whereabouts. They feared that he would lose the fragile peace of mind that he had regained if he knew that she was right there on the Gaski's farm, tending sheep at the south end of their property.

"She remembers nothing of her time as Malissa," Shondral assured him. "Would you kill a new-born babe? For that is what she is."

Jeorg looked away, not wanting her to see the indecision in his eyes.

A few days later, Endel and Maol declared Jeorg strong enough to travel to Alba. The Uamhans, too, would travel to the port town and looked forward to meeting the Council Triad; Uamh and Alba had much to share.

It was also long past time for Jon and Shondral to return to School although the day-to-day routine would suffer badly in comparison to their recent adventure. They wondered if their story would be entered into the Archives. What had happened was certainly 'of significance to Alba,' and to all Méadhon for that matter, but would the Historians accept it? *Could* they? Lifefire was an astounding discovery; it would change everything. And not everybody would be happy about that.

Aird insisted that Arthon and Elli join them. Mila had proved to be a quick learner and a hard worker, and the Gaskis could leave the farm in her care for a few days. It also seemed prudent to keep someone who so closely resembled Malissa far from curious eyes. When Mila was approached about staying, she confided to Elli that she would be glad for the quiet and solitude; too many people, she had said, made her nervous. It was settled.

Arthon procured brightly painted wagons and high-stepping horses. They departed for Alba in fine style—Elli would have it no other way.

***

Mila meandered through the meadow. She felt more peaceful now that the others had left. They were so busy all the time; it grated on her nerves. She was quick to remind herself that she was grateful to them for saving her, although she was puzzled about why, exactly, she needed saving in the first place.

In her dreams, when she could remember them, she was a much different person—a person she didn't recognise but was drawn to even though that person scared her. She shrugged away such thoughts; it was too beautiful a day.

She perched on a sun-warmed rock from which she could keep an eye on her charges. The Gaski's flock of sheep browsed through the abundance of greenery, grazing contentedly. Their fluffy white wool mirrored the fluffy white clouds that were almost too bright to look at.

She shaded her eyes with a raised hand and, in the distance, saw a speck in the sky which resolved itself into a hawk on the hunt. The bird circled nearer, the sunlight glinting on its tail feathers and wingtips. Mila watched it gracefully soar through the perfect sky.

The hawk's stoop, when it came, startled her with its intensity. Outstretched claws snagged in the vole's hide; its squeal of fright and pain shattered the serenity of the meadow. With powerful downbeats of its wings, the hawk lifted its prize into the air and arrowed toward the trees on the perimeter of the meadow. The faint cries of the vole stilled and the day returned to its former tranquility.

But Mila was anything but tranquil. She replayed the scene over and over in her head: the hawk, the claws, the savaging of the prey. Her mouth pooled with saliva.

THE END

Titles by Peggy Hogan

For a Song
In which a singer saves the world

Milo's Burden
Sometimes you have to make it right—no matter the cost

Coming Soon

An Unusual Girl
Seeing the future can ruin your day

Comments on *For a Song*

For a Song imaginatively created an alternate reality, but one in which, like our own world, pure ideology takes those hungriest for power far from their good intentions, with disastrous consequences for everyone. The plot was suspenseful, funny, and was carried along with a beautiful sense of wonder from page 1.

Chris Benjamin, Author of *Drive-by-Saviours* and *Indian School Road*

You have such a lovely turn of phrase—paints pictures in one's imagination! A pleasure to read.

Karen Jans, Reader

I finished *For a Song* today and was mesmerized by the adventures of Blat. I could not imagine how you could conceive this diverse cast of characters and exquisite plot for the story. I just loved your book.

RJL, Reader

It's brilliant! I was hooked. I carried it in my purse, read it when I could, made excuses to be alone with your story. It was such a joy to read.

Dianne Deans, Reader